Also by the Author

The Erin O'Reilly Mysteries

Black Velvet	*Hair of the Dog*
Irish Car Bomb	*Punch Drunk*
White Russian	*Bossa Nova*
Double Scotch	*Blackout*
Manhattan	*Angel Face*
Black Magic	*Italian Stallion*
Death By Chocolate	*White Lightning*
Massacre	*Kamikaze*
Flashback	*Jackhammer*
First Love	*Frostbite*
High Stakes	*Brain Damage*
Aquarium	*Celtic Twilight*
The Devil You Know	*Headshot* (coming soon)

Tequila Sunrise: A James Corcoran Story

Fathers
A Modern Christmas Story

The Clarion Chronicles
Ember of Dreams

Celtic Twilight

The Erin O'Reilly Mysteries
Book Twenty-Five

Steven Henry

Clickworks Press • Baltimore, MD

Copyright © 2024 Steven Henry
Cover design © 2024 Ingrid Henry
Cover photo © 2024 under license from Shutterstock.com (Credit: Silent O/Shutterstock)
NYPD shield photo used under license from Shutterstock.com (Credit: Stephen Mulcahey/Shutterstock)
Author photo © 2017 Shelley Paulson Photography
Spine image used under license from Shutterstock.com (Credit: diggers1313/Shutterstock)
All rights reserved

First publication: Clickworks Press, 2024
Release: CWP-EOR25-INT-P.IS-1.0

Sign up for updates, deals, and exclusive sneak peeks at clickworkspress.com/join.

Ebook ISBN: 1-943383-023-5
Paperback ISBN: 978-1-943383-024-2
Hardcover ISBN: 1-943383-025-9

This is a work of fiction. Names, characters, places, organizations, and events are either the products of the author's imagination or used in a fictitious manner. Any resemblance to actual persons, living or dead, is purely coincidental.

For Kira, Mari, Brook, Noah, and the rest of the AAC.

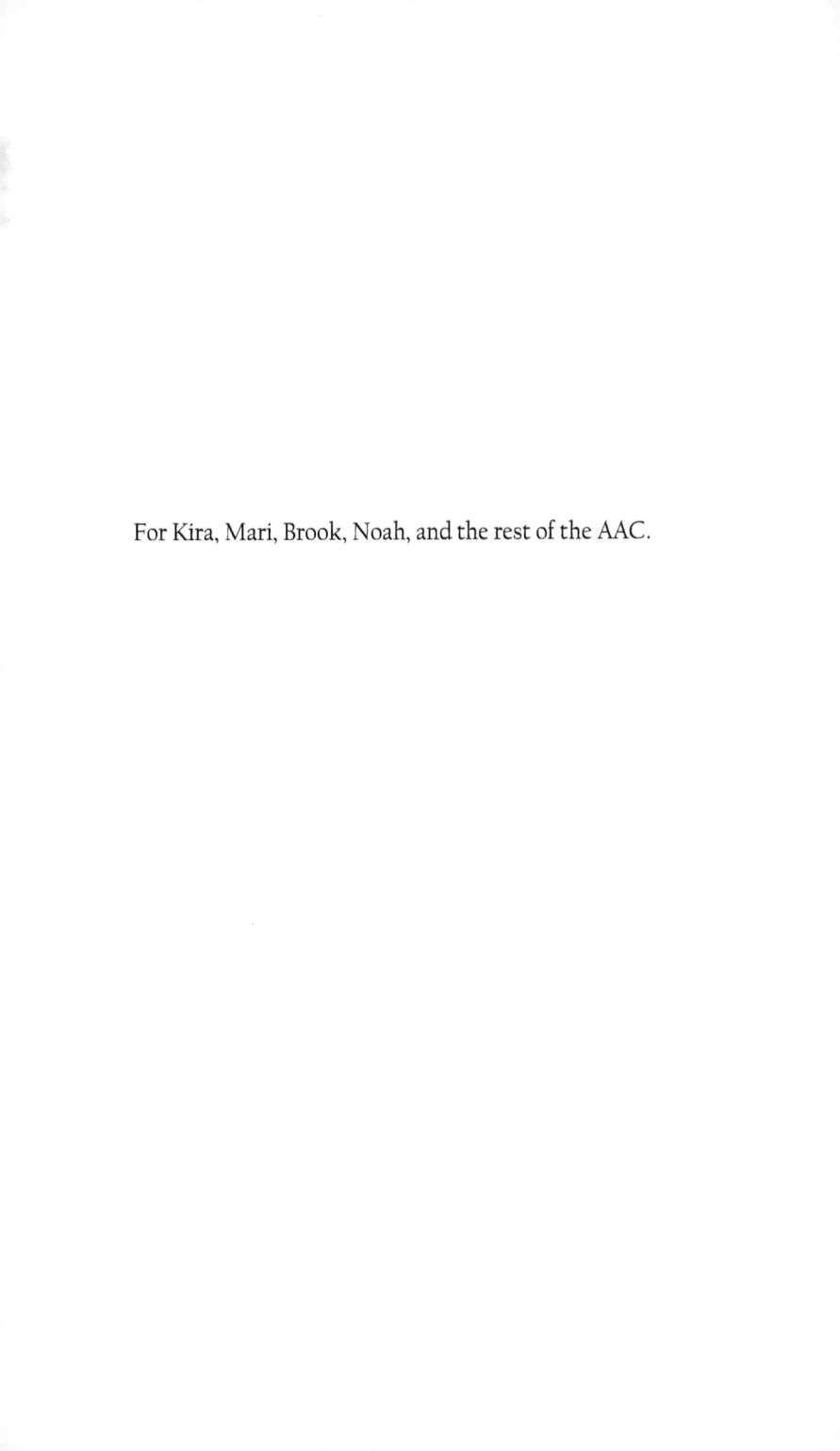

Celtic Twilight

Combine 1 oz. Irish whiskey, 1 oz. hazelnut liqueur, and 1 oz. Irish cream in a shaker 2/3 filled with ice. Shake until thoroughly chilled. Strain into a chilled cocktail glass over crushed ice.

Chapter 1

"My God," Erin O'Reilly said, taking in the scene. "Eleven years on Patrol, another year and a half wearing a gold shield, and I've never seen anything like this. You've been a cop longer than I have. What do you think?"

"It's pretty bad," the veteran cop beside her admitted. He rubbed his gray mustache. "You think there's any survivors?"

"Hard to tell," Erin said. The room was strewn with debris. Crumpled bits of paper, boxes, and bodies lay everywhere. The kids were the worst. When an adult went down that was bad enough, but in addition to the young man sprawled on his back, there were three children. The oldest couldn't be more than ten. One of the kids was a little girl. She was still clutching a black, fluffy puppy in her arms. Another dog lay nearby, a scraggly unkempt mutt.

"Better send in your K-9," the old man said. "To make sure."

"Good idea," Erin said. "Rolf?"

The German Shepherd was at her hip, instantly alert and attentive. His enormous ears perked forward and his head cocked a little to one side, listening for instructions.

"*Such!*" Erin ordered, pointing at the carnage. It was the

German word for "seek" and it triggered Rolf's search-and-rescue training.

The dog sprang into action, nostrils flaring, leaping forward and snuffling at the bodies. When he came to the girl, he thrust his muzzle against her cheek.

She squealed and batted the snout aside. "Rolfie, no!" she giggled. "Your nose is cold!"

Rolf sat back on his haunches and barked once, sharply, to let Erin know he'd found someone.

"Good boy," Erin said, grinning. "Sorry, kiddo. I thought maybe you were dead."

Sean O'Reilly, Erin's dad, chuckled. His mustache twitched. "Dinner's just about ready, kids," he said. "I hope you didn't wipe yourselves out. Mary's got a real feast laid on for us."

The bodies on the living room carpet began to stir. Two were O'Reillys: Anna and Patrick, Erin's niece and nephew. The other kid was Ben Jordan. Trying to explain the connection made Erin feel like she was setting up a tedious joke. His mother was the girlfriend of Erin's boyfriend's bodyguard. But Ian Thompson had been an honorary O'Reilly ever since he'd been very nearly killed protecting the family, so he, Cassie, and Ben were more than welcome in the household, particularly at Christmas.

The young man who'd been playing with the kids was Ian himself. He rolled onto his feet with the same casual efficiency with which he always moved. "Need anything, sir?" he asked Sean.

"The kitchen's got too many cooks as it is," Sean said. "Between Mary, Shelley, Cassie, and Sarah, I think they've got it covered. Our job is to stay out of the line of fire."

"Roger that, sir," Ian said. He'd never entirely stop being a Marine.

"Maybe you could pick up some of that wrapping paper,"

Erin suggested. "I can't believe how far it scattered."

"Seen frag grenades with a smaller blast radius," Ian said, scooping up handfuls of the stuff. The kids had almost literally dived into the pile of presents under the tree. They'd been overstimulated, especially once the dogs got in on the action, and a late-morning nap had been inevitable. Now it was time for the big family dinner.

A veritable caravan of cars had made its way from New York City all the way to Sean and Mary O'Reilly's house in the upstate boonies. Erin had brought Rolf and her boyfriend Morton Carlyle in her unmarked NYPD Charger. Ian had driven Carlyle's Mercedes, into which he'd packed Cassie, Ben, and his dog Miri. Then Erin's brother Michael and sister-in-law Sarah had arrived in a brand-new BMW, of which Michael was absurdly proud. Sean Junior, Michelle, Anna, Patrick, and their Newfoundland pup Lucy had come in a minivan Junior had borrowed from one of his colleagues at Bellevue Hospital. Erin's youngest brother Tommy had been dropped off, along with his guitar, by a complete stranger who'd happened to be passing in a VW minibus.

The line of parked vehicles stretched all the way down the O'Reilly driveway. Erin had lobbied hard to have the family Christmas in the city, and not just because of the logistics of moving all those people all those miles. A major NYPD operation was about to go down, in approximately fifteen hours, and she had to be there when it did. It was the culmination of months of tense, dangerous undercover work. People had gotten hurt. Some had died. Now the end was finally in sight, and she'd been pulled away from the scene of the action.

What a crime lord like Evan O'Malley couldn't manage through intimidation or violence, Mary O'Reilly had accomplished by just being herself. She'd insisted on hosting Christmas, with all her children present, and there'd been no shifting her. The one trait Erin was sure she'd inherited from her mom was her stubborn streak.

Erin was putting up a cheerful front, but she wasn't feeling the holiday spirit. She was utterly exhausted. The nervous tension was really getting to her. She had a fearsome headache from a combination of fatigue, stress, and the impact of a crooked cop's bullet to the side of her skull. She'd promised Carlyle, the NYPD, and herself that once this whole thing was over, she'd take a couple weeks off. She'd get some real rest and make sure nothing was seriously wrong with her brain.

Christmas was a fluffy distraction, nothing more. She was glad to see her family, of course, and the kids' excitement had brought plenty of smiles to her face, but she could feel the fragility of her joy. Her smile felt like a clown's makeup, plastered across her lips. *Fifteen hours*, she thought for the second time in five minutes. Then a blaze of blue and red emergency lights, the thunder of ESU boots on bad guys' doors, and that would be it.

What if they missed one? What if just one of Evan O'Malley's top guys slipped through the net? Evan probably wouldn't dare retaliate against a police detective, but what would he do once he learned Carlyle had betrayed him? The only safety her lover had was if they made a clean sweep.

The best thing would be to keep Carlyle out of town for the next twenty-four hours, but that was no good. It might make Evan suspicious. Mobsters had fantastically sensitive antennae. Paranoia was a way of life for them. And Evan was *smart*.

"Erin, darling?"

Carlyle gently touched her arm. She jumped at the contact, spinning toward him. His face was calm, collected, and pleasant. How could he be so unaffected? He'd been a gangster for twenty years. His whole life was about to be ripped up by the roots.

"What?" she asked, marveling at how steady her own voice

sounded.

"We're at the table," he said. "If you'd care to join us?"

"Oh," she said. "Yeah, I'll be right there."

* * *

Mary O'Reilly was one of those old-school, traditional-minded women who thought the best way of showing love was by showering enormous quantities of food onto her family. Erin firmly believed that if her mom heard the world was about to end, the first thing Mary would do would be to fire up the oven and start baking so her family would meet Jesus with full stomachs.

"Erin, honey," Mary said, partway through the feast. "You're hardly touching your food. Is something wrong?"

"Leave the girl alone," Sean said. "She's fine."

"You're pale, too," Mary persisted. "I hope you're not ill."

"Mom, she got shot," Sean Junior said. "In the *head*."

Mary shuddered. "I know," she said. "And it's so awful! But I thought it wasn't anything serious."

"Getting shot in the head is always serious," Erin's brother replied. "I think maybe we can defer to the ER trauma surgeon on this, don't you? I see a lot of GSWs, but not very many to the head."

"Why not?" Anna piped up. Erin's niece was a very bright, inquisitive girl; sometimes a little too inquisitive for her parents' liking.

"This isn't exactly dinner-table talk," Michelle said.

"GSW stands for Gun Shot Wound," Anna said proudly. "It's what cops say when somebody gets shot."

"And just where did she learn that, I wonder?" Michelle said, giving Erin an icy look.

"Don't bad guys get shot in the head sometimes?" Anna

pressed.

"Good guys, too," Ian said quietly. "Incoming fire doesn't discriminate."

"Isn't that the truth," Cassie said. She was a physical rehab nurse for the Veterans Administration. That was how she'd met Ian.

"Then why don't they go to the hospital?" Anna demanded.

There were a few seconds of silence.

"Because most lads don't make it that far with bullets in their heads, darling," Carlyle said gently.

Anna blinked. "Oh, right," she said. "Because they're D-E-A-D, right?"

"She got third in the Fourth Grade spelling bee," Sean Junior said, trying to put a positive spin on his daughter's words.

"I didn't know how to spell 'catastrophe,'" Anna said. "I put an 'f' in it. But I remembered 'appalling' has two 'p's and two 'l's."

"That word list is really making me wonder what they're teaching these kids," Michael said, drawing a laugh from most of the adults.

"They're just trying to get them ready for the real world," Erin's dad said.

"Do you still want to be a cop, Anna?" Ian asked. Erin had noticed he was much more talkative with kids than with grown-ups.

"Yes," Anna said. "And a ballerina. Maybe a gymnast, too."

"Sounds like a plan," Ian said.

"What about you" Anna asked.

"Me?" Ian sounded surprised.

"What do you want to be?"

He blinked. "Was a Marine," he said.

"But you're not anymore," she pointed out.

"I wouldn't be so sure about that," Cassie interjected,

getting another laugh.

"That's true," Ian said. "Now I work for Mr. Carlyle."

"Driving his car?" Anna asked.

"Affirmative."

"Is that what you're always going to do?"

"Long as he needs me."

"Why do you carry a gun?"

There was another silence.

"Protection," Ian finally said.

"And it's a good thing he does," Erin's dad said gruffly, surprising Erin. "Otherwise things might've gone differently with that guy last summer."

"Think maybe I'll hang it up one of these days," Ian said.

"Why?" Anna asked.

"Not good for me," he said. "Carrying makes me feel like I'm still in combat. Might be time to make a change."

Cassie gave him a warm look and squeezed his hand, saying a lot without words.

"Not yet, though," Ian added. "Mr. Carlyle might need me a little longer."

"Perhaps not so very long," Carlyle said quietly.

Erin shot him a sharp glance. That was exactly the sort of thing he shouldn't be saying right now, even to her family. He wasn't supposed to know the precise timing of the O'Malley takedown, for just this reason. She didn't think anybody in the room was going to say anything, but loose talk was always dangerous.

"What would you do?" Michael asked. "Career-wise, I mean."

"Don't have many job skills," Ian said. "I'm patient. Pretty good under pressure. Steady hands."

"College degree?" Michael asked.

Ian shook his head. "Joined the Corps out of high school."

"It's a tough job market," Michael said. "You could maybe do corporate security. I know some guys. I could make some calls."

"Thanks," Ian said. "But I'm good for now."

"We should probably be getting back," Erin said to Carlyle. *Fourteen hours*, she thought.

"Don't rush off, Erin," Mary said, catching her words. "We see so little of one another these days."

"Sorry, Mom," Erin said. "I have work. It's the Job, you know?"

"On Christmas?" Mary pouted.

"Crooks don't take holidays off," Erin said.

"We can stay a bit longer, surely," Carlyle said. "We've the afternoon in front of us."

"Okay," Erin said. "But traffic's going to be a beast when we get close to the city. I don't want to get stuck. Six o'clock and we're out of here. No later."

"Yay!" Anna said.

"Ian's going to help me build my Lego castle," Patrick said. It was the longest sentence he'd spoken since arriving. Michael had given him a big, expensive box of the plastic blocks and the kid was positively giddy about it, which for Patrick meant he was actually smiling and would sometimes talk in front of a group.

"That's right," Ian said. "Ben's going to help, too."

Ben nodded eagerly. He loved Legos.

"Besides, we still have pie," Mary announced, to no one's surprise.

"And we can crack open one of those bottles our friend brought," Michael said, grinning at Carlyle.

"With pleasure," Carlyle said. He'd given every adult couple a bottle of Glen Docherty-Kinlochewe whiskey, the finest Scotch Erin had ever tasted. It was from a microbrewery in the Highlands and almost impossible to find in America, but Carlyle knew a lad.

"Can I have some?" Anna asked.

"Ask me again in ten years," Sean Junior said.

"Awww," Anna said, sticking out her lower lip.

"It doesn't really taste good," Ian said in a stage whisper.

"Why do grown-up drinks always taste nasty?" Anna asked.

"It's what we expect from life," Tommy O'Reilly said. "It's a bitter, awful experience. The only thing worse than living is dying."

His words hung in the air.

"I'm going through an emotional stage in my songwriting career," Tommy explained. "I'm getting in touch with my existential angst."

"Well, I don't know about the rest of you," Erin's dad said. "But that's definitely putting me in the holiday spirit. Tommy, how about you get out that guitar and play us something Christmassy. None of that emo, Goth, punk, whatever it is you usually do."

"I play acoustic guitar in coffee shops," Tommy said in wounded tones. "I'm not a punk."

"More of a hippy, then," Sean Senior muttered into his mustache. "That isn't any better."

"I've heard it said that music as an avocation is a marvelous thing," Carlyle interjected. "But music as a vocation often leaves a great deal to be desired."

* * *

"Christmas is for kids," Erin said as she steered the Charger south toward the Big Apple. It was eight o'clock and they were about halfway home. The sun had gone down at four-thirty. A little light sleet was falling. She'd have to be careful on the road.

"You'll hear no argument from me," Carlyle said. "Though

it's grand to see your family all together."

"Do you miss yours?" she asked.

"My family's here," he said. "Ian and yourself, begging your pardon."

"That's not what I meant," she said, squinting through the windshield. "I'm talking about your mom and your brother."

"I've not seen either of them going on twenty years," he said. "And to be brutally honest, I imagine they're well quit of me."

Erin checked her mirrors. The Mercedes was hanging well back. Ian, careful as ever, was giving plenty of following room to account for the bad conditions. "I can't imagine your mom doesn't miss you," she said.

"There's the family we're born into and the family we choose," he said. "Of the two, I'm glad to spend the holidays with the one I've found. I hope Corky's had a pleasant day. The poor lad's got no one but me."

"And that out-of-town girl," Erin said. She didn't think her car was bugged, and in ten more hours it wouldn't matter anyway, but she still didn't name Teresa Tommasino. Teresa was the key witness in the murder case against Valentino Vitelli's son. Corky Corcoran had gotten a little too close to her while protecting her from the Mob. He'd left her somewhere in Mexico, but he'd left his heart there too.

"Ah yes," Carlyle said. "I imagine he's rather lonesome this evening. Perhaps I ought to ring him up."

"We've got plenty of time before we hit Manhattan," she said. "Just remember, not a word about the other thing."

"It seems rather harsh to keep him in the dark," Carlyle said. "But I see your point. While he knows it's coming, it's best he doesn't know just when. No one's ever accused James Corcoran of being close-mouthed."

He took his phone out of the inside pocket of his suit coat, dialed, and set it to speaker. It rang once, twice, three times, four.

"He can't be stumbling drunk already," Carlyle muttered. He poised his thumb to hang up.

"Evening, Cars," Corky said breezily. "How's about you, mate?"

"A merry Christmas to you, Corks," Carlyle said. "I'm motoring toward you as we speak, in the company of the lovely Miss O'Reilly."

"Merry Christmas, Corky," Erin said.

"Surely the two of you've better things to be doing, particularly with one another, than jabbering to a scunner like myself," Corky said. "If you're lacking for ideas, I've a few I can suggest. Though I'd best add, they're not safely done while behind the wheel of an automobile. Not that I haven't tried it from time to time."

Erin made a face. "No thanks," she said.

"I was just thinking of you, lad," Carlyle said. "And hoping you're keeping well tonight."

"Just grand, thank you," Corky said. "In point of fact, you've caught me at a slightly awkward moment. I've some business to attend to, and it's with lads unaccustomed to being kept waiting."

"Nobody too dangerous, I hope," Erin said.

"It's the Teamsters, if you must know," Corky replied. "They've been a bit fluthered ever since their local vice president took the express stairway from his office."

"I remember that," Erin said. She'd been right next to the crooked Teamster when the man had taken a twelve-story nosedive out his own window.

"I'm just showing the flag at their Christmas party, letting the lads know everything's under control," Corky said. "We wouldn't want any of those big, rough fellows being too upset."

"Certainly not," Carlyle agreed. "Just so long as you're not stewing in loneliness. It's bad form to get drunk alone, even for an Irishman."

"As to that," Corky said. "I've a grand evening planned for afterward. After the party, I'll be coming back to my flat. I'll draw a nice, hot bath with some of those scented bubbles, light some candles, crack a bottle of red wine, and romance a fair colleen."

"Corky!" Erin snapped. "I thought you weren't doing any of that!"

"Erin, a detective oughtn't to jump to conclusions," Corky said with mock severity. "I've a touch more class than that. I won't be entertaining any lasses in the flesh. I can woo just as effectively from a distance, I'll have you know. I've a good waterproofed phone in hand for just such an eventuality. You'd be surprised how much you can accomplish with the power of voice alone."

Carlyle put a hand over his mouth to stifle a chuckle. Erin grimaced.

"And that's more than I need to know about that," she said.

"In point of fact, there's her on my call waiting now," Corky said. "Kindly don't disturb me, unless you're truly dying to know what I get up to in the bath by my lonesome. Ta."

Before Erin could think of anything to say to that, Corky hung up. Carlyle tucked his phone away.

"There's our answer, darling," he said. "We needn't worry about Mr. Corcoran, at least no more than usual. I'm rather glad to hear of his plans. He'll be home and out of trouble before midnight. That's one less thing for us to worry about."

"Yeah," Erin said. "That only leaves about six hundred other things that could go wrong."

The Charger rolled through the darkness, eating up the miles toward New York City. They'd be home before ten, assuming nothing happened. That would leave six hours to go.

Chapter 2

Ian peeled off to take Cassie and Ben home. He'd meet Carlyle at the Barley Corner once he'd seen them safely to their door. Erin continued on toward the pub.

"Remember, just act normal," she said.

"As opposed to what, precisely?" Carlyle replied.

"You know what I mean," she said. "You're not supposed to know it's happening tonight. Don't do a single thing different from usual."

"I'll close up at two, same as always," he said. "Then I'll retire to my flat for a bit of late-night reading, never imagining armed men will be storming it in the wee hours."

"They'll have the combination to your keypad," she said. "Because I'll give it to them. I won't be there."

"Of course not," he said. "You'll be arresting one of the other lads, the ones likely to offer resistance. Will you be handling Pritchard, O'Malley, or Finnegan?"

"Vic called dibs on Finnegan," Erin said. "And Webb may pull rank so he can collar Evan. I guess that leaves Pritchard for me."

"Be careful," Carlyle said. "The Snake's got a pair of fangs on him. He's a dangerous man."

"They're all dangerous men," she said.

"Gordon Pritchard more than most."

"I took down Mickey Connor," she reminded him. "Pritchard can't be worse than him."

"He's different," Carlyle said. "He's smaller, aye, and less explosive in temperament, but he's just as fast and a born killer. The lad's got ice water in his veins, and he's a sight smarter than Mickey ever was. Mickey liked to kill with his hands for the sheer pleasure of it. Pritchard's more pragmatic. He'll use guns, bombs, fire, or whatever will get the job done. Don't give him a single chance or you'll regret it."

"I'll keep that in mind," she said. "I wish we didn't have to haul you downtown."

"It's the best thing for everyone," he said. "It's a shame to taint my clean record, but things may get a trifle chaotic on the street. A holding cell may be the safest place for me to spend the next few hours. Just make certain I draw Corky for a cellmate, rather than Kyle Finnegan."

Erin shuddered. "Finnegan's a nutjob," she said. "We'll be keeping a really close eye on him. We don't want him eating any of the other inmates."

She pulled up to the curb outside the Barley Corner. The pub's lights glowed warm and welcoming, though it didn't look heavily populated.

"I guess all the goons are home with their families," she said.

"Would you care to come in for a few minutes?" Carlyle asked. "Perhaps a glass of something to cheer your heart?"

Erin was tempted, but she shook her head. "I'd better get to the Eightball," she said. "I'm about to go on duty, so no booze tonight. Coffee will be waiting at the station."

"I'll see you once it's over, then," he said.

"Catch you on the flip-side," she said. Suddenly, as she

looked at him, she felt a wave of fear so strong it almost made her physically ill. She actually felt dizzy. It was just her head wound acting up, she told herself. Erin O'Reilly didn't believe in evil omens.

"Goodnight, darling," Carlyle said. He opened the passenger door and started to climb out of his seat.

"Wait," she blurted.

He paused. "What is it?"

"I love you," Erin said.

"Aye, darling," he said. He bent toward her and kissed her lightly on the lips. "And I love you. It'll all come right in the end, no fear."

Then he walked through the Barley Corner's front door and disappeared into the golden light of the pub. And Erin drove on into the cold Manhattan night.

* * *

The rest of the Major Crimes squad was already in their second-floor office. Lieutenant Webb was staring at the whiteboard and frowning. Zofia Piekarski was sitting at her desk, talking on the phone. Vic Neshenko had just emerged from the break room. He had a can of Mountain Dew in one hand, a donut with red and green sprinkles in the other, and a fuzzy Santa hat on his head.

"Now I know where the party is," Erin said.

"The hat was Zofia's idea," Vic said. "She thinks I need to get in the holiday mood. I keep telling her I'm jolly, but she doesn't believe me."

"Let's hear your best Santa Claus laugh," Erin said.

Vic gave her a flat, cold-eyed stare. "Ho. Ho. Ho," he growled in a guttural baritone.

"And that's going to follow me into my nightmares," she

said. "Please don't ever do that again."

"I dunno what everyone's worried about," he said. "This is gonna be the best Christmas ever, and I'm counting the one when I was twelve and Mom finally thought I was old enough to have my first BB gun."

"You didn't shoot your eye out, did you?" Piekarski asked. She'd hung up the phone and was enjoying their back-and-forth.

"Do you have any idea how hard it is to shoot your own eye out with an air rifle?" Vic retorted. "I might've been a dumb kid, but I did have a basic knowledge of firearm safety, and that included not staring down the damn barrel. I just used the thing for target shooting and for hunting pests."

"What kind of pests?" Piekarski asked.

"The usual," Vic said. "Rats, pigeons, Polacks."

"Shut your pie-hole, you Russian jackass," Piekarski said. "Just for that, you're not getting laid when this shift's over."

"Seriously?" Vic said. "Russia's been screwing Poland for *centuries*, Zofia. It's as much our national pastime as Baseball is for Americans. You want to throw all that tradition away?"

Zofia showed him a sweet smile and the middle fingers on both hands.

"She's bluffing," Vic confided to Erin. "We're gearing up for the biggest felony bust of any of our careers, and you know how she gets jazzed on the action. You'll see. We won't even be done with half the arrest reports and she's gonna drag me into an interrogation room for a little *debriefing*."

Webb cleared his throat, loudly and meaningfully. Erin and Vic looked at him.

"If you've gotten the nonsense out of your systems," the Lieutenant said, "we've got some work to do."

"How are we looking?" Erin asked.

"Evan O'Malley's hosting a party uptown," Webb said. "We've got eyes on it right now. It'll probably run until midnight. Then we think he'll go back to his apartment. Finnegan's at the party. No idea where he's going afterward, but we'll have a revolving tail on him. Maggie Callahan's there, too. Pritchard was, but he just left."

"Where'd he go?" Erin asked sharply.

"Relax, O'Reilly," Webb said, holding up a hand. "Everybody's under constant surveillance, Pritchard included. He's in motion right now, but it's not a big deal. The surveillance is compartmentalized, so even if O'Malley learns about one or two of the units, he'll just think it's standard Organized Crime Task Force reconnaissance."

"ESU knows they're moving tonight," Vic put in. "I just talked to Lieutenant Lewis. They're standing ready. But they don't know who they're hitting yet, or why."

"Good," Erin said. Everyone was assuming Evan O'Malley had ears in the Department.

"Corcoran's at a Christmas party for the Teamsters," Webb went on. "Our last report said he was, and I quote, 'Drinking like a goddamn fish.' As for Carlyle…"

"He's at the Barley Corner," Erin said.

"We know," Webb said meaningfully, which gave her a little shiver. She hadn't noticed the NYPD watchers, but apparently they'd seen her drop Carlyle off.

"Zofia's been coordinating the last-minute stuff for the little guys," Vic said. "How's that coming?"

"No problems," Piekarski said. "But we've got to leave most of the logistics work to the local commanders. There's just too many guys for us to juggle from here."

"How many arrests are we making?" Erin asked.

"One hundred sixty-three," Webb said.

"This is gonna be one for the textbooks," Vic said. "We're gonna be front-page news all over the damn country. Medals and commendations for everyone."

"That's assuming nothing goes wrong," Erin said. "What do you need me doing?"

"Get in contact with Sergeant Brown," Webb said. "We've got people from Vice setting up to take down the prostitution wing of the organization. We don't really care about the girls."

"Nobody cares about the girls," Erin said sourly.

"Not what I meant," Webb said. "We don't care whether the girls get arrested or not. We want the pimps, and they're harder to pin down. Make sure Brown's got enough manpower, and find out if he needs anything else. If he does, take it direct to Captain Holliday. He's at home, but reachable by phone all night."

"Why isn't he here?" Erin asked.

"He's keeping up appearances," Webb said. "The man has a wife and children. How would it look for him to be sitting in his office late on Christmas day?"

"We're here," Vic pointed out.

"We're just a squad of sad losers," Webb said. "Nobody will think twice about us."

"Speak for yourself," Vic said indignantly.

"How many of the people you love are outside this room right now?" Webb asked.

"My mom," Vic said. He paused. "Okay, my brother, too. I guess."

"Hey, Vic?" Erin asked. "What happened to your dad?"

"He died," Vic said. "When I was seventeen. Cancer."

"That's rough," she said.

"It is what it is," he said, shrugging. "Something's gotta get you."

* * *

If Erin ever started to feel too optimistic about her life, or the direction of the world, or human nature in general, Sergeant Brown was always ready to balance her out. Tad Brown was in charge of Precinct 8's Vice squad, which meant he spent his time dealing with the seediest, ugliest parts of police work. Erin avoided his office—a windowless converted closet—as much as possible.

"I wasn't sure you'd be here tonight," she said, poking her head through the doorway and trying to ignore the stuffy, stale smell that hung in the air.

"How come?" Brown replied. He was doing paperwork on a few inches of clear space on his cluttered desk.

"It's Christmas night," she said. "Don't you have a family?"

"You've got a family," he said. "You're here."

"Are you married, Brown?" she asked. His hands were bare of rings, but that didn't mean much. A lot of cops left their wedding bands at home.

"Not anymore," he said. "What's up?"

"Just making sure you're up to speed on tonight's op," she said. "Are you clear on the objectives?"

"Standard pest control," Brown said, shrugging. "I've got my list of offenders, I've got officers keeping tabs on them. They're out on the same old street corners doing the same old business. Christmas doesn't matter to those boys. You know I once busted three guys in Santa suits for solicitation? On the same street corner? One was actually doing the business, the other two were waiting their turn. It was just like being in a shopping mall, only in reverse. See, in the mall there's little girls lining up to sit on Santa's lap, while on the corner there was a little girl and three Santas in line..."

"Yeah, I get the picture," Erin said with a grimace. "Any questions?"

"Just one." Brown scratched the old, puckered scar on his face. "These guys on my list, they're all O'Malley's boys."

"That's not a question, Sergeant," she said.

"Are we targeting Old Man O'Malley?" Brown asked bluntly, staring at her.

"Why do you say that?" Erin replied, trying not to give anything away. She had no information suggesting Brown might be dirty, but she was taking no chances.

"Because if we're not, this is worse than pointless," he said. "Look, prostitution is a filthy business. You know it, I know it, the girls sure as shit know it, and so do the pimps and the johns. But it's impossible to get rid of. We'd have to castrate half the guys in New York, and even then we'd have the tourists to worry about."

"Tempting thought," she said.

"Isn't it, though?" Brown said with slow relish. "That'd take care of the repeat offenders at least. But O'Malley's people aren't so bad, as pimps go. Oh, they're scumbags, don't get me wrong. They'll get girls hooked on smack and keep them on a chemical leash, they'll slap them around, they're abusive assholes. But compared to some of the gangs out there, these guys are practically running a convent."

"Are you approaching a point?" Erin asked. "Because I have a lot of stuff to take care of tonight."

Brown held up a hand. "Patience, Detective. It's better if you don't rush. Know who told me that? A hooker who called herself Candi. Liked sucking on lollipops. Pretty girl. She OD'd two weeks after I had that conversation. I was the one who ID'd the body. We found her behind a dry cleaner. Where was I?"

"Convents," Erin said dryly.

"Right," Brown said. "The O'Malley whore apparatus is in a certain amount of disarray at the moment. What with Vicky Blackburn getting whacked, and Red Rafferty in the hospital..."

"I know," she said even more dryly. She'd been there when Declan Rafferty had been shot by a rogue DEA agent, and she already knew more than she wanted about Veronica Blackburn's death.

"They don't even have anyone big calling the shots right now," Brown said. "The only guys left to bust are the street-level pimps, and those guys are friggin' cockroaches. Stomp on as many as you like, there'll always be more. And if we wipe the O'Malley guys off the street, the guys who replace them will be more of the same, only worse. O'Malley's kind of a prude, you know?"

"Yeah, he's a real model of ethical behavior," Erin said.

"Hey, this is a Major Crimes case, so it's none of my damn business," Brown said. "I just wanted to make sure you big shots have thought this one all the way through. After all the lights and sirens and newspaper headlines, people are still gonna be living on those streets, and some of those people screw for a living. They're not going away."

"We're not social workers, Brown," Erin said. "We're cops. Are you saying we *shouldn't* arrest these jerks?"

Brown rubbed his scar again. "Nah, by all means, let's haul them in," he said. "I mean, it's not like our jails are overcrowded or anything. But keep in mind, if we get rid of the minor offenders we'll have major offenders filling the void."

"Do you need anything?" she asked. "More uniforms? I can throw some bodies your way."

"Nah, we're good," Brown said. "I'll be heading streetside myself to lend a hand. I'd say it's good for my health getting out of the office, but I know better. I've never been stabbed in the office."

"How'd you get that scar?" Erin couldn't resist asking. "I met a detective down in Brooklyn with one that's almost identical. She told me she got it from a pimp."

"Might be the same pimp," Brown said. "Those guys can turn nasty when you try to slap the cuffs on them. There's no such thing as a routine bust, O'Reilly. On the street, we're always three seconds and one bad decision from dead."

"That's a comforting thought," she said. Her phone buzzed, cutting off whatever else she wanted to say. "Be safe out there," she said instead, stepping out of Brown's office and fishing the phone out of her pocket.

"You too, Detective," Brown said as the door swung shut between them.

"O'Reilly," Erin said into the phone.

"If you're available, I'd like to talk to you," said a man with a smooth, polished voice.

"Lieutenant Keane," she said, getting the name out with difficulty. Of all the officers in the building, the Internal Affairs chief was the one she least wanted to talk to.

"Well?" Keane asked, with an undercurrent of slightly malicious amusement. "I hope I'm not intruding. Please come to my office at your earliest convenience."

I'd rather shove thumbtacks under my fingernails, she thought. "I'll be right up," she said.

Chapter 3

It never mattered what time Erin saw Lieutenant Keane. Day or night, rain or shine, it was all the same: he was always immaculately dressed, hair neatly combed, not a hint of stubble on his chin. A beard would never grow without his permission; it wouldn't dare. His suit looked freshly dry-cleaned and pressed. His necktie was perfectly knotted. And he was *smiling*.

Some animals looked like they were smiling. They were the really toothy predators: sharks, alligators, and hyenas. The way to avoid being taken in was to stop looking at the mouth and look at the eyes. Keane's mouth was curled up in a friendly way, but his eyes might as well have been lurking in a Louisiana bayou, scanning the swamp for careless tourists.

"Good evening, Detective," Keane said.

"Merry Christmas, sir," Erin said, keeping her own voice and expression carefully neutral. Did Keane have a family? She always pictured him going to sleep in a dark motel room. Or maybe a coffin.

"Yes, of course," he said. "Big night for you, isn't it?"

"Yes, sir." She stared at a patch of brickwork just above Keane's left shoulder, studying the rough bricks, considering the slight variations in color between them.

"I suppose you're wondering what I'm doing here," he said.

"No opinion, sir," Erin said. She was proud of that answer. She'd learned it from Ian Thompson.

Keane's smile grew fractionally wider, but still stopped short of his eyes. "I have no tactical responsibilities," he said. "Tonight's festivities are a tactical problem for ESU and Patrol Division. And, of course, Major Crimes and the Organized Crime Task Force. *Real* cops, I suspect you'd call yourselves."

He paused, but he hadn't asked a question, so she didn't say anything.

"You've played your cards admirably close to your chest," he went on. "I'll admit, I wasn't sure you were up to the task of dismantling Evan O'Malley's organization from within. But it was worth a try, and the opportunity provided by your... *unorthodox* relationship with Morton Carlyle couldn't be passed up. It was a question of making use of it or of allowing it to torpedo your career."

Erin felt her jaw tighten. She kept her mouth shut.

"I thought I was in the loop, so to speak," Keane said. "Imagine my surprise when I learned you and former Detective Stachowski had cast your net wider than initially planned. Why is the Lucarelli Mafia family involved?"

His voice, which had been quiet and almost melodious, suddenly hardened as he fired the question at her.

"There was a peripheral agreement between O'Malley and some of the Lucarelli leadership, sir," Erin said.

"What agreement?" Keane demanded. "On what subjects?"

"I don't have authorization to share that information with anyone who doesn't have the need to know, sir," Erin said stonily. God bless Ian and all the time she'd spent with him.

There was nobody like a United States Marine for building a polite wall between you and a rear-echelon officer. Show no anger, take no offense, and tack "sir" onto the tail of every single sentence.

"And you don't think I need to know?" Keane's voice was growing colder, his diction more clipped.

"No, sir."

"Why not?"

"As you said, sir, this is a tactical operation."

"Who, precisely, is being targeted in the Lucarellis?" Keane demanded.

"I'm not at liberty to say, sir."

"Damn it, O'Reilly, this will all be over by morning anyway!"

It was rare to see Keane lose his cool. Erin was surprised how much she enjoyed it.

"I guess your question will be answered then, sir," she said.

"I'm asking you now."

"Captain Holliday has tactical command," she said. "Why don't you ask him, sir?"

It was the turn of Keane's jaw to tighten. "You know perfectly well he won't tell me a thing he doesn't have to," he grated out.

"If that's true, sir, I could probably get in trouble for revealing information he'd prefer kept quiet," Erin said. It wasn't necessary to point that out. Both of them already knew it. She just couldn't resist.

"If we're on the subject of information we'd prefer to be kept quiet, there's a few things you ought to remember," Keane said softly. His momentary lapse of control was gone, leaving no trace. "I can think of at least two things you very much do not want publicly aired. One of them pertains to the New York Police Department. The other, unless I'm very much mistaken, bears on the Lucarellis."

Erin tried very hard not to flinch, and thought she succeeded. The NYPD incident was what had happened to Detective Lenny Carter. Erin had effectively told Keane to take care of Carter personally, off the record. She hadn't seen any choice in the matter. Carter knew too much, and he'd expose her to Evan O'Malley unless he was silenced. She had no idea what Keane had done with Carter. Nobody had seen or heard from the dirty detective since that snowy December day. That action had tied Erin to Keane much closer than she wanted, so it was no surprise he'd bring it up now. But when he mentioned the Lucarellis, he had to be talking about Teresa Tommasino.

How could Keane possibly know about Teresa? The official story was that she was dead, a witness to a Mafia murder who'd died in a car bomb outside the JFK Hilton. The Medical Examiner's report, filed by the scrupulously honest Dr. Sarah Levine, and the Bomb Squad's investigation, headed by explosives expert Skip Taylor, had said as much. The *New York Times* had reported it, as had every other media outlet. It had made the national news.

What was not common knowledge was that Erin and Carlyle had planted the bomb and staged the whole thing. The bomb was more of a special effect than an assassination device, and Skip had helped Carlyle design it. The body that had been torn apart was a Jane Doe from the city morgue, provided by Levine. The operation had been a conspiracy, aided and abetted by Captain Holliday. Teresa was very much alive, somewhere in Mexico, having been spirited away by the lovestruck Corky Corcoran. But the Lucarellis didn't know that. They thought Erin was a dirty cop who'd killed Teresa at the behest of Valentino Vitelli.

She had her answer, or thought she did. Keane had ears on the street, including someone inside Vitelli's organization. Vitelli was running the remnants of the Lucarellis, who'd been thrown into chaos by the death of their don—a death Erin had personally witnessed, though she'd had no hand in it. But if Keane knew the street story of Teresa's murder, that meant he thought he was talking to a Mob assassin now. Why hadn't he arrested her, or at least investigated her?

Keane's eyes remained as alien and unreadable as a crocodile's. "If I were in your position, Detective, I would choose my words and actions tonight with exceptional care," he said quietly.

Are you threatening me? That was the traditional thing to say, but it was also stupid. For one thing, it was obvious. Of course he was. To call attention to it would be clumsy and would just make her look like a blustering idiot. For another, it might force her to take a stand. While the threat remained ambiguous, she had a little breathing room.

"I'm not aware of any large-scale action against the Lucarelli organization, sir," she said, falling back on Carlyle's tried-and-true technique of telling the literal truth and using it to mislead the other guy. What she'd said was true. Only one Lucarelli—Old Man Vitelli—was being targeted tonight, and it wasn't for racketeering. It was for ordering Erin to kill the woman who could put his son in jail for the rest of the kid's miserable life.

"So tonight is about the O'Malleys?" Keane pressed.

"They've always been the target, sir," she said. "But if you need further clarification, the Captain's said he's reachable. Why don't we call him and—"

"That won't be necessary," Keane interrupted. "I only wanted to make sure you understand your own position. You wouldn't want to get carried away by the momentum of this operation and take action you'd regret. It's so easy, when working a long-term undercover assignment, for your worldview to get a little muddy. Lines get blurred. I'm sure you've done everything with the best of intentions, and with your long-term goals in sight. I hope you'll continue that wise pattern of behavior."

"Absolutely, sir," Erin said, wondering exactly what he meant.

"Let's hope tonight's operation is executed with a minimum of collateral damage," he said. "And if there's anything you feel I ought to know, please don't hesitate to contact me immediately. That will be all, Detective. Good luck and good hunting."

"Thank you, sir," she said, taking the opportunity to get the hell out of Keane's office.

* * *

"The Captain wants everyone in position by two-thirty at the absolute latest," Webb said when Erin and Rolf came back downstairs.

"That means we'd better be streetside by two," Vic said. "Just in case."

"I still think I ought to come," Piekarski said.

"And I'll remind you once again, Officer Piekarski, that your temporary assignment to Major Crimes is for medical reasons," Webb said.

"Not just medical," Piekarski said. "I'm getting experience for when I get my gold shield. Besides, I'm not due until March."

"This isn't up for discussion," Webb said. "And this isn't a democracy, so while I'll listen to your opinions, they carry exactly as much weight as I want and not an ounce more."

"We need someone in the office manning the phones," Erin said, trying to soften Webb's order. "If anything unexpected happens, you'll need to coordinate our response."

"Yeah," Vic said. "The Captain's gonna be on the street, same as the rest of us."

"So you're saying an old fogey like Holliday can run around busting bad guys, but because I got knocked up I have to sit here and play house," Piekarski said, pouting. "What about Vic? He's as responsible for this as I am."

"I'd leave Neshenko, but he hasn't been housebroken," Webb said, deadpan.

Vic had his Sig-Sauer field-stripped on his desk. He was cleaning the pistol and pretended not to hear Webb. "Hey, Erin?" he said.

"Yeah?"

"You ever get your Glock fixed? Remember how it misfired last time you needed it?"

"I'm not likely to forget," she said. "I got a new one from the armory."

"Did you test-fire it?" Vic asked. "You know, even with the same make of pistol, there's little differences that can screw with you if you're not used to the new piece. You want to make sure you've got it dialed in the way you want it."

"I took it on the range," she said. "Relax."

"When's the last time you cleaned and oiled it?"

"Vic!"

"What?"

"Stop it."

"Stop what?"

"Fretting. You sound like my mom on my first day of grade school."

Vic blinked. "Your mom double-checked your guns before putting you on the bus? Jesus, where'd you go to school? I thought Brighton Beach was bad!"

"Don't worry about him," Piekarski said to Erin. "He gets like this when he's nervous."

"Who says I'm nervous?" Vic snapped. "I used to kick down doors with ESU every damn day. I just don't want anything to go wrong."

"Nothing's going to go wrong," Webb said.

The others all stared at their commanding officer in horrified disbelief. It was the worst of all possible jinxes.

"Please tell me he did not just say that," Vic muttered. Piekarski crossed herself.

"I'll handle the O'Malley arrest in person," Webb said, ignoring their reaction. "O'Reilly, you'll be with me. Neshenko will be in charge of taking Finnegan. Lieutenant Lewis and his team will tackle Pritchard. He's probably the most dangerous individual, so we want our top ESU guys on him. But watch out for Finnegan, Neshenko. He's unpredictable."

"By which you mean he's bat-shit crazy," Vic said. "I know. I saw him eat a guy's face."

"Those are the three absolutely essential targets," Webb went on. "With luck, we'll catch all the others, too. With the exception of a very few people, nobody knows the full extent of the operation. The other Patrol and ESU elements all think they're serving specific, individual warrants with no connection to anything bigger. That should eliminate any chance of O'Malley thinking he's under coordinated attack until it's too late. We've got a good plan and good people carrying it out. Everything's going to be fine. In the morning we can read all about it in the *Times*."

"I don't read the *Times*," Vic said. "Except sometimes the Sports section."

"Having seen your reports, I can believe it," Webb said. "I'm surprised you can read anything."

"I've got a college degree!" Vic protested. "Just because I went to community college instead of some fancy Ivy League bullshit school doesn't mean you gotta shit all over my education."

"I'd love to hear where you think I went to school," Webb said. "Do I look like a Harvard man?"

"Where *did* you go, sir?" Erin asked.

"UCLA," Webb said. "I majored in psych. If I'd known where I was going to end up, I would've done a concentration in abnormal psychology."

"Yeah, that would've been helpful cracking perps in interrogation," Erin said.

"Perps?" Webb echoed. "I'm talking about handling the nutcases in this squad."

Vic had picked the wrong moment to take a sip of Mountain Dew. His snort of laughter sprayed it clear across his desk. He spluttered a curse and started wiping down his pistol.

* * *

It ought to snow on Christmas; white, soft, magical flakes. But New York had experienced one of the worst blizzards in its history earlier that month and they'd expended their allotment of enchantment. What they were getting now was what the weather guys called "wintry mix," a nasty slurry of cold rain and sleet that left puddles of slush and sheets of black ice everywhere.

Erin drove Webb toward O'Malley's Tribeca apartment, going carefully. They were early; it was about one in the morning. She was allowing a lot of extra driving time. Her Charger had good tires, but it would be far too easy to spin out into another late-night motorist. She squinted through her rain-spattered windshield, trying to see through the glare from the streetlights. The wipers were going, but the little droplets kept freezing on contact with the glass and couldn't be wiped away.

"Is all this shit going to cause problems with our timetable?" she asked.

"It shouldn't," Webb said. "If anything, it'll make it harder for the bad guys if they try to make a run for it."

"I guess so," Erin said. "They'd probably get fifty yards and wrap themselves around a lamppost."

"You think O'Malley's going to run?" Webb asked.

She'd been thinking about that. "No," she said. "He's an old gangster. The young ones try to run or fight. He'll try to beat us in court."

"He doesn't have a chance," Webb said. "The case is airtight. DA Markham is practically drooling over it."

"Evan doesn't know that," she pointed out. "He doesn't know we have everything."

She was referring not only to Corky and Carlyle having switched sides, but also to Evan's ledger. The meticulous accounting of his criminal empire had been well hidden. It had taken months for her to discover he'd been using the brain of his ward Maggie Callahan as a data repository. Maggie's mind didn't work like a normal human's; she was the only person Erin had ever met who possessed a truly photographic memory. Corky had been the one to convince Maggie to write down an emergency backup of her mental files—a backup that was now in the possession of the New York District Attorney's office.

"He also thinks he has leverage on you," Webb said.

"Yeah," she said, smiling grimly. "I'm kind of looking forward to when he tries to drag me down with him. It's like when a guy tries to shoot you and the gun clicks empty."

"I had a man shoot at me with blanks once," Webb said. "It wasn't much of a relief when I found out afterward."

"Who's our backup?" she asked.

"Half a dozen ESU," Webb said. "We'll have Patrol units on perimeter duty. We're ready to come heavy, but the plan is to just knock politely and show him our warrant. If you're right, he'll come quietly. No muss, no fuss."

"And we can't tip our hand," she said.

"We're setting up down the block," Webb said. "We've prepared a cover story of a high-risk warrant nearby, in case O'Malley has people monitoring the airwaves and ESU assignments."

"I guess the planners thought of everything," she said.

"That's why this took so long to set up," Webb said dryly. "It's been hard on you. I honestly don't know how you manage without cigarettes."

"There's always whiskey," she said. "What's your brand, sir?"

"Jim Beam. Johnnie Walker for special occasions."

Erin made a face. "That crap? Tell me you at least spring for the Blue Label."

"Red," Webb said. "I need to pay alimony and child support on a Lieutenant's salary, remember? I can't afford the good stuff."

"My brother Mike said I was crazy to become a cop," she said. "He told me the private sector's where the money is. He was right, dammit. Crime may not pay, but neither does law enforcement."

"Not if you're doing it right," Webb agreed. "Tell you what, after this is all over, you can have your boyfriend get me a drink on the house. Top-shelf whiskey."

"What makes you think he'd do that?" Erin asked, grinning.

"It's the least he can do," Webb replied. "We're keeping him out of jail, aren't we? Not to mention protecting him from a large number of unpleasant, violent people who'll want to hurt him. And speaking of unpleasant people, take the next left and pull into that parking garage. The rest of the team should be showing up soon, if they're not already here."

Erin unloaded Rolf and walked him around the garage for a couple of minutes. The K-9, unlike Vic, was thoroughly housebroken, and parking garages were an odd sort of no-man's-land, halfway between indoors and outdoors. But Erin said it was okay, so he cocked a leg on a support column. Then he trotted up to the next level with her, where they found a group of ESU officers standing around a black SUV. Their commander was talking with Webb.

"Hey, O'Reilly," one of the officers said, raising a gloved hand in greeting.

"Five Cent!" she said, recognizing Officer Nichols, one of Vic's old ESU buddies. "Merry Christmas."

"Now I have a machine-gun," Nichols quoted, hefting his assault rifle. "Ho, ho, ho. Campbell says hi, and he's sorry he can't be here."

"How's he doing?" she asked. Officer Campbell had been badly injured in a botched assassination attempt on a judge earlier that autumn.

"Pretty well," Nichols said. "He had to get a bunch of skin grafts on account of the burns, but the docs say he's doing better than expected. He might even get cleared for duty sometime next year."

"That's great news!" she exclaimed.

"Yeah," Nichols said. "He says to tell you if you want to set one or two of these bastards on fire for him, it wouldn't be the worst idea."

"Yes, it would," Webb said. "There'll be no lighting perps on fire. That's an order."

"Goddamn bosses, always spoiling our fun," Nichols said, pretending to scowl.

"Let's move this inside," the ESU Lieutenant said. "We've got a place lined up next door with good visual lines on the target building."

Erin found herself in an empty corporate office, apparently part of an architectural firm. The Lieutenant laid out a set of blueprints on a drafting table.

"O'Reilly, I understand you've been inside," he said. "Are these plans accurate?"

Erin spent the next fifteen minutes going over the floor plan of Evan's penthouse, describing the layout from memory. She noted the positions where guards had been on her prior visits, and what sorts of weapons they'd been carrying. The ESU guys listened attentively, asking a few questions but mostly just absorbing the information.

"Shouldn't be too bad," the ESU Lieutenant said. "The elevator's the only really dicey spot."

"Ready-made kill-box," Erin said, giving Ian's favorite description of an elevator car.

"But assuming this guy's not ready to go to war with the NYPD, he won't hit us in the elevator," the Lieutenant said. "All the same, we'll stop two floors down from the penthouse. We'll hold the elevators there and take the stairs the rest of the way. Full tactical gear. Nobody take any chances. I'm damned if I'll be delivering death notices on Christmas."

"Too late for that, boss," one of the ESU guys said. "Midnight was an hour and a half ago. Christmas is over."

"You know what I mean, Booth," the Lieutenant growled. "I don't want any surprises, I don't want any accidents, and I don't want any friendly casualties. You get me?"

"Yes, sir," came the chorus of replies.

"Lieutenant Webb and Detective O'Reilly will be coming in with us," he went on. "Because this is some sort of big, fancy Major Crimes case. And we'll have O'Reilly's K-9, which might be useful. Any questions?"

"Can I say 'yippie-ki-yay' when we bust the bad guys?" Nichols asked, still in a *Die Hard* frame of mind.

"Only if you're barefoot," the Lieutenant replied. "Okay, we're greenlit at 0400. We'll move into the lobby at 0355, which means I want boots on the street at 0350. You've got till then to nap or jerk off or whatever the hell you do when you're not earning your paychecks."

The tinny, recorded strains of "Jingle Bells" sounded from Webb's direction. He patted his trench coat and fished out his phone. "Sorry," he said, bringing it to his ear. "Webb. Talk to me."

There was a short pause while he listened to the voice on the other end.

"I don't see why you're calling me, sir," he said. "That doesn't sound like a Major Crimes situation. And besides, you know what we're doing right now."

There was another pause. Erin watched her commanding officer and waited, fighting an irrational, crawling dread seeping up from her stomach. Rolf, at her side, nosed her hand. She absentmindedly rubbed his ears.

"I see," Webb said. "Yes, I'll send O'Reilly right away. I'd better stay here. Yes, Neshenko should be available, too. Yes, sir, I'm aware of the time constraints. I'll keep you posted."

He hung up and turned to Erin. "We've got a problem," he said.

"I was afraid of that," she said. Her throat was suddenly very dry. "What's up?"

"That was Captain Holliday," he said. "We have a possible home invasion. Patrol units responded to a report of shots fired in an apartment. One casualty, multiple GSW. I don't know if he's alive or not."

"I'm with you, sir," Erin said, mystified. "That sounds like a job for our Homicide boys. Or Robbery, if the victim's not dead. And we really don't have time to screw around. Not tonight. Why is this our problem?"

Webb sighed. "It's James Corcoran," he said. "Somebody broke into his place and shot him."

Chapter 4

Erin threw caution out the window. She drove way too fast for the conditions, the Charger fishtailing through the slush at every corner. She used lights, siren, the whole deal. Webb wouldn't wait on her. The clock on her dashboard read 2:08. If she hadn't gotten back by four, the operation would proceed in her absence. The genie was out of the bottle. Too many people knew too much. Given even a few hours, Evan might put the puzzle together. She couldn't take that chance.

She compounded her bad driving by using her phone. Her first call was to Carlyle.

"I rather thought we were observing radio silence, darling," he said mildly.

"Never mind that," she snapped. "Are you safe?"

"I'm sitting on my couch with a glass of Glen D and a good book," he said, a hint of confusion cracking his façade. "I can't imagine being safer. What's the matter?"

"Someone just tried to clip Corky," she said. "I'm on my way to his place now."

"What's his condition?" Carlyle asked, immediately becoming all business.

"I don't know. And I don't know what's going on. This could be internal, or it could be an attack from some other gang. Either way—"

"I'm in some danger, aye," he said calmly. "No fear, Ian's downstairs with Ken Mason and enough firepower to storm Belfast. I've a stout steel door between the night and myself. Don't worry about me."

"Don't let anybody up there," she said. "Not until the cavalry comes."

"Understood. Take care, darling. You're in a sight more peril than I at this moment, I'm thinking."

"Copy that. I have to go."

"Of course. God be with you. And with us all. Let me know how Corky is, when you can."

She hung up on Carlyle and dialed Vic one-handed, keeping an eye on the road. Someone honked at her, really leaning on the horn. She didn't know why and didn't care.

"Erin," Vic said. "What the hell is going on?"

"No idea," she said. "You heard from Webb?"

"Just got off the phone with him. I'm on my way. Jesus, this throws everything up in the air."

"No it doesn't. We proceed as planned."

"You think so? Erin, there's a damn war going on tonight and we're gonna be right in the middle of it!"

"You don't know that," she said. "We don't know anything yet. Let's see what we have on site before we jump to conclusions. You have the address?"

"Sure. Do you know if the cocky little ginger bastard bought it or not?"

"He's on our side, Vic," she said angrily.

"He's on his own side," Vic retorted. "Always has been, always will be. Forget about it. The only thing we need to worry about is what this does to us."

"And you say he's the selfish one," she said and hung up before he could reply.

She spent the rest of the drive listening to the police-band radio and trying to figure out what was going on. According to the emergency chatter, James Corcoran had been taken by ambulance to Bellevue Hospital. His condition was critical. Erin was still having trouble believing it. She knew a single bullet was enough to punch anybody's ticket, but Corky had an aura of carefree invulnerability about him. He was quick, clever, and the luckiest son of a bitch she'd ever known.

He was also reckless, thrill-seeking, and had spent better than two decades in one of the most dangerous jobs in the world. Nobody's luck lasted forever. On reflection, it was surprising nobody had managed to kill him before now.

Corky kept two apartments in Manhattan. One was comfortable, cozy, and the place he actually lived. The other was glitzy and glamorous, the pad where he took women he wanted to impress and undress. Given the conversation she'd had with him earlier that night, Erin wasn't surprised Webb had pointed her to Corky's love nest.

The ambulance was long gone by the time she arrived, but a pair of NYPD blue-and-whites were idling out front, their flashers lighting the night. A handful of civilians were rubbernecking nearby, but not many. The hour was too late, and the weather too unpleasant, for all but the most hardcore curiosity hounds. As Erin parked her Charger behind one of the squad cars, she saw Vic's Taurus roll up, lights ablaze. Before she'd finished unloading Rolf, Vic popped out of his car and hustled toward her. For all his apparent unconcern about Corky, he'd really hauled ass to get there as fast as he had.

They showed their shields to the Patrolman in the lobby, who pointed them to the top floor. Erin didn't need the directions; she'd been here before. But she didn't say so.

On the ride up, Vic drew his Sig and press-checked it, ensuring a round was chambered.

"Geez, Vic," Erin said. "We're not the first cops on scene. It'll be secured."

"Says you," Vic said grimly. "Goddamn it, this is all because of Webb's bullshit about everything going smooth. I've already had one more surprise than I want tonight. Anything else happens, I'm gonna be ready."

Erin fought down a surge of paranoia and left her own Glock in its holster. Jittery nerves were plenty dangerous without adding loaded guns to the mix. She still flinched when the elevator bell dinged and the doors slid open, but all she saw was another uniformed officer waiting for them.

"Follow me, Detectives," he said, leading the way to Corky's door.

Rolf, padding at Erin's side, lowered his head and snuffled at a dark stain on the carpet.

"That looks like blood," Vic said.

"Yeah," Erin said, kneeling and examining the dark red droplets. "Fresh, too. It's still wet."

"Just don't taste it," Vic said.

"Why would I do that?"

He shrugged. "Cops on TV do it sometimes."

"Blood? Seriously?"

"I might be getting them confused with vampires."

"Vampires," Erin muttered, rolling her eyes and continuing to the door. It stood open. She took a deep breath and stepped through the doorway, having no real idea what she'd find.

Rolf's nostrils flared. Erin caught the scent too; a floral, soapy odor, with the coppery stink of blood adding an edge to the smell. The air was humid and warm. The lights were dim. Corky had adjustable bulbs so he could set the mood just right.

"Where'd it happen?" Vic asked.

"Kitchen," the uniform said, cocking a thumb. "Through there."

The kitchen was more brightly lit. Its walls were white, the appliances showing the sheen of well-kept stainless steel. Everything was clean and tidy. Well, almost everything.

"Wow," Vic said. "That's a lot of blood."

Erin stared. "No kidding," she said. "See the spatter on the wall?"

"At least two exit wounds," he said. "So the shooter had to be standing about where we are."

They turned to consider the wall next to the door. "Whoa," Erin said. A steak knife was embedded in the drywall at about the height of her head. A few inches to one side, another bloodstain stood out against the white plaster.

"Looks like our boy got a couple hits in," Vic said. "Or one, at least. What the hell was he doing, throwing silverware?"

"Corky doesn't carry a gun," Erin said distractedly. She was studying the pattern of bloodstains. "See that hole in the wall, right in the middle of that stain?"

"Too narrow for a bullet," Vic said. "I'd say that was a blade. Jesus, do you have any idea how hard you've got to throw a knife to put it straight through a guy? It couldn't have gone into the chest, not unless he was flinging a friggin' machete. The blade wouldn't be long enough and he'd have to have muscles like the Hulk to get enough force behind it."

"I'm thinking hand or arm," Erin guessed. "Then our shooter ripped the knife free. See that arc of blood? He flung it away, so it would've landed right about…"

"There," Vic said, pointing to the corner of the kitchen. A bloody knife lay on the tile, an exact twin of the one stuck in the wall.

"The blades came from the knife block," Erin said, nodding in the direction of the counter. Sure enough, two steak knives were missing.

A man cleared his throat behind them. Erin turned to see a Patrol sergeant.

"Help you with anything, Detectives?" he asked. He lowered his voice and went on, "Sergeant Carton. I'm in charge of the detail that was setting up on this mope."

"You were watching the apartment?" Erin asked. "Did you see anybody suspicious go in or come out?"

"We weren't really paying attention to that," Carton said. "My orders were to go in and scoop this boy up at four o'clock sharp. We didn't think anything was gonna happen before then. I was on a coffee break. Officer Pollard told me something was hinky."

"Hinky how?" Erin asked.

"The lights were blinking," Carton said. "On and off, in a pattern. Three long, three short, three long."

"SOS," Vic said. "Morse code."

"I thought that was weird," Carton said. "But our orders were, we don't go in until four. So we talked it over a couple minutes."

Erin gritted her teeth and bit back some angry words. While they'd been discussing what to do, Corky had been bleeding out on his kitchen floor.

"Anyways, I figured we better do something," Carton said. "So Pollard and me came in. The door wasn't locked. We found our guy on the floor next to the light switch, passed out. I called a bus, and they showed up quick, but he'd lost a hell of a lot of blood."

"Where was he hit?" Erin asked. "How bad?"

"Arm and chest," Carton said. "Arm's busted, but that's small potatoes. The chest is the bad one. Medics said he had a collapsed lung."

"And they took him to Bellevue?"

"That's what I heard. He was still breathing when they got him in the bus, more or less. They were using a bag on him. He'll have gone straight into surgery."

Vic nodded. "Your brother working tonight?" he asked Erin.

"Yeah," she said. "He would've gotten back from my parents in time for the graveyard shift."

"Then Corcoran's got as good a chance as anybody," Vic said. "Your brother's one hell of a doc."

"I know," Erin said, giving him a grateful look. Vic might not like Corky, but he understood the Irishman was important to Erin.

"Hey," Carton said. "I was just wondering, if we were picking this guy up on a warrant, like I was told, how come he was using the lights as a signal?"

"What do you mean?" Erin asked.

"He'd have to know somebody was watching," Carton said. "Otherwise, what's the point? And if he knew we were watching him, then what's going on here?"

"Forget about it," Vic said. "It'll all make sense sooner or later. In the meantime, we just do our jobs and don't ask too many questions."

"Copy that," Carton said doubtfully.

"Okay," Erin said. "We've got blood that probably belongs to the shooter. He's wounded, so if we're lucky he may already be at a hospital himself. We can match the blood. This should be pretty simple—"

She paused. A faint ringtone was audible.

"Where's that coming from?" Vic asked.

Carton pointed down the hallway. "Bathroom?" he guessed.

"I'm on it," Vic said. He hurried out of the room.

Erin was trying to think. Once they had a suspect, they'd be able to put him at the scene easily enough. But they were on a really tight clock. If the attack on Corky had anything to do with the upcoming bust, the whole operation might be in jeopardy. She had to solve this within the next couple of hours, or at least eliminate some of the possibilities.

She heard Vic's voice emanating from the bathroom. "Who is this?" he asked. After a moment, he asked it again.

There was a short pause. Then Vic said, "Lady, this is the NYPD. Identify yourself. What was that? Just a second."

Vic came back into the hallway, holding a cell phone. He had a funny look on his face. "It's some woman," he said to Erin. "Says she'll only talk to you."

Mystified, Erin took the phone out of Vic's hand. "This is Detective O'Reilly," she said.

"Detective," a female voice said. "It's me."

That wasn't much help. "Ma'am, I don't have time to screw around," Erin said. "Tell me your name."

"I shouldn't say it. But you know me."

Erin was tense and distracted. She wasn't thinking clearly, or she would've figured it out before that. *Teresa*, she thought. *Teresa Tommasino. God damn it, Corky, what did you do? Did you compromise the case for this girl? What did you tell her?*

"Oh," Erin said aloud. "I see."

An awkward silence stretched between New York and Mexico, or wherever the hell Teresa was calling from.

"You shouldn't be calling here," Erin said, speaking carefully. "You shouldn't even have this phone number. Where are... no, never mind. I don't need to know. Why are you calling? Are you in trouble?"

"What's happened to James?" Teresa demanded. An edge of raw panic in her voice was obvious to Erin, even over a so-so phone connection.

What should she tell her? Unable to think of anything suitable but innocuous, she decided on the truth.

"James Corcoran was shot earlier this evening."

"Is... is he...?" Teresa stammered.

Erin fell back on her training and experience. This wasn't the first time she'd had to inform an acquaintance of a loved one's misfortune. "He's in critical condition at Bellevue," she said briskly. "He's in surgery right now."

"How badly is he hurt?" Teresa asked.

"He's critical," she said again. "It'll be touch and go. We've got a good doc working on him."

"Who shot him?"

"Wiseguys, obviously," Erin said. "They hit him at home, and we think he tagged one of them pretty good. Now, ma'am, you really should get off the line here. Unless there's any information you can give me about what happened?"

"Please," Teresa said, with a hitch in her voice. In that hitch Erin recognized all the fear she had for her own man in the life he'd chosen.

"Yeah?" Erin asked.

"Is... is he going to be okay?"

Teresa's desperate, loving hope and fear tore at Erin's heart. She closed her eyes and took a steadying breath. Corky really did love her, and the feeling was obviously mutual.

"Oh God," Erin said. "He wasn't kidding about you, was he. You and he... Jesus. What a mess. Okay, look. I know the surgeon. He's my brother, as a matter of fact. There's no one I'd rather have holding the knife if someone I care about goes on the table. Corky caught two slugs; one in the arm, one in the chest. He's got a collapsed lung, a broken arm, and he'd lost a lot of blood by the time the paramedics got to him. He's damn lucky to be alive. But he made it to the hospital, so I'd say his chances are better than even."

"Thank you, Detective," Teresa whispered.

"Now, you know it's dangerous for you to have any contact with anyone here," Erin said, lowering her voice. "Is this a number you can be reached at?"

"Yes."

"I'll call you in a day or two, let you know how he's doing. Don't call again. Don't do anything. Just hang tight in the meantime, okay?"

"Okay."

"Now we've got to go run down the son of a bitch who did this. I need to go. Talk to you later."

Erin hung up.

"What was that all about?" Vic asked.

She shook her head.

"One of Corky's side pieces?" he asked.

"Something like that," she said.

"Well that's just great," Vic said. "Friggin' wonderful. Exactly what we need right now. Is this gonna be a problem?"

"I don't think so," she said. She turned her attention to the uniformed officers. "Sergeant?"

"Yeah?" Carton replied.

"Describe what you found when you got here."

"Like I said, Corcoran was lying on the floor by the light switch, white as a sheet. He wasn't conscious."

"What was he wearing?" she asked.

"Bathrobe," Carton said. "Silk, I think. Looked expensive. All covered with blood. No shoes, no socks. Nothing on underneath. We're talking full commando."

"The bathtub's full," Vic reported. "More like overflowing. Bathroom floor was pretty wet. Looks like our boy was having himself a bubble bath. Got a couple candles lit in there, too. Nice romantic evening. Are we sure our shooter's a guy? Because it sure looks like he was entertaining a chick. Maybe we oughta see about jealous husbands in the area."

"That's not what happened here," Erin said.

"You sure?" Vic asked. "Because from what I remember, he's got no problem screwing married ladies."

She shot him a look with daggers in it. He hadn't mentioned her sister-in-law's name, but he was obviously thinking about her. Michelle O'Reilly, an otherwise sensible woman, had flirted with having an affair with Corky. It had ended about as badly as it could have, with a bunch of people dead or hospitalized, including Erin herself.

Her glare was having no effect on Vic, so she just snorted and turned her attention back to the kitchen. A bottle of red wine stood on the counter next to a single wineglass. The label on the bottle read Castello Vicchiomaggio, which meant nothing to Erin. The bottle hadn't been opened. A drawer was a few inches ajar. It looked to contain miscellaneous kitchen implements, including bottle openers and corkscrews.

"One glass," Erin said. "Not two. He wasn't expecting company."

"I found his phone next to the sink," Vic said. "In the bathroom. I guess that's why he didn't call 911."

"He must have two phones, then," Carton said.

"At least two," Erin said. "But why do you say that?"

Carton pointed. On the floor, almost hidden under the refrigerator, lay a Smartphone.

Erin pounced on it, pausing just long enough to snap a picture of it and pull on a pair of disposable gloves. Then she drew it out into the light.

"It's broken," she said. The screen was a spider-web of cracks. It still lit up, but it was demanding a security code or a fingerprint.

"Locked out?" Vic asked.

"Yeah," she said.

"We can take it to the hospital and run Corcoran's finger over it," he suggested.

"If it's his phone," Erin said.

"You think it's the shooter's?"

"Yeah," she said. "Think about it. Corky's drawing a bath. He leaves the water running and comes out here to get himself some wine."

"Some *good* wine," Sergeant Carton interjected. "That's a damn fine chianti. Runs a couple hundred bucks a bottle."

"You know wine?" Erin asked, startled. She would've pegged him as a beer or whiskey man.

"The wife," Carton said with a sheepish shrug. "She does these wine tastings. We took a trip out to California a couple years back, Napa Valley. It's not really my thing, but I picked up some trivia hanging around her."

"Whatever," Vic said. "So our boy starts pouring himself some two-hundred-dollar wine, because he's a schmuck with expensive tastes. But he never pops the cork, because the shooter tries to pop him. How'd the perp get in, you think?"

"The door wasn't locked, like I said," Carton said. "He could've just walked in."

"The door wasn't locked because he left that way after nailing Corcoran," Vic said. "We saw the blood in the hallway. Sheesh. They're never giving you a gold shield, buddy."

"Take it easy, Vic," Erin said. "Maybe our shooter had a spare key. Maybe Corky was careless and left his door unlocked. Maybe the perp's good with a lockpick. Whatever. He gets the drop on Corky and comes into the kitchen with a gun. Corky's caught off guard."

"Not just with his pants down," Vic said. "No pants at all. Bad idea bringing nothing but your dick to a gunfight."

"It'd be worse leaving it at home," Carton said, which drew a snicker from Vic.

"They have a conversation," Erin said thoughtfully. "It goes sideways and the gun comes out. Corky doesn't have a weapon on him, but he's standing right next to the knife block. He grabs a couple of steak knives and throws them. One misses, one connects and pins the perp to the wall. The shooter puts two in Corky, yanks out the knife, and makes a run for it."

"I dunno," Vic said. "Why do you think they talked? How do you know our shooter didn't just start blasting?"

"The phone," she said. "He must've had it in his hand. Otherwise it wouldn't have flown across the room like that."

"And why didn't he finish Corcoran off?" Vic asked. "If I'm gonna kill a guy, I'm gonna make damn sure he stays down. Anybody worth shooting twice is worth emptying the clip into."

"He was hurt," Erin said. "We don't know how seriously, but it was bad enough that he left a blood trail in the hallway. Try this on for size. They have a confrontation, it escalates. Corky throws a knife. It doesn't hit the other guy, but either it knocks the phone out of his hand or the shooter drops it while he dodges. Then the shooter starts firing as Corky tosses another knife into him. I think that knife must've disabled his gun hand, but not before Corky got hit."

"Our bad boy drops his gun," Vic said, nodding. "He gets his arm free with his other hand, but it messes up his good hand. Maybe he's no good with his off-hand, or maybe he's just in a shitload of pain. Getting stabbed will do that to you. Either way, he figures Corcoran's toast and he'd better get out of there, so he beats feet. Yeah, I can see that. I guess he forgets about the phone."

"Or he can't see where it fell right away," Erin said. "Anyway, we know Corky stayed up long enough to get to the light switch to send up his SOS. I think the shooter didn't want to stick around and get turned into a pincushion. Corky's dangerous with a blade, even wounded."

"Knife versus gun, the gun usually wins," Vic observed.

"And it did," she replied. "The shooter left under his own power. But I think it was a near thing. I'm going to set Rolf on his trail."

"The shooting was at least half an hour ago," Carton said. "Your boy's long gone by now."

"Maybe," Erin said. "But you know the best way to find someone, Sergeant Carton?"

"What's that, Detective?"

"You start by looking," she said. She turned to her K-9 and pointed to the blood on the kitchen wall. "Rolf? *Such!*"

Chapter 5

If a police K-9 wanted to track you, he'd probably succeed. Sweat, saliva, dirt, skin cells; people were constantly shedding little bits of themselves onto their environment. But blood was easier than most substances. Even a short-nosed human could follow the scent of fresh blood.

Not that humans could tell the difference between one another on the basis of their blood. They were, after all, only human. But that was why they had dogs like Rolf.

Without conscious thought or effort, the Shepherd analyzed the bloodstain on the kitchen wall. He filed it away in the large part of his brain reserved for odors. If he ever smelled this human again, he'd recognize it as unique among the billions of people on the planet. Rolf drew the scent deep into his nostrils. Then he started moving.

He went at a brisk trot, keeping to a speed his partner could match. They'd trained for endless hours together, practicing until they could practically read one another's thoughts. It might look like magic to an observer, but it was science, biology, breeding, and years of experience.

Erin followed Rolf straight out of the apartment and down the hall. She wouldn't have needed the dog for this part of the pursuit. Their target had been bleeding significantly. The trail of dark droplets was ragged but sustained. They traced it past the elevators to the stairwell, where a bloody smear marred the doorknob.

Vic caught up with them as Erin carefully opened the door with her leash hand, Glock ready in the other. "Stairs?" he said in surprise. "We're on the twelfth friggin' floor and he's hurt! Why didn't he take the elevator?"

"I'm just following the blood," Erin said. "Don't ask me what our guy's thinking."

"I left the unis securing the scene for CSU," he said. "I didn't see any shell casings in the kitchen, so either our boy collected his brass or he was using a revolver."

"I'm guessing revolver," she replied as they reached the eleventh-floor landing. "If he'd been willing to take the time to retrieve his shells, he would've grabbed his phone while he was at it."

"That's what I think, too," he said. "I bet he left in one big hurry. Corcoran must've put the fear of God into him. Fighting a shooter to a draw with goddamn kitchen knives. I'm no fan of the guy, but I gotta say, I'm impressed."

"Corky's fast," Erin said as they passed the tenth floor. "Really, really fast. Remember the fight in the sugar factory?"

"You're right," he said. "I'd forgotten about that. He took on a guy who was rocking a friggin' MP5. And he won! Even if I hadn't been there, he would've taken him out. Too bad he's an asshole gangster."

"Nobody's perfect," Erin said. "Rolf! *Bleib!*"

Rolf skidded to a stop, one paw raised, looking quizzically at his partner. They hadn't caught up with their target yet. But humans had their reasons, and he was a good boy, so he waited for the chase to continue.

Erin pointed. A first-aid box hung open on the wall, next to a fire extinguisher. Ripped-open packaging littered the floor, sticking to a sizable pool of half-dried blood.

"That's why he went this way," she said. "He knew there'd be an aid kit somewhere and he didn't want to be bleeding when he hit the street."

"We won't have a blood trail anymore," Vic said. "Is that gonna be a problem?"

"Not for Rolf," Erin said proudly. "*Such*, kiddo!"

With that, Rolf was off once more. His prey wasn't dripping blood now, but that didn't mean a thing to him. Even if the target hadn't still had a fresh wound, Rolf knew the human's other odors by now. He headed downstairs once more.

"Here's what's bugging me," Vic said as they jogged down the concrete steps. "Corcoran brought knives to a gunfight. Okay, I get it. He's good with a blade and he's a cocky bastard. But who brings a phone when the blades and bullets are flying? What was the shooter gonna do, take a selfie with him?"

"Beats me," Erin said. "I'd love to get a look at that call history."

"You'll have to wait on the CSU guys for that," Vic said. "You do know this is a waste of time, right? Even that punk Carton said so. A foot chase in Manhattan, going after a guy with a half-hour lead? He's long gone."

"Maybe," she said again. They were halfway to the ground by now and Rolf was still eagerly leading the way.

"How much do we care?" Vic asked.

That made Erin pause for a moment, which brought Rolf up short when he hit the end of his leash. The dog gave her a reproachful look.

"What do you mean?" she demanded. "This is attempted murder! If Corky dies at the hospital, it's straight-up Murder One!"

"I know that," Vic said with exaggerated patience. "I've got a gold shield too, remember? But I also know we're in the middle of a major organized-crime takedown. Corcoran's sure to have seen the guy's face. Why don't we let this sit until he comes out of surgery? Hell, he probably knows the guy! We grab him in a day or a week or whatever. Bam! Easiest collar we'll have this month!"

"Yeah," Erin said slowly. "He probably does know him. Rolf, *bleib.*"

The K-9 sank back on his haunches and stared at her, waiting for his partner to come to her senses. They had a clean, fresh trail laid out in front of them. A bad guy was waiting at the end, somebody he might get to bite. Even if he didn't, he'd still get his rubber Kong ball, and that made everything worth it. There were no Kong balls in this stairwell. Why were they standing around?

Erin holstered her gun and pulled out her phone. She brought up Piekarski's number and pressed it. Sometimes stairwells had too much concrete and the signal got scrambled, but this call went through fine. Piekarski picked up before the third ring.

"Major Crimes," she said.

"It's me, Zofia," Erin said. "Are we missing anybody?"

"How do you mean?" Piekarski asked.

"O'Malleys," Erin said. "Any bosses, or any muscle guys? Do we have eyes on all of them?"

"Last I heard."

"That's not good enough," Erin said. "I need confirmation. Where are Gordon Pritchard and his goons? Don't assume anything. I need you to actually talk to the boots on the ground."

"That's going to take a little while," Piekarski said. "I hope you're not in a hurry."

"About like usual," Erin said grimly. "Go as fast as you can."

"Copy that," Piekarski said. "Will do."

"You think it's an O'Malley guy?" Vic asked as Erin put her phone back in her hip pocket.

"I hope not," Erin said. "Because if it is, we might be blown."

"Then we gotta move *now*," Vic said. "Pull the trigger. Jump on the rest of the O'Malleys. Drag them all downtown."

Erin shook her head. "We can't," she said. "The op's too compartmentalized. The whole point was that almost nobody could know what we were doing until it was all over. There's no centralized communications network. Sure, we can get the word out to everyone, but it'll take so much time it won't matter. Evan can probably talk to his people faster than we can talk to ours."

"Not if we shut him up," Vic said. He grabbed his own phone.

Erin tried not to jump up and down with impatience. They were wasting time, time they didn't have. Vic held up a finger, which she seriously considered bending back all the way to his wrist.

"Lieutenant?" Vic said. "Neshenko here. Got O'Reilly on my elbow. Yeah, it's a goddamn mess. I'll explain later. I'm putting you on speaker now. We got a time-sensitive situation."

"No kidding," Webb said. "Talk to me."

"We need to isolate Evan O'Malley," Vic said. "I'm talking total radio silence. Landline, cell, the works."

"That's not protocol," Webb said. "It could tip O'Malley off."

"The guy's, like, a hundred years old," Vic said. "It's after two in the morning. He's asleep!"

"He's sixty-three," Webb replied. "And he's not the only person in his apartment. What's going on?"

"Will you just trust me, sir?" Vic said in exasperation.

"We've got a bad guy on the loose who might blow the whistle on the whole operation," Erin interjected. "We need to keep him from talking to Evan. We're not sure who it is, so we have to cut the wires on Evan's end."

"Understood," Webb said. "There's a risk. It means changing our plan on the fly. I'll talk to ESU and see what we can do."

The call disconnected.

"Good thought, Vic," Erin said. "Let's keep moving."

"It may not matter," he said as they continued down the stairs behind Erin's eager K-9. "Suppose you're a mobster and you think the cops are coming down hard on your gang. Would you call your boss and talk to him about it? On a New York telephone line?"

"No," she admitted. "I'd assume his phone was tapped. But they might have a code set up for situations like this, or a special set of burner cells. It's better to keep Evan under a blackout. If he notices, we'll have a problem, but he might not."

They reached the ground floor of the apartment. Rolf scratched at the door and whined quietly, tail wagging. Erin saw a faint smear of blood on the knob. She yanked the door open and the detectives spilled out into the lobby.

"We could've taken the damn elevator," Vic muttered. "It would've saved time."

Erin ignored him. Rolf was leading them out onto the street. She zipped up her jacket and hunched her shoulders, wishing for a moment she was back in a Patrol uniform. Those came with hats. Vic pulled a wool watch cap over his scalp and followed her outside.

Rolf lunged to the left along the sidewalk. Erin and Vic took half a dozen jogging steps after him. Then, as they came out from under the awning that hung over the apartment's entrance, Vic's foot caught a patch of black ice. His feet went up, his head came down, and he slammed into the concrete with an impact Erin could swear she felt through the sidewalk.

"Jesus, Vic!" she said, dropping to one knee beside him. "Are you okay?"

"Shit," he said in a quiet, breathless voice. He held up a hand. "I'm good. Just give me a boost."

"You sure?" she asked. "Maybe you should lie there for a sec, see if anything hurts."

"Help me up," he growled. "Or I'm dragging you down with me."

She extended her own hand, braced herself as well as she could, and helped him to his feet. The back of his jeans and jacket were soaked, but he didn't seem to be hurt.

"That does it," he said. "After I put in my twenty, I'm getting the hell out of this goddamn town. I'm going somewhere warm. Tahiti, maybe. Or Hell."

"I think one of those is more likely than the other," Erin said. "You good?"

"Just cold, wet, and pissed. Forget about it."

Chasing a half-hour-old trail down a Manhattan sidewalk in freezing rain was an exercise in discomfort and futility. Erin knew it. Vic knew it. Rolf was the only one who didn't accept the obvious truth. The Shepherd kept trotting along, tail lashing wetly, drops of icy water flicking from its tip with every wag. If the weather bothered him, he wasn't admitting it.

The K-9 angled abruptly down the steps into a subway entrance. Erin followed with a sinking heart. It was nice to be out of the rain, but this pursuit was headed for a dead end. Sure enough, Rolf came to a stop on the platform. He snuffled at the concrete for a few moments and whined unhappily.

"The shooter got on a train," Erin said.

"No shit," Vic said. "That's why we get to carry gold shields; on account of our brilliant deductions. What do we do now? Check the subway security cams?"

"It'll take too long," she said.

"We gotta get an ID on this mope," he argued. "You have a better idea?"

Erin's phone buzzed. She saw Piekarski's name on the screen and quickly put the call through.

"Talk to me," she said.

"Gordon Pritchard," Piekarski said, not wasting any time. "He was at the Teamsters' Christmas party earlier tonight. He left just after Corcoran. His detail was on him, a couple of Lewis's ESU guys, but he went into a café and didn't come out. Our guys were watching the door, but they didn't have eyes directly on him."

"Why not?" Erin asked sharply.

"Does it matter?" Piekarski retorted. "They had his car in the garage down the block. I asked them to double-check, just to make sure. One of them went in, plainclothes, and scoped the place out. Pritchard's car's still there, all right, but he's gone."

"Son of a *bitch!*" Erin said. "He's the most dangerous guy in the O'Malleys! He's the one Evan uses when he needs people killed! He must've made his surveillance."

"Looks like it," Piekarski said. "I'm sorry, Erin. Is he the guy who shot Corcoran?"

"Maybe," Erin said. "He could've dumped his tail, then headed for Corky's place. I need to know what the Snake knows and why he might've gone after Corky. You have Lewis's number?"

"Yeah." Piekarski rattled off the digits. "Do you know where Pritchard is now?"

"No," Erin said. "But I've got a good idea where he's going. Thanks, Zofia." She hung up.

"I'll call Webb," Vic said. "If Pritchard's on his way to O'Malley's, he could be there any moment now."

"And that's where we're headed," Erin said, turning away from the empty subway platform. "We don't have to follow if we know where he's going."

"*If* that's where he's going," Vic said darkly.

"Where else would he go?" Erin asked.

"I can think of a couple places," he said. "The hell away from New York, for starters. He used to hang out in Jersey, didn't he?"

"That's true," she said. "He might go back to his old stomping grounds, especially if he's hurt badly."

"And there's one other good possibility," Vic said, glancing around. They were alone on the platform. "If he knows about Corcoran, there's a good chance he knows about you and Carlyle."

"Shit," Erin said. "You're right. But he can't get at Carlyle, not tonight. He's buttoned up in our—his—apartment. That place is a fortress. Ian's downstairs, ready for trouble, and he's got one of his former Marine buddies with him. Carlyle will be fine."

"If you say so," Vic said. "You're the one who says Pritchard's this super-dangerous psycho killer."

"Damn it," Erin said. "You convinced me to worry. I'd better make sure the place is secure."

"This is no time for a booty call," Vic said. "Just drop him a line and tell him to watch out. Thompson's a vigilante asshole, but he's a competent one."

"Leave my booty out of this," Erin said. "I'd like Rolf to have a sniff around the place. He knows Pritchard's scent now."

"Have it your way," Vic said. "I'll catch a train and link up with Webb. You go to the Corner and look after your sugar daddy. But remember we're on a clock."

"If either of us finds Pritchard, we call it in," she said. "And we keep Evan in the dark as long as we can. Otherwise he and his guys will scatter and we'll never get all of them."

He nodded, his face serious. "Good luck, Erin," he said.

"You too, Vic."

Then she was running up the stairs, back into the cold, wet night. Rolf was right beside her.

Chapter 6

"Everything's quiet here, darling," Carlyle said over the phone. "I'm still sitting on my couch, sipping fine whiskey, reading Patrick Taylor while I wait for your lads to knock on my door. Have you ever read him?"

"No," Erin said, squinting through her spattered windshield. "I don't get much reading time these days."

"You ought to," he said. "The lad writes about rural Ireland, a wee village called Ballybucklebo. He's telling the tale of a country doctor, name of O'Reilly, if you can believe it. The lad spins a fine tale."

"Listen," she interrupted. "We think Snake Pritchard shot Corky."

"Really?" Carlyle's voice sharpened. "Erin, how badly hurt is the lad?"

He'd been doing a good job disguising it, but his concern came through clearly now. Corky was Carlyle's best friend, his lifelong mate all the way back to their Belfast childhood. Erin realized that until he'd learned who the likely attacker was, Carlyle had mostly managed to convince himself Corky was fine. After all, the redheaded Irishman had more scars and narrow escapes than anyone else she knew, and had taken them in stride.

"He's critical," she said. "Collapsed lung."

"Sweet Jesus," Carlyle murmured. "This bloody world we're living in. Can I get in to see him, do you think?"

"Don't worry about him right now," she said.

"Erin, the lad's closer than a brother to me. You can't tell me something like that and expect me to shrug it off."

"He's getting the best care we can give him," Erin said. "My brother saved Ian's life and I'm betting he'll save Corky's. We have to worry about you."

"I told you, I'm safe enough."

"From Pritchard? Are you sure?"

Carlyle hesitated only a moment. "Aye," he said. "Though I'll be certain to warn Ian. The Snake won't be able to simply walk in. He may be good, but he's no match for Ian in a straight fight. Not many are."

"He won't come looking for a straight fight," Erin said grimly. "Pritchard's an assassin. He'll come from behind, from the dark, from some direction you won't expect."

"That's as may be, darling. But unless you're aware of some glaring gap in my security, I'll be safest lurking here. But if you think I'd better be on the move..."

"No," she said. "That'd be more dangerous. He might already be watching the Corner."

"Pritchard's not the bogeyman," Carlyle said. "He can't be everywhere at once and he can't turn invisible. He's naught but one lad, no matter his reputation. Have you any idea where he is?"

"None. We tracked him to the subway. He left his car to shake his tail. So he's on foot, and he's injured."

"Corky marked him? I'm glad to hear it. Is it serious?"

"No way to know. I think his gun-hand is screwed up."

"His left, that'd be," Carlyle said. "He's not been much good with his right since it was burnt."

Pritchard, like Corky and Carlyle, was Belfast-born. As a teenager, he'd been involved in a demonstration against the British that turned nasty. The British Army had fired rubber bullets to disperse the crowd, who had retaliated with rocks and Molotov cocktails. As Pritchard had been in the act of flinging a petrol bomb, an unlucky bullet had shattered the glass bottle in his hand. Blazing gasoline had coated his right arm and the right side of his face, horribly scarring him.

"Then maybe he won't be able to do much," she said. "But tell your guys to keep their eyes open. I'm pretty sure he'll either go for you or he'll try to get to Evan."

"Then he knows," Carlyle sighed. He sounded suddenly very tired, almost resigned.

"He knows *something*. Maybe he just had a personal beef with Corky."

"Pritchard wouldn't dare move on Corky for a petty quarrel," Carlyle said. "He knows or suspects treachery. Nothing less would satisfy Evan."

"Webb is cutting Evan's phone lines and setting up cell jammers," she said. "We're still on schedule. An hour and a half and Evan will be in custody. He won't get away."

"And Pritchard?"

"We'll catch him," Erin said with more certainty than she felt.

"I'd best speak with Ian now," Carlyle said. "I'll see you soon, darling. And remember, Pritchard may be after you, too. One eye over your shoulder."

"Copy that."

* * *

Even gangsters needed a little time to sleep off their booze before sunrise. The Barley Corner closed at two in the morning, so the pub was dark and quiet as Erin pulled into the garage across the street at quarter to three.

She kept her head on a swivel as she parked. The garage was as secure as such a place could be. Two of Carlyle's guys were on the gate, and she knew the NYPD had the Corner under surveillance. The place had security cameras covering bottlenecks and one-way spike strips at every entrance. But she trusted her own eyes, and Rolf's nose, more than any of these.

Despite her jumpy nerves, the garage was deserted. She walked quickly but warily down to street level. A few pedestrians were in sight, hurrying to finish their late-night business, doing their best to deflect the sleet with hats and umbrellas. Not a single person set off Erin's street instincts.

But those instincts were humming like high-voltage power lines. What did Pritchard know? It had been enough for him and Corky to try their best to kill one another. She had to assume it was Teresa Tommasino, or else Corky's deal with the District Attorney. Nothing short of treachery would be enough for Pritchard to risk Evan's wrath by unilaterally dispatching one of his top lieutenants. The O'Malleys were too short of captains these days to throw them away over petty bullshit.

If he knew about Teresa, then he was on to Erin and Carlyle, too. The three of them were a package deal. It was common underworld knowledge that Erin "Junkyard" O'Reilly and "Cars" Carlyle had blown the woman apart. It was a safe assumption that if Erin had faked the hit, she'd faked everything and wasn't the dirty cop Evan thought she was.

But how far was Pritchard prepared to go without Evan's sanction? Erin wished she knew the man better. How loyal was he to Evan? The smart play, if he knew the O'Malleys were burned, was self-preservation. Maybe he was already outside the city limits and running for his life. If so, she was worrying about nothing. Once he got clear, if he did, he wouldn't come back.

Unless one day he did.

She could only plan so far ahead. The first step was to make absolutely certain the Barley Corner was secure. She crossed the street as fast as she safely could, trying to remember everything she'd learned from Ian and from the NYPD's tactical training regarding snipers and fields of fire. It was a little silly and she knew it. Pritchard was wounded. He wasn't lying in wait somewhere with a rifle and a telescopic scope. The man had no military experience. He was no sharpshooter. He was a violent thug, willing and able to kill; no less, but also no more.

"*Such*," she murmured to Rolf, who obediently started snuffling. An enormous number of people had walked the sidewalk in front of the Barley Corner. No particular scent caught his notice. He glanced up at her and wagged his tail, receiving an ear rub for his troubles.

Erin made a snap decision and went to the front door instead of the back. The alley felt dark and threatening. She felt for her keys, keeping her eyes up and alert. One of the best times to ambush a woman was when she was fishing out her keys, distracted and stationary.

She got the door open a few inches and slipped through, Rolf snaking his way in a half-step behind. The door swung shut and she flipped the deadbolt with a sigh of relief. The main room of the pub glowed faintly in an eerie red-tinted twilight, illuminated only by the EXIT sign over the door. Chairs and stools were upended atop tables, a naked forest of spindly wooden legs. Rolf sniffed the air and barked sharply, shattering the silence.

The man materialized out of the shadows, less than two yards away. He moved in perfect silence, his dark jacket and slacks blending with the near-blackness. If not for the K-9's keen nose, Erin would have walked right past him.

Her heart tried to jump straight up her throat and out over her tongue. She spun toward him, hand falling to the grip of her Glock, mouth opening to give Rolf his "bite" command, knowing it was already too late.

"Sorry, ma'am," the shadowy figure said. "Didn't mean to startle you."

Adrenaline spiking her system, Erin let out the panicky breath she'd sucked in. "God damn it, Ian," she said. "Don't do that!"

"Sorry, ma'am," Ian Thompson said again.

"And don't call me 'ma'am.'"

"No excuse," he said. "Mr. Carlyle said you'd be coming, but to keep a low profile."

"Who else is here?" she asked.

"Mason's in the office, watching the cameras. Mr. Carlyle's upstairs. Mr. Sullivan and Ms. Tierney left together, about ten minutes ago."

"Sullivan?" Erin repeated. "Who's that?"

"The bartender," Ian said. "Thought you knew him."

"You mean Danny?"

"Affirmative."

Erin realized she'd never actually caught Danny's last name. He'd always been simply "Danny." It was a reminder how little she really knew about many of these men. Danny wasn't an O'Malley, didn't even have a criminal record. He was just the bartender.

"Nobody else?" she asked.

"Only you and Rolf."

"Are you staying all night?"

"Usually don't, but Mr. Carlyle said there might be trouble. Won't be a problem."

She smiled at him. Her heart was starting to slow down again after the jolt it had taken. "Thanks, Ian. I feel a lot better just knowing you're here."

Ian nodded and melted back into the shadows. It was uncanny. She was looking right at him, but she could hardly make out his silhouette. He had a stillness that made her eye slide past him. She tried to imagine what he'd been like as a Marine Scout Sniper, out in the field. He must have been a terrifying enemy.

Her fingers did their familiar dance over the keypad next to Carlyle's apartment door. The lock clicked open. The weight of the reinforced door and its heavy bolts was heavy and reassuring. She'd told Ian the truth; she was feeling enormously better already.

"It's me," she called. "Where are you?"

"Living room, darling," Carlyle replied.

She found him there, whiskey bottle and shot glass on the coffee table, book on the couch next to him. He was relaxing, which meant he'd removed his suit coat and taken off his necktie. He was still wearing a silk button-down shirt under a fine Italian vest. His legs were sheathed in trousers that probably cost more than anything in Erin's wardrobe.

"I thought I'd find you in a robe and PJs," she said.

"I'm planning on being arrested tonight, if you recall," he said mildly. "It didn't seem polite to ask your colleagues to wait on me while I dressed. Tell me about Corky."

Erin explained how she'd found the apartment. Carlyle listened, steepling his fingers in front of his face.

"That sounds like Pritchard, sure enough," he said when she'd finished. "Though he made a rather serious mistake, letting Corky get so close to a rack of knives. What I can't figure is how he tumbled to the truth."

"Maybe Corky got careless," Erin said. "He's been talking to her. Teresa, I mean. On the phone. Pritchard might've bugged his apartment."

Carlyle shook his head. "If he'd known ahead of time, he'd have told Evan. Then Corky and I would both be dead, and maybe you along with us. Nay, the Snake found something tonight. Where was he?"

"The Teamsters' Christmas party," she said. "Same as Corky."

"Something the lad did there must have piqued Pritchard's suspicions," Carlyle said. "Or his curiosity, at the least. I don't suppose Corky said anything to you?"

"He was already at the hospital by the time I got to his place," she said. "From the sound of things, he won't be talking anytime soon. Listen, I'm going to take a quick look around and make sure everything's okay here. Then I need to keep searching for Pritchard. As long as that guy's out there, we're in danger."

"I've told you over and over, darling, I'm perfectly safe," Carlyle said. "You know the security in this place as well as I. So does Pritchard. He'll not try anything here, not until he's desperate."

"I think he's pretty goddamn desperate," she retorted. "Tell me about him. How does he operate?"

Carlyle shrugged. "He's a killer," he said. "Guns, knives, explosives, he's a dab hand at nearly everything. He served with the Brigades in Belfast, you ken, as I did. But all I really did was manufacture devices. He was out there on the sharp end, doing damage. He always did have a particular liking for fire."

"Even after he got torched?"

"Aye. The lad gets a certain thrill out of the stuff. The last time I saw him at Evan's flat, Evan had a fire burning on his hearth. Pritchard's eyes had a funny gleam in them and he couldn't stop watching the flames."

"You think he's a firebug? An arsonist?"

"I think he'll do whatever's likeliest to put his target in the ground," Carlyle said. "And he'll stick at naught."

"How fireproof is this building?" she asked.

"It's stone," he said. "It's an older building, but it's up to code. I suppose the woodwork in the pub might burn, but we've sprinklers and extinguishers."

"If you were going to attack this place, how would you do it?"

Carlyle rubbed his chin. "The best way would probably be—"

The world lurched and tilted with a tremendous noise. It was so loud that Erin felt more than heard it, the wave of sound crashing through her, rattling her teeth and flinging her off her feet. All the lights went out at once. She was tossed into the darkness, slamming face-first into the living room floor.

Chapter 7

"Erin? Are you all right?"

Carlyle's voice had a ringing, tinny quality. He might be right next to her, or twenty feet away. She had no way of knowing.

"I'm fine," she said. Her tongue felt thick in her mouth. "I can't see."

"Nor I," he said. "The power's gone."

She smelled smoke and a thick, nasty chemical odor. *Natural gas*, she thought. A smoke alarm was plaintively beeping.

Something cool and wet thrust itself under her arm, accompanied by an anxious snuffling. Rolf. The dog seemed unharmed. He nudged her again, more urgently.

"Where are you?" she called.

"On the couch," Carlyle said. "I'm not hurt. What was that?"

"Gas main," she said distractedly, rising to her hands and knees. Something wet was dripping onto her upper lip. She licked it and tasted blood. She'd hit her nose against the floor, but seemed otherwise unharmed.

"Gas main," he repeated.

"Yeah. Can't you smell it?"

"I'm smelling a great deal of smoke at the moment," he said grimly.

"We need to get out of here," she said. The smoke was getting thicker in the air. She couldn't see it but she could taste it, oily and sooty, coating the inside of her mouth.

"Grand idea. Fire escape, or stairs?"

She tried to think. It wasn't easy in that smoky darkness. "Stairs," she said. "If this is a trap, Pritchard might be watching the escape."

Erin got out her phone and turned on its flashlight app. Carlyle's face looked pale and unhealthy in the cold, blue-white LED light. Rolf's pupils threw back the light in flashes of green. The air wasn't as smoky as she'd feared, but wisps were drifting through the room.

"Where's it coming from?" she wondered as she led the way toward the staircase. There was no point in dialing 911; the officers observing the Corner would have already called in the blast.

"Central air vents," Carlyle said. "I'm guessing the fire's in the cellar, near the furnace. That's where the gas line comes in."

"And that's where the air ducts come from," Erin agreed. "The main floor may still be okay. Rolf, *fuss!*"

The K-9 placed himself at Erin's hip. He watched her, moving in tandem, just as if they were on a training exercise. But his ears were flat against his skull and he whined softly. He'd been in a fire before, and come out of it badly scorched. Rolf wasn't scared of much, but he couldn't bite flames.

Erin wanted to run like hell. One of Ian's military sayings played through her head. *Slow is smooth and smooth is fast.* It was better not to rush. When you panicked was when you started making mistakes. She took the steps one at a time, keeping one hand on the railing and the other tight on her phone. Rolf wasn't on leash. That was okay. He wouldn't leave her side unless she told him to.

She stopped at the foot of the stairs and put out a hand. Carlyle's door was sturdy and would take a while to heat up, but she still might be able to feel the warmth if a fire was raging on the other side. She felt nothing but wood paneling over cool steel core. Ready to slam it shut if she saw or felt fire, she pulled the door a few inches open.

Ian Thompson was standing right outside. His back was to her. He was holding a pistol in both hands, covering the room. Erin saw no open flames, but the smoke was much thicker down here. It flowed through the open doorway in a choking cloud.

"Ian!" she called.

"You good?" he asked without turning his head.

"We're fine. You?"

"No casualties. Mason's clearing the back for our exfil. Basement's on fire. No contact with hostiles."

Ian gave his situation report in clipped, concise sentences. He might as well have been describing the weather, or the Yankees' pitching prospects.

"Let's go," Erin said, laying a hand on his back so he'd know where she was. Carlyle was right behind her, Rolf at her side. The little group walked briskly to the back hallway. On the left was the basement door, on the right the restrooms and Carlyle's back room, where the O'Malleys played cards and held private meetings.

Smoke was boiling up from the crack under the basement door. The door itself hung slightly askew, wrenched out of frame by the force of the blast. Wisps of smoke were rising between the floorboards in the pub, too. The floor might collapse, or the whole building might come down.

Ian got to the back exit. He pulled the door open just enough to let in a breath of the December night. "Mason?" he called.

"Here," the other former Marine replied. "Alley's clear."

"On me," Ian said, gliding out the door into the alley.

"Close it," a voice rasped just behind Erin's ear.

Her heart gave a sickening lurch. Even before she turned her head, she knew what she'd see. How the hell had Pritchard gotten in? How had he snuck up behind her? Why hadn't Ian seen him? Why hadn't Rolf smelled him?

"Now!" Pritchard snapped. "Or the colleen gets it."

Carlyle didn't flinch. "Go, lad!" he called to Ian as he pushed the door closed.

"Bolt it," Pritchard ordered.

Carlyle slid the deadbolt into place. "Evening, Gordon," he said quietly. "I assume you've an explanation for this intrusion?"

Erin and Carlyle turned around. Pritchard was standing in the restroom doorway. He was holding a pistol in his black-gloved right hand; a snub-nosed revolver. It wasn't much of a gun, probably a .32, smaller and lighter than the backup gun Erin had clipped to her ankle. The short barrel meant it wouldn't reliably hit anything outside twenty yards. But he was a lot closer than that, and the small hole looked plenty big when it was pointed at her.

Ian would be moving. If he couldn't get in through the back door, he'd be circling around to the front. It would take him a couple of minutes at most to get the door open and flank Pritchard. And when he did, he'd come heavy. The police surveillance team would also be doing something. They were under orders to wait until four o'clock to serve the warrant, but the explosion would have forced them into action. Uniforms and fire trucks were probably already on their way. The clock was ticking.

Carlyle knew that, which helped explain his calm, quiet demeanor. He was playing for time, trying to run that clock down.

Gordon Pritchard looked like he was having a rough night. His left hand was wrapped in a blood-soaked handkerchief. His black hair, usually slicked back, was disheveled. The old scars on the right side of his face were a patchwork of livid lines. But his eyes were dark and expressionless as ever.

"Corky's dead," he said.

When the Molotov cocktail had exploded in his hand all those years ago, he'd inhaled some of the flaming vapor. The scar tissue that coated the inside of his throat made him sound like he had a perpetual cold. It also robbed his voice of any emotional inflection. He talked like a robot with bronchitis.

Neither Erin nor Carlyle corrected him. Erin was thinking about the dog at her hip and the gun on her belt. The last time she'd sicced Rolf on a man who was pointing a weapon at her, she'd taken a bullet to the skull that probably should have killed her. Rolf was fast, but no dog could outrun a lead slug.

"Did you shoot him?" Carlyle asked.

"Yeah," Pritchard said.

"Why?"

Pritchard's mouth twisted in a lopsided half-smile. "Because of a girl, of course," he said. "A real stunner. She was all over him at the Teamsters' party. Blonde, big tits, small dress. He blew her off."

"You shot Corky because he *didn't* screw a bimbo?" Erin asked.

"It got me thinking," Pritchard said. "Corky never turns down a free piece of ass. He'd been acting weird lately. Wasn't stepping out with anyone. And he'd gotten real chummy with Maggie Callahan."

"Wait a second," Erin said, silently willing Ian to hurry. The smoke was really getting thick. She could hear the crackle of flames somewhere nearby. NYPD first responders had to be en route by now. The first Patrol units would arrive in a matter of moments.

"What you've got to say, say it quick," Pritchard said.

"You think Corky's screwing Maggie?" she replied. "You're nuts!"

"Of course not," Pritchard said. "Maggie doesn't put out. But Corky had a girl, a secret one. And he was working his way in close with the boss's bookkeeper. And I had cops on me tonight. But you know all that."

"I'm really confused right now," Erin said. "What's this got to do with Carlyle and me?"

"Corky was a damned rat," Pritchard said. "And so are you, Cars."

"You're making wild accusations, lad," Carlyle said. "Put that gun away and let's continue this conversation somewhere a bit safer. This building's aflame, if you didn't notice."

"I know all of it," Pritchard said. "Corky fell for that Italian chick. She's the one he's been seeing. I know you didn't kill her. And that makes you a traitor."

Carlyle shook his head. "You're talking about the hotel job, I take it," he said. "You're pointing a gun at me, so I'll grant you the benefit of the doubt. Even if you're speaking the truth, for the sake of argument, that would mean I'd cheated Valentino Vitelli, not Evan O'Malley."

"You're saying you didn't know what Corky was up to?" Pritchard demanded.

"You set fire to my pub on *suspicion*?" Carlyle shot back. "How dare you! This is my livelihood and my home! The woman I love sleeps here!"

"Is that wop chick alive or not?" Pritchard asked. "I'm only asking once."

"She got in a car I blew to bloody bits!" Carlyle exclaimed. "I did the job I was asked to do! Now you're telling me you've murdered my best mate and torched my home. You're the one who's going to have to explain to Evan just what you've done."

"Funny thing," Pritchard said. "I tried calling him from a pay phone, after I finished with Corky. They've still got those, you know. The call didn't go through. Between that and the surveillance, it's got me thinking—"

Ian Thompson came through the smoke behind Pritchard. He had his Beretta in his hands, level and steady, trained on the back of the man's head. Because of the smoke and the dim lighting, he'd had to get dangerously close. He was only a few steps from the cluster of people.

His finger slid inside the trigger guard. Erin tried not to react. If she ducked or stepped away, it would tip Pritchard off. She had to trust Ian not to hit her or Carlyle.

The floorboards splintered beneath Ian's feet. He pitched forward, the gun flying from his hand, and clutched at the floor. There was a crackling crash. A table tumbled into the hole. A cloud of sparks spun up toward the ceiling.

Pritchard's head snapped around. He was experienced enough to keep his gun aimed at Erin and Carlyle, but he had to see what was happening at his back.

"*Fass!*" Erin shouted. At the same moment, she let her legs buckle and dropped to the floor.

Pritchard's revolver went off. Erin didn't know where the bullet went, but it didn't hit her. Rolf snarled and lunged, a blurred silhouette of fur and fangs.

The K-9 caught Pritchard high up on the chest. He was supposed to grab the man's gun arm, but Pritchard twisted like a startled snake and somehow got his left forearm under the dog's chin, holding him back. Rolf's teeth clicked shut less than an inch from Pritchard's face.

The O'Malley enforcer wasn't a big man. He was five-foot seven and weighed in around one-sixty. Rolf was ninety pounds of muscle and focused ferocity. The Shepherd plowed Pritchard clean off his feet. The two of them tumbled and rolled across the floor.

Ian was holding onto the broken ends of the floorboards with the grip of desperation. He saw the struggling man and dog hurtling toward him and wrenched himself to the side. He lost his grip with one hand and held on with the other as Rolf and Pritchard flashed past him. One moment they were there, then they toppled through the hole, into the column of smoke and sparks.

No, Erin thought, but the sound that came out was closer to a wail than a word. She couldn't believe it. Rolf was gone.

Chapter 8

The first rule of being in a burning building was to *get out of the building*. Forget the family photo albums. Forget the heirlooms. Forget the cash, the keepsakes, the clothes, the computer. Just run. Save the kids. Save the pets if you could, but if you got out and they didn't, you did not go back for them. The firefighters would try, if they got there in time, but an unprotected person running into a fire was just asking to die.

Erin knew the rule as well as any first responder did. *Fuck that*, she thought. Rolf wasn't a pet. He was her partner. He'd gone through fire for her more than once. Now he might be injured or dying down in Carlyle's basement, and she was damned if she'd leave him there.

Carlyle was running to help Ian. She didn't bother going with him to look into the hole. They had no way to lift a dog ten feet straight up. The only chance Rolf had was if she could get down to him.

A fire extinguisher was mounted on the wall next to the basement door. She wrenched it clear, pulled the safety pin, and jerked the door open.

It was like sticking her face into an open oven. The blast of heat was incredible, blurring her vision. She could hardly see anyway, on account of the billowing smoke. She pulled the trigger on the extinguisher, sending a blast of foam down the stairwell. It would make the steps slippery, but it might also keep her from getting incinerated.

Erin turned her head away and sucked in the biggest breath she could. Then she started down.

She'd hadn't yet been a police officer on 9/11, when the World Trade Center came down. Her dad had been stationed in Queens and hadn't been at the site, though he'd lost friends there. She'd often wondered what those officers' last minutes had been like: groping through smoky stairwells, feeling the fire around them, knowing that if they died, Hell couldn't be much worse.

She had near-zero visibility. Her most important sense was touch, helping her shy away from the more intense patches of heat. She tried to remember the layout of the Corner's cellar. It was mostly used for storage, and she was unhappily aware that most of the storage was high-proof alcohol. If those bottles got too hot, they'd explode like grenades. Carlyle had a workshop down here, but his bomb-making days were behind him, thank God. He didn't keep explosives in the building; at least, she hoped not. If he did, her angry ghost was going to have a talk with him about it.

The floor had given way over one of the storage rooms. It ought to be about fifteen feet to her left. She trailed her left hand along the wall. The rough old bricks were hot to the touch. With her right hand she fired short bursts from her extinguisher, clearing a path.

She was holding her breath. She'd heard Navy SEALs could do that for something like three or four minutes, but she wasn't in that kind of shape. She had a minute, maybe a minute and a half. Then she'd gasp like a landed fish, suck in a lungful of smoke, and keel over. Rolf might come if she called, but she didn't dare waste the air. Besides, he was likely as not injured and unable to walk.

With the power out, there was no point looking for a light switch. It would have been pitch-black if not for the flames. It seemed like the entire place had caught fire. Through streaming eyes, Erin saw weird, translucent flames rippling across the ceiling. It was strangely beautiful and terrifying.

Dizzy, disoriented, sweat evaporating from her skin as quickly as it flowed, she made it to the storeroom. The door was open. The room beyond was strewn with broken glass and flaming debris. Several cases of Carlyle's top-shelf whiskey had been broken open by the blast, then ignited. A dark lump lay on the floor in the middle of a jumbled wreck of wood and cardboard. She stumbled toward it.

Flames reached hungry, inquisitive fingers up around the inert, furry shape. Erin played the extinguisher on the floor, driving the fire back. She saw Rolf lying on his side. His mouth was open slightly, his tongue dangling limply. She saw no sign of Pritchard.

It was time to go. She dropped the extinguisher, which was nearly empty anyway, and bent over the dog. She didn't think there was any way she could carry a dead-weight German Shepherd all the way back to the stairs, not on half a lungful of air, but she was damned well going to try.

"Erin!" someone shouted from above. Confused, she glanced up and saw Carlyle and Ian's faces peering down at her.

"Rope!" she called hoarsely. It was a mistake. She used up the last of her stored air, drew in a reflexive breath, and started coughing. She went to her knees, then her belly. Smoke and heat rose, so the best air was at floor level. She sucked in a breath that had only a little smoke in it.

"Hold my legs!" Ian shouted, which made no sense to Erin. Then she saw his upper body swing down, arms and head upside-down. Carlyle, out of Erin's field of view, must be bracing his lower half. Ian reached toward her and beckoned with both hands.

She understood what he wanted, but didn't think it would work. Rolf was ninety pounds, a big weight for anybody, much less someone dangling in midair. But what else could she do? She wedged her arms under Rolf, gritted her teeth, and lifted.

She almost didn't manage it. Rolf's body kept trying to slither through her grasp to the floor. Ian's hands were at about the height of her head. It wasn't enough to cradle Rolf in her arms. She had to lift him up. Tottering, straining, she gave it everything she had and hoisted the dog overhead.

Ian's hands came around Rolf's midsection. Erin, with a silent prayer, let go. Then she planted her own hands under the dog and pushed, trying to help however she could.

Ian's entire body went rigid with strain. Slowly, incredibly, his slender abdomen curled. He and his burden went up, up, up. Ian was trembling from exertion, but he didn't let go and he didn't stop. With a final effort, he edged Rolf over the rim of the broken floorboards.

The really amazing thing wasn't the feat of strength, something way beyond anything Erin had thought the lean former Marine could do. The amazing thing was that after doing it, without resting or even hesitating, he uncurled again, reaching for Erin.

She considered making a dash back for the stairs. But the smoke had only gotten thicker, the heat more intense. She'd never make it. So she extended her arms and gripped Ian's hands in hers, being sure to get a good, firm grip around his wrists. Then she jumped and he pulled.

She was heavier than Rolf by a good fifty pounds. But with a desperate effort, tendons standing out on his arms and neck, Ian was able to get her about halfway through the hole before his muscles started giving out.

Erin felt him start to go, felt the tremors in his overstressed muscles. She held on with one hand and let go with the other, grabbing at the edge of the floor. Splinters drove wickedly into her palm and she winced, but she held on. Using that arm as a lever, she hauled herself the rest of the way out onto the floorboards next to Rolf and Ian. She rolled onto her side and gasped for air, which was another mistake. The fire was still burning and she inhaled a full breath of smoke. She coughed so hard she started retching, hacking up dark mucus and half-curling into a fetal position.

Fresh, cold air washed over her. Voices, strange ones, were all around her. Hands took hold of her, half-carrying, half-dragging her across the floor and out into the night. The sleet was still falling. It was wet, cold, and miserable. After the fire and smoke, it was pure heaven.

"Rolf," she coughed. "My K-9." Her throat was raw. She sounded just like Gordon Pritchard.

"We've got your dog, lady," a man said. "Don't worry. You take it easy. Everything's going to be fine. The fire department's on their way."

They laid her on a thin blanket on the sidewalk. Erin didn't mind the hard surface. The cool concrete felt good: solid, soothing, reliable. She looked to one side and saw Rolf, lying on his own blanket. The dog's mouth still hung open. He was panting shallowly. When he saw her looking at him, his tail thumped twice.

"Good boy," she rasped. "Good, good boy. *Sei brav.*"

His tail thumped harder.

* * *

The fire engines had arrived by the time Erin was able to fully take in what was happening. She, Carlyle, Ian, Mason, and Rolf congregated in the back of an ambulance, where a couple of paramedics checked them over. Two uniformed policemen stood just outside, watching them. Ian and Mason had been armed when the cops had gotten to the scene. Both men were decorated former Marines, both were licensed to carry firearms, but the NYPD took a dim view of handguns at scenes of suspected arson and Mob violence. The situation was tense. The cops had an understanding with the veterans that they weren't under arrest as long as they didn't try to leave.

Nobody had seen Gordon Pritchard since Rolf had tackled him into the basement. The FDNY had shut off the gas, and the Barley Corner's sprinkler system had engaged, so the fire didn't look like spreading, but the basement had been completely engulfed.

"I have to go," Erin rasped. She barely finished the sentence before another coughing fit immobilized her.

"Not a chance, lady," one of the paramedics said. "You've got smoke inhalation and some minor burns. You really ought to go to the hospital for a full checkup. You might have serious damage to your lungs."

"I don't have a choice," she said weakly. "Things to do."

"The thing you need to do right now is rest," the medic said. "You could have died in there."

"Story of my life," Erin muttered. She took a sip from a bottle of water the medic had given her, cleared her throat, and hawked a mouthful of sooty mucus onto the street.

"You needn't do anything," Carlyle said. "The situation's well in hand."

"Pritchard blew up your bar!" she protested.

"Looks like the last thing he'll do," Ian said. "Nobody came up those stairs after you went down."

"The lad's done for," Carlyle agreed. "He'll be no further trouble to anyone. Besides, the time's going on three. Another hour and it's all over."

"Somebody's going to tell Evan," Erin said. "About your bar. When they can't get in touch..."

"If anyone's awake, they'll be confused," Carlyle said. "Whatever action they take, it'll be hesitant and none too quick."

"O'Malleys aren't a military unit," Ian added. "No discipline, weak chain of command."

"Who're you guys talking about?" the paramedic asked.

"Forget about it," Erin said. "Official NYPD business." Her throat was sore, but she was already feeling much better. Rolf had bounced back, too. He was lying next to her, leaning his head against her leg, but she could tell his energy was returning. The rubber ball in his mouth was helping his mood a great deal.

"Pritchard's dead," Carlyle said. "And if he isn't, he soon will be. If anyone thought otherwise, the firemen would be digging in my cellar as we speak. They're standing back, which suggests no one's alive in the place."

"Yeah," Erin said. She reached out and took his hand. "I'm sorry."

"For what?" he asked, startled. "Pritchard was no friend of mine."

"For your pub," she said. "It's ruined."

"It's insured," he said. "We'll rebuild, no fear. I'm from Belfast, remember? During the Troubles, a pub would get blown up every other week or so. We'll be shuttered a few months, but we'll reopen in finer shape than we were."

He spoke lightly, but Erin saw the pain in his eyes as he looked at the smoke pouring out of what remained of his pride and joy. The Barley Corner was the one thing he'd built in America that he'd been genuinely proud of.

"I have to call Webb," she insisted. "This will be all over the radio net by now. I'm surprised he hasn't already called me."

She dug out her phone, swiped the screen, and saw seven missed calls and half a dozen texts. "Shit," she said. "I had it silenced. I kept thinking about all those times in the movies when someone's trying to be quiet and some idiot calls them."

Five calls and three texts were from Webb. The others were from Vic. The texts were all speculation regarding Erin's location and physical wellbeing.

She called Webb first. He must have had his phone in his hand. It hardly had time to ring before he picked up.

"Talk to me," he said.

"I'm fine, sir," she said.

"You don't sound fine," he said. "Your place got blown up?"

"Yes, sir."

"Deliberately?"

"We have to assume."

"Agreed. Word just went out a few minutes ago. Someone's going to call O'Malley with the news. When they can't get through to him, they'll do something, and probably show up in person."

"That's what I just said," Erin replied.

"We're going now," Webb said. "Before anything else happens."

"It's early," she said. "What if—"

"The genie's out of the bottle," Webb interrupted. "We move now or we lose them. I've looped the Captain in and he's already given the green light. This was his call. For all he knew, you might have already been dead. I'm still with ESU. We're taking the target down in five."

Erin closed her eyes. Webb and Holliday were right, she couldn't argue it, but after all their preparation, suddenly everything seemed slapdash and rushed. "What do you want me to do, sir?" she asked.

"Sit tight and wait for the Bomb Squad," Webb said. "I don't have much time. Just tell me one thing. Neshenko said the Corcoran shooting was Gordon Pritchard. Was he behind the explosion, too?"

"Yes."

"Did you get him?"

"We don't have a body, but Ian says he didn't make it out of the basement."

"As soon as you can, get people in there and confirm it," Webb said. "I have to go. Good luck, O'Reilly."

"You too, sir."

She hung up, thinking it was all wrong. She ought to be there, looking Evan O'Malley in the eye. This was supposed to be her big moment of triumph and all she felt was cold, wet, filthy, and sick.

"You bastard," she whispered, even though Pritchard couldn't possibly hear her. "You goddamn bastard."

* * *

It took the Bomb Squad another twenty minutes to show up. With only thirty-three active members, they lacked the citywide coverage of the FDNY. Erin didn't know who was on duty that night, so was gratified to see Skip Taylor hop out of the van almost before it stopped rolling.

"Skip!" she called, waving to him.

The EOD technician, hearing his name, hurried to the ambulance. "Erin!" he called. "What can you tell me?"

"Somebody blew the gas main," she said.

"How do you know?"

"I was upstairs when it happened."

Skip put his hands on his hips and shook his head. "You're lucky," he said. "The whole building could've come down. That's good construction there, solid foundations. What is it with people trying to blow this place up?"

"It is a Mob bar," she pointed out.

"And I'm the proprietor," Carlyle added.

"There is that," Skip said. "Who'd you piss off this time, Cars?"

"Another former IRA lad," Carlyle said. "A fellow name of Pritchard. He hasn't the training I've had, but he's a natural talent with fire and suchlike. I expect he used a simple incendiary device."

Skip nodded. "Is there likely to be a secondary?" he asked. "Or anti-tampering?"

"I doubt it," Carlyle said. "This was laid on in a hurry."

"We'll be careful anyway," Skip said. "I've got plans for my thumbs when I retire. I'd like to keep them."

He put two fingers between his teeth and whistled sharply. The rest of his team congregated around him.

"Okay, guys," he said. "This one's a probable arson. Watch yourselves. We'll start with the gas line, as soon as the fire's all the way out. We won't need the bomb suits or the robot. Just normal protective gear."

"I hate waiting on other guys," Erin said sourly as the Bomb Squad suited up.

"Ninety percent of my time in the Corps was waiting," Ian said. "Got good at it."

"Are you okay?" she asked.

"Squared away," he said.

"It was dangerous, you going down there," Carlyle said to Erin.

"I didn't have a choice," she said. "It was Rolf."

"I didn't say you did the wrong thing," he said, smiling thinly. "And I know you'd have done the same for Ian, or myself."

"And you'd do it for me," she replied. "Ian, that was incredible. I've never seen anybody do anything like that before. How the hell did you lift Rolf, let alone me?"

Ian shrugged. "All those crunches had to be good for something," he said. "Got my core in good condition."

"Did you pull a muscle or anything?"

"I'm good."

"Would you admit it if you had?"

"Probably not."

"Ian, do Marines understand there's such a thing as pain?"

"Of course we do," he said, straight-faced. "Happens to other people."

Glass shattered. The firefighters had broken one of Carlyle's prized green stained-glass windows to ventilate the space. A hose team started pouring water through the new hole. Erin felt a stinging in her eyes that was partly smoke and partly not.

"I'm sorry," she said again. "I'm so damn sorry."

"I love the Corner," Carlyle said, speaking mostly to himself. "But Mr. Taylor's wrong. It's built on a rotten foundation. I don't know why I thought I could keep it. Maybe it's better this way. Maybe it's no more than the place deserves."

"Don't say that," she said. "It's a good bar. Even with all the money laundering and gambling and mob hits. You'll rebuild it, you said so yourself. And this time it'll be clean."

"Are you implying something about the hygiene in my establishment, Miss O'Reilly?" Carlyle asked with mock severity.

"I'm saying something about the moral tone of the place," she replied.

"Maybe Gordon Pritchard did me a favor," Carlyle said softly.

"The world runs on favors," Erin reminded him. "A wise guy told me that once."

"Anyway, the blighter's gone now," Carlyle said. "May he rest in peace. And it's over."

"Not yet," Erin said. All over the city, she knew, men with guns were knocking on doors and groggy gangsters were stumbling out of bed, deciding to run, fight, or come quietly. And her brother and his trauma team were trying their best to keep Corky Corcoran alive; assuming they hadn't already failed.

Frustration boiled up in her. It wasn't supposed to go like this. She was supposed to be in on it, slapping the cuffs on Evan O'Malley, looking him in the eye. That had been the plan. What the hell was she doing instead? Watching the Barley Corner burn.

"God *damn* it!" she hissed, clenching her fists. She felt like a hotshot ballplayer who'd been drafted into the All-Star Game. It was the bottom of the ninth, two outs, a couple runners were on base, and the game was on the line, and she was warming a bench with her ass.

The sun would be coming up in about four hours. It seemed more like four days.

Chapter 9

Containing a fire could be relatively quick and easy. Putting it all the way out was a long, slow process. The reasoning went that as long as nobody was still alive in the burning building, and the physical property was already burned, or at least smoke-damaged, there was no reason for firefighters to do the heroic stuff you always saw them doing in movies. The FDNY was quite content to stand outside and rain water into the building until they were satisfied it was safe. They called it "surround and drown."

Erin couldn't really blame them for that. Cops were told not to take stupid chances either. But it was awfully frustrating to just stand around as her boyfriend's livelihood burned, wondering how many thousand dollars' worth of expensive liquor was literally going up in smoke. She stood next to Carlyle in a borrowed NYPD raincoat and watched the Barley Corner smolder.

"Excuse me, sir?" a Patrolman said.

"What is it, officer?" Carlyle asked politely.

"Are you Morton Carlyle?"

"Aye, that's me."

"Sir," the Patrolman said, "I'm going to have to ask you to turn around and put your hands on the side of the ambulance."

"What?" Erin burst out, taking a step toward him. "What the hell for?"

"Please stand back, ma'am," the uniform said. In spite of his polite words, he had a hand on the grip of his sidearm. He hadn't taken it out of its holster, but his body language was clear. Erin had seen it plenty of times; hell, she'd *done* it plenty of times.

"Sir?" Ian said quietly. He hadn't moved an inch, but Erin could see the sudden tension in him.

"It's all right, lad," Carlyle said. "I'm not looking for trouble." He placed his hands on the cold, wet metal of the ambulance's side. The uniform came toward him, accompanied by three more cops.

"Mr. Carlyle," he said. "I'm placing you under arrest for—"

"God damn it, stop!" Erin interrupted. She'd recognized the face under the uniformed cap. They were in Precinct 8's Area of Service, and she'd gotten to know most of the officers at the Eightball. "It's me, Polikowski!"

Officer Polikowski blinked. "O'Reilly?" he said. "That you?"

"Of course it's me!" she snapped. "What do you think you're doing?"

"Following orders, ma'am," he said, shifting uncomfortably. "The Captain gave me specific instructions. It didn't go through normal chain of command, but I thought maybe you'd know about it, seeing as you're here. We're to take Morton Carlyle into custody. The charges are racketeering, money laundering, gunrunning, and Murder One."

Erin stopped short. Her brain had finally caught up with what was going on. The explosion and fire had blown it clean out of her mind, but Carlyle was supposed to get arrested tonight. That had always been the plan. He had an immunity deal, and he'd skate on the charges, but the NYPD still had to take him in. It was important both for the look of the thing and for Carlyle's physical safety. He was, after all, part of the O'Malley senior leadership.

"Oh," she muttered. "Right. Yeah. I get it."

"Worth, keep an eye on those other two," Polikowski said, nodding toward Ian and Mason.

"Identify yourselves," Worth said. He didn't like the look of the two former Marines. He was an experienced street cop, conditioned to pick up danger signs, and these guys were setting off all kinds of warning signals.

"Thompson, sir," Ian said crisply. "Ian. Former sergeant, USMC."

"Mason," his comrade chimed in. "Kenneth. Former lance corporal, USMC. Semper fi."

"Thank you for your service," Worth said automatically. He glanced at his partner. "We got anything on these two?"

"Nope," Polikowski said. "All we have is the one warrant. Who are you guys, anyway?"

"Already answered that, sir," Ian said.

"What were you doing at this bar after closing time?" Polikowski pressed.

"Security, sir."

"Guess you weren't doing a very good job," Worth snickered.

"No excuse, sir," Ian said. He was looking straight ahead, no expression on his face.

"Whatever," Polikowski said. "All we want is your boss. You're free to go."

"Rather stick around," Ian said.

"That wasn't a suggestion," Polikowski said. "Scram."

Ian didn't move. "Heard it was a free country," he said softly. "Standing on a public street."

"Give it a rest, Polikowski," Erin said. "He's fine."

"I've got no friggin' idea what's going on," Polikowski said. "Because they don't tell me shit. But that's okay. I've got my orders, I've got my guy, and I'm taking him in. You want the rest of this mess, Detective, it's all yours."

He patted Carlyle down with quick, efficient movements. Then he pulled Carlyle's arms around behind his back and cuffed him.

"Is that really necessary?" Erin couldn't resist asking.

"I don't know how you do it in Major Crimes," Polikowski retorted. "But on the street, when we arrest a mope, we don't do it on the honor system. What's it to you, anyway?"

Erin bit her lip and said nothing. This was all part of the plan, she reminded herself. It didn't mean a damn thing. But it still tore at her heart watching the man she loved marched off in handcuffs. When Polikowski loaded him into a squad car with the usual motions, putting a hand on his head so he didn't bang it on the doorframe, she surprised herself by having to blink back tears.

"Something I learned in the Corps," Ian said.

Erin jumped. She hadn't heard him move, but he was right there beside her.

"What's that?" she asked.

"Brass makes lots of plans," he said. "Even the good ones, a lot of the time people get hurt. Don't usually finish an op without a couple casualties."

"Are you sure you're okay?" she asked.

"Absolutely," Ian said. "Sorry I went through the floor. No—"

"If you say 'no excuse,' I'll punch you in the face," she said, not quite meaning it.

"Should've had him," Ian said. "Wasn't ready for smoke. Should've had IR goggles. Could've drawn a bead from further out."

"Ian, nobody's blaming you for not being equipped for a shootout in a burning building," she said. "Any idea how Pritchard got in?"

"Probably had a key," Ian said. "Still should've seen or heard him."

"He was pretty sneaky," Erin said.

"Hard to sneak up on me," he replied. "Doors were secure until the explosion. Gas line comes in the basement. To blow it, he had to have gotten in some other way."

Erin slapped her forehead. "Son of a *bitch!*" she swore. "God damn it!"

"What?" Ian asked.

"The bootlegger's entrance!" she exclaimed. "Remember? In the alley?"

Ian's face, usually expressionless, twitched in a slight wince. "You're right," he said. "Not many people know it's there. Forgot Pritchard was an insider. He could've known about it."

The Barley Corner was an old pub. Its history went back to before Prohibition. When it had been a speakeasy, the owner had installed a secret entrance that accessed the basement. It had remained as a curiosity through several remodelings, but the O'Malleys had used the Corner's cellar for smuggling, and Carlyle had kept the secret entrance for that purpose. Erin herself only knew about it because Carlyle's homicidal one-time ward, Siobhan Finneran, had once used it to escape an NYPD ambush.

"Don't your cameras cover the alley?" she demanded.

"Wasn't watching the cameras," Ian said. "Was standing guard in the bar. Besides, he'd need to know the secret latch. Didn't know we were expecting an attack from inside. Mason could've caught it, but he doesn't know about that entrance. Not his fault. He was watching the doors. My mistake, no excuse."

Erin didn't hit him. She hadn't really wanted to. She sighed and shook her head.

"Not that it makes any difference now," she said wearily. "He did what he did."

"Mason," Ian said.

"Yeah, Sarge?" Mason replied.

"You cover the alley after I flanked the position?"

"Until I got detained by local law. They took my pistol and made me wait here."

Ian nodded. "Nothing else you could do," he said.

Erin looked at him. "What're you thinking?" she asked.

"Slim chance," he said. "Pritchard might've got out the way he got in. Wounded, all that smoke, not likely. Either Mason or NYPD would've spotted him."

"Yeah," Erin said. "You're probably right."

"Orders?" he asked.

"I'm not your boss," she reminded him.

"Was talking about chain of command earlier," he said. "Take my orders from Mr. Carlyle. If he's taken out, you're next in line."

"And what if I'm out of the picture?" she asked.

"Personal initiative," Ian said.

"I have to get back to the Eightball," Erin decided. "They'll need me with all the shit that's going on. I'll talk to the cops here and warn them about Pritchard, but I'd like you to hang around just in case."

"ROE if I see him?"

"Rules of engagement? Tell the cops and have him arrested! Jesus, Ian, don't you think you've been in enough gunfights in New York? Anyway, like you said, he's probably toast."

Erin left instructions for the officers on scene to apprehend Pritchard if he was found alive, or to contact her the moment they found his remains. Then she crossed the street to the parking garage and loaded Rolf into her Charger. There was no reason to waste more time here. The fire looked like it had been stopped before it could get into the upstairs apartment, so her belongings were probably okay, but whether they were or not, she couldn't do a thing about it until the fire department cleared the site.

The police-band radio was alive with chatter. Some of it was the ordinary late-night business of the NYPD. Emergencies were a twenty-four-seven concern, and just because a major police operation was in progress didn't mean random idiots weren't crashing their cars, stabbing their spouses, or burning down their apartments. Between three and four in the morning was a relatively dead time, but people called 911 at all hours. Erin caught bits and pieces of relevant news, but not enough to form a real picture of what was going on. It was just a few minutes' drive to the Eightball. She'd find out the situation once she got there.

The Precinct 8 station house looked like Grand Central Station at rush hour. The first thing Erin noticed was the hulking black shape of ESU's Lenco Bearcat, an armored behemoth that would have been more at home on a battlefield than on an urban street. It stood directly in front of the main entrance, tinted windshield glowering at the squad cars clustered around it. Erin saw three TV news vans, four guys holding shoulder-mounted camera rigs, and several dozen gawking bystanders. Police officers scurried in and out of the building, all of them looking extremely busy.

"Goddamn ambulance-chasers," Erin muttered as she guided the Charger past the Channel 6 van and into the station's basement garage. "Don't they ever sleep?"

Rolf had no opinion. He stared out at the gathered vehicles, his eyes shining with the reflected glow of headlights and emergency flashers.

On her way up, Erin passed a group of officers in tactical gear. They were wrestling with three very large men. The cops had the advantage of numbers, but the sheer size of their prisoners gave the other guys the edge in weight. One of the officers had lost his helmet and his left eye was swollen shut. Several other combatants also sported various injuries. Even though the three big guys were in handcuffs, they were putting up one hell of a fight.

Erin didn't hesitate. "Rolf! *Fass!*" she snapped. Wishing she still carried a Taser or even a nightstick like she had in her Patrol days, she charged in on the heels of her dog.

Rolf had been dropped through the floor and lit on fire earlier that night. He hadn't had nearly enough sleep. He was wet, scorched, and singed. None of that made a bit of difference. The moment he heard his favorite command he was airborne toward the nearest target, a fur missile tipped with teeth.

The guy weighed at least two-eighty, more than three times Rolf's body mass. That didn't matter either. In Einstein's famous equation, as Erin had learned in school, mass might be important but velocity was what you squared.

The prisoner was in the process of head-butting one of the cops, disregarding the man's riot helmet, when Rolf slammed into him from behind. He gave a startled grunt, which cut off abruptly as his skull collided with the helmet much harder than he'd intended. He went down like a sack of spuds and stayed on the floor, the dog triumphantly grabbing his arm and wagging happily.

Erin's target was a tougher proposition. He was equally large, and knew how to fight in spite of his restraints. As she jumped on his back, he planted a knee in the crotch of the cop on his right. That officer folded up with a gasp. Erin snaked an arm around the man's neck, trying for a headlock. It wasn't a strictly regulation hold, but as long as she didn't cut off his airway it was legal. Her feet were dangling several inches from the ground. Ignoring her completely, he pivoted and kicked another cop in the belly. The cop's vest took some of the impact, but the poor guy was launched across the hallway. He bounced off the cinderblock wall and dropped.

The guy Erin was holding had been facing away from her and she hadn't seen his face. Up close to the man, smelling sweat and cheap cologne, she saw a familiar spider-web tattoo on his neck. His build and hair were familiar, too.

"Wayne!" she shouted in his ear. "Knock that shit off!"

Wayne McClernand paused in the act of stomping on one of the downed cops. "Erin?" he said, confused. "What're you doing here?"

"I work here!" she shot back.

Wayne wasn't the brightest truck driver in the Five Boroughs. He blinked and tried to sort out what was going on. "Yeah," he said slowly. "But what're you doing helping these guys?"

"I'm a cop, remember?" she said. "Stop fighting!"

"They started it!" he objected.

One of the other officers, seeing Wayne's distraction, took the opportunity to whack him on the kneecap with his baton. It had no effect whatsoever. Wayne absentmindedly shouldered the man aside, flinging Erin around on his back like a ragdoll. She gritted her teeth and hung on.

"They're—we're *allowed* to start it!" she said.

The cop with the nightstick had recovered enough to take another swing at Wayne. The stick caught him just below the shoulder, narrowly missing Erin's own arm. Wayne flinched slightly.

"Stop that!" he said to the cop. Then, to Erin, "We was coming along quiet, but then one of these bozos hit Express!"

"So you guys started fighting cops," Erin said through gritted teeth. She was still holding on, but it felt so futile she was considering giving it up.

"I told you, they started it!"

"Look, Wayne, give it a rest," she said. "You can't fight the whole NYPD. You're only making things worse for yourself."

Wayne body-slammed the cop with the nightstick again. The smaller man went flying, sprawling flat on his back on the hallway floor.

"You've always been straight up with me," Wayne said. "You want me to take it easy? Fine. Have it your way. You can get off me now."

Erin let go and slid down Wayne's back to the ground. "You're stronger than I thought," she said.

"I do a lot of weights," he said. He looked down at the three cops he'd flattened. "Sorry, guys. Wasn't nothing personal. I got upset 'cause you beat up my buddy. And you put the cuffs on too tight."

"I can loosen them," Erin said. Like most officers, she carried a key that would fit NYPD-issue handcuffs.

"Nah, don't bother," Wayne said. He bunched his shoulders and flexed. With a metallic *spang*, the chain between the bracelets snapped. He brought his hands around in front of himself and rubbed his wrists, each of which was still encircled by a steel cuff.

"Holy shit," one of the downed officers said, fumbling for his gun.

"Wait a second," Erin said. "You could've done that anytime you wanted, and you fought these guys with your hands tied behind your back?"

"Sure," Wayne said, shrugging. "Rules say you can't shoot a guy once you've got him in cuffs. No hard feelings, guys?"

The man he'd kneed in the crotch muttered a series of expletives he'd probably learned from the Harbor Patrol. He was still bent double and was holding himself.

"This is all a misunderstanding, anyway," Wayne said. "Right, ma'am?"

"I'm sure it'll all get sorted out," Erin said. She could hardly stand to look Wayne in the eye. He'd helped her more than once and had always been a gentleman. Despite his massive strength, he really wasn't a violent guy, but he was one of the O'Malleys and he was getting hauled in like all the others.

"That's what I figured," Wayne said more cheerfully. "Look, guys, I'll go wherever you say and I won't be no more trouble. But just so we're clear, I'm gonna want my lawyer before I say anything, okay?"

Erin left the other officers to finish sorting out Wayne and his buddies. Rolf was happy enough to have gotten his teeth into another bad guy, but she was feeling depressed. First Corky, then the Barley Corner, and now this. She'd been dreaming about this day for months, but it had never felt like this in her imagination. This was more like a fever dream, a high-temperature nightmare.

She went up the stairs in a foul mood, her nostrils still full of the reek of smoke and natural gas. As she passed the lobby, she took no notice of the milling crowd of perps and uniformed officers. Her only thought was to get up to Major Crimes. Maybe there'd be some order and sanity there.

"Detective O'Reilly!"

The use of her name and the bright, perky female voice saying it cut through the background noise. Erin paused, one foot poised on the stairs, and turned to see who'd called. She saw a model-perfect face, wearing full makeup in defiance of the early hour, framed by salon-styled blonde hair. The woman thrust a microphone toward her.

"Detective O'Reilly," Holly Gardner said again. The Channel 6 newswoman gave her a megawatt smile. "Would you care to comment on the nature of your relationship with alleged mobster Morton Carlyle?"

Chapter 10

"The NYPD doesn't comment about ongoing investigations."

The reply jumped automatically off Erin's tongue, before she'd even had time to fully process Holly's question.

"So Mr. Carlyle is a subject of an NYPD investigation?" the reporter asked, eyes lighting up.

Erin silently cursed. "I didn't say that," she said.

"I asked you about your relationship with him," Holly said. "You gave me an official response to a personal question."

"Oh, if it's a personal question, that's different," Erin said.

"So you do have a comment?" Holly leaned forward eagerly.

"You can take your personal question and shove it up your personal garbage chute," Erin said. "That's off the record, unless you want me to ram your question up there with your goddamn microphone. On the record? No comment."

As Erin continued up the stairs, Rolf trotting beside her, she heard Holly talking for the benefit of her cameraman.

"Emotions are running high at the New York Police Department's Eighth Precinct in the early hours of December Twenty-Sixth, where one of the largest law-enforcement operations in the city's recent history is apparently coming to a head. Details are still sketchy…"

The newswoman's voice faded mercifully into the background as Erin reached the second-floor landing and walked into Major Crimes. But it was no refuge. The room was humming with activity. Captain Holliday had left his office and stood in the middle of the space, holding three conversations at once: one with another Captain Erin didn't know, a second with a pair of stone-faced guys wearing FBI windbreakers, and a third on a cell phone he held against his left ear. Instead of the normal whiteboard, Major Crimes now had three, covered with names, addresses, and photographs. Somebody had set up a long folding table by the windows and stocked it with sandwiches and soft drinks. Zofia Piekarski was actually standing on her desk above a milling crowd of uniforms, shouting at them.

"Jesus," Erin said quietly. Either the squad didn't need her at all, or they desperately needed her. She had no idea which. She glanced down at Rolf, who returned her look and wagged his tail uncertainly. A late-night snooze on his blanket next to Erin's desk appeared to be out of the question.

Captain Holliday was a tall man. He made eye contact with Erin over the heads of the crowd, somehow managing one more bit of multi-tasking. Still holding his phone in his left hand, he beckoned her over with his right. Erin sighed and threaded her way over to him. As she approached, Holliday said something into his phone and dropped it into his hip pocket like a gunslinger holstering a six-shooter.

"Detective O'Reilly, Captain Delano," Holliday said. "Agents Vickers and Pope, FBI."

"Pleased to meet you," Delano said. He was a soft-spoken, smoothly handsome man who looked like the Hollywood version of a policeman: square jaw, blue eyes, perfect hair.

"Captain Delano is a special advisor to the Commissioner," Holliday explained. "He's here to oversee the operation."

"As an observer, that's all," Delano said. "I don't want to step on any toes. This kitchen already has plenty of cooks in it. Congratulations, Detective."

For what? Erin thought. *Getting my boyfriend arrested after watching his bar burn down, or getting his best friend shot?* "Thanks," she said. "It's been a busy night so far."

"So I understand," Holliday said. "Is everyone all right? You look like you've been through it."

"James Corcoran's been shot," she reported. "Morton Carlyle's in custody and Gordon Pritchard's missing, presumed dead. Pritchard snuck into the Barley Corner and blew up the gas line in the basement"

"Yes, I was just on the phone with FDNY," Holliday said dryly. "Was the Bomb Squad on scene when you left?"

"Yes, sir. Skip Taylor's in charge there."

Holliday nodded. "Good. He's the best we've got."

One of the FBI guys, either Vickers or Pope, stepped forward. "Do we need to notify ATF?" he asked. "Or Homeland?"

"I don't think so," Erin said. "Whatever explosive he used, it's already gone off and our top bomb guy is on it. I think the Feds would just get in the way."

"No disrespect, Detective, but your dog smells like a bonfire," Holliday said. "He looks a little singed. Do you need to get him checked out?"

"Rolf's fine," Erin said. Rolf couldn't speak English, so sometimes she had to lie on his behalf. It was only a little lie; he'd definitely have echoed her words if he could talk.

"Hmm," Holliday said, unconvinced. He eyeballed the dog.

Rolf stared back at the Captain, admitting no weakness. He'd just jumped on a bad guy a few minutes ago and was ready to do it again.

The best way to cover a lie was by changing the subject, which was what Erin did. "Why'd the Agency send you guys over here?" she asked the Feds.

"Liaison," Vickers or Pope replied.

"After all, one of our guys was arrested earlier this morning," the other one added.

"Freddy Giusto," the first one said.

"It's about time," Erin said under her breath.

"We couldn't just slap the cuffs on a Federal agent," Holliday explained. "So I've been in touch with the Bureau. They're handling it in-house. Special Agent Giusto was arrested at home by an FBI team, on racketeering charges. It seems he was on the Lucarelli payroll for quite some time, but we can't prove that. What we can prove is that he's also been taking money from Evan O'Malley."

"Dirty agents tarnish the entire Bureau's image," Vickers or Pope said. "We're glad to clean house."

"Especially since it's only one agent," his partner interjected. "Unfortunately, your own department appears to have been more heavily infiltrated."

"That's an Internal Affairs matter, and is being dealt with," Holliday said calmly.

"What about O'Malley himself?" Erin asked. "And his other top guys?"

"Officer Piekarski is coordinating at a tactical level," Holliday said. "She'll have the most up-to-date information. Dismissed, Detective."

Erin walked over to Piekarski's desk and looked up at the petite officer. Piekarski's face was flushed and she was breathing hard. Some of her blonde hair had come loose from its tight bun and was flopping across her forehead.

"Zofia!" Erin called.

"Oh, hey, Erin," Piekarski said. "How's it going?"

"You tell me."

Piekarski reached down. Erin helped her to the floor.

"Everything's gone nuts," the other woman said, leading the way to the whiteboards. "The whole timetable's shot to hell. All kinds of crazy shit is going on. You smell like cheap barbecue, you know that?"

"If you're asking whether I know I've been in a fire, yeah, I was aware of that," Erin said.

"Anyone hurt?"

"We think Gordon Pritchard's dead."

"I talked to Vic a few minutes ago. He said Pritchard's the one who put Corcoran in the hospital."

"And tried to burn down the Corner with Carlyle, Rolf, Ian, and me in it," Erin said. "I'm not going to cry at his funeral. How's Corky doing?"

"Last I heard, he was in surgery. Critical condition."

Erin nodded. It was neither better nor worse than she'd expected. "Evan O'Malley?"

"Webb and ESU grabbed him and everybody else in his apartment. They're on their way in now."

"They have to shoot anybody?"

Piekarski shook her head. "It was a clean takedown."

"How about Finnegan?"

"We got him, too. Vic missed out on it. He was running interference at O'Malley's place. He figured Pritchard might mess with the setup there, but I guess that asshole came after you instead."

"A snake can't be two places at once," Erin said.

"Huh?"

"Forget about it. Valentino Vitelli?"

"A unit down in Brooklyn got him at his favorite restaurant. Who the hell goes to a restaurant at four in the morning?"

"I bet he was eating pancakes," Erin said, remembering Vitelli's favorite dish at Lucky's Restaurant. "Ricotta pancakes with strawberries."

"Pancakes, huh? Nothing would surprise me tonight. Anyway, with Pritchard out of the picture, looks like we've landed all the big fish and practically all the little ones. We're hoping to finish the sweep in the next hour."

"Good." Erin tried to smile.

"Maggie Callahan got scooped up by a couple units," Piekarski added. "Someone seems to think she's important."

"She is," Erin said. "I hope she's somewhere safe."

"Absolutely. The last I heard, she was at JFK on her way to an undisclosed location, courtesy of the US Marshals' Service. Full witness-protection suite."

"Good," Erin said again. The smile was getting harder to muster up.

"Jesus, Erin," Piekarski said. "You look like you got run over by a truck. A truck that was on fire. I called that all-night deli down the street and had them send over some food. Why don't you grab something and sit down for a bit?"

"Plenty of time to rest once I'm dead," Erin said hollowly.

"When's the last time you took your pulse?" Piekarski retorted. She took hold of Erin's shoulders and steered her toward the refreshment table. "I'm prescribing you a Reuben and a Diet Coke."

"You're not a doctor."

"If your brother was here, he'd agree with me. Except doctors don't agree. They concur. I think that's pretty much the same thing, only more expensive. Sit. Eat."

"What I really need is a shower," Erin muttered. "But I don't have a change of clothes, and the rest of my wardrobe probably smells just as bad."

"Can't help you there," Piekarski said. "I'm wearing maternity sizes these days, and you're too tall for anything of mine. Don't you keep extras in your locker?"

Erin sighed. "When I wore a uniform, I kept a set of civvies at the station. But now that I'm plainclothes, sometimes I forget."

"Do you want to talk about it?"

"About what?"

"The fire. Dispatch sent two engines, plus a bus. The city shut off the gas to the whole block. Now you and Rolf show up looking like you smoked a couple exploding cigars."

"No." Erin picked up a sandwich, not even bothering to check what was between the pieces of bread, and took a bite. She paid no attention to the flavor.

"No?"

"No, I don't want to talk about it." Erin washed down her mouthful with a swig of Diet Coke. That, at least, tasted familiar.

"We've got Evan O'Malley," Piekarski said.

"Yeah, I know. You just told me."

"You don't seem like you heard me." Piekarski reached out and gave her shoulder a shake. "We won. *You* won. Relax."

"He'll know by now," Erin said.

"I'd hope so," Piekarski said. "If he didn't know he was under arrest when they slapped the cuffs on him, he's not as smart as everyone says. Erin, what's the matter?"

"Just tired, I guess," Erin said. She kept eating mechanically, knowing it was a good idea to get something in her stomach. "Did Finnegan come quietly?"

"As far as I know. Vic's gonna be pissed. He told me he was really looking forward to nailing that bastard in person. And he thought Finnegan would put up a fight."

"How many times did he mention the face-eating thing?" Erin asked.

"Ten or twelve," Piekarski said. "Did he really do that? Eat a chunk of a guy's face?"

"Yeah. Vic and I watched it happen."

"So he's as crazy as they say?"

"Maybe."

Erin's phone buzzed. She took it out and saw the name KEANE on her screen. She grimaced, but it wasn't a good idea to ignore a call from Internal Affairs. Holding up a hand to quiet Piekarski, she put the phone to her ear.

"O'Reilly," she said.

"You're in the building, I take it?" Lieutenant Keane asked. No greetings, no preliminaries, just straight to the point.

"Yes, sir," she said.

"My office. Now."

Erin started to answer, but he'd already hung up. She stared at the phone.

"That was weird," she said.

"What?" Piekarski asked.

"Tell Holliday I just got called upstairs," Erin said. She considered leaving Rolf behind, but decided she might need the moral support. He'd make Keane's office smell like burnt fur, but that didn't bother her one bit.

* * *

In contrast to Major Crimes, the Internal Affairs office was dark and quiet. That made some sense; IAB tended to keep more reasonable hours than most branches of the Department. Erin wondered whether Internal Affairs officers were out on the street right now, busting the cops on the O'Malley payroll. The only lights were the red EXIT signs and the lamplight under Keane's door. Erin approached it, took a breath, and knocked.

"Enter," Keane said.

He was sitting behind his desk, tie neatly knotted, no trace of stubble on his chin. His eyes reminded her of black shotgun barrels.

"Close the door," he said.

Erin obeyed.

"You have a problem, Detective," he said.

I've got a bunch of problems right now, Lieutenant, Erin thought. *One of them is sitting in your chair, wearing a suit that's too nice for a cop and not flashy enough for a gangster.* "I'm pretty busy tonight, sir," she said. "Is this important?"

"Valentino Vitelli was arrested a short while ago," Keane said. "Are you aware of that?"

"Yes, sir," Erin said, falling back on her usual tactic when called on the carpet.

"He's not a member of the O'Malleys," Keane continued.

That wasn't a question, so Erin didn't say anything.

"The charges against him include bribery, racketeering, drug trafficking, and conspiracy to commit murder," Keane said. "Is that accurate?"

"Those are the charges, sir," Erin said.

"Mr. Vitelli has some interesting things to say about you, Detective. Would you care to guess what those things are?"

"Perps say lots of things, sir," she said, staring steadily past Keane's left ear and avoiding looking into his face. "That doesn't make them true."

"Detective, look at me," Keane snapped. His voice, normally cool and collected, suddenly cracked like a pistol shot.

Startled, Erin met his eyes. "What?" she demanded.

"He's charged with conspiracy to murder a woman named Teresa Tommasino," Keane said. "A schoolteacher from

Brooklyn. An innocent woman who was being kept in protective custody by United States Marshals, prior to her death by car bomb outside the JFK Hilton."

"I remember the incident, sir," Erin said.

"I'd be surprised if you'd forgotten," Keane said. "Since you drove the vehicle to the hotel and were standing next to it when it exploded. Mr. Vitelli is claiming you killed Miss Tommasino."

"I didn't kill her, sir," Erin said, unflinching. She was looking right into Keane's double-barreled stare. Let him read whatever he wanted in her eyes. She was telling the truth.

"He says Morton Carlyle built a bomb and installed it in the car, which you checked out from the impound lot."

"Why would we do that?" Erin asked.

"As a favor to Vitelli," Keane said. "Miss Tommasino was the prosecution's key witness in the murder of Isabella Romano, the girlfriend of Vitelli's son. Miss Tommasino claimed to have seen Gabriel Vitelli leaving Miss Romano's apartment, covered in blood and carrying a bloody knife. Her death badly weakened the case against the younger Vitelli."

"So Vitelli confessed to ordering someone to kill a witness?" Erin asked.

"You seem to misunderstand the situation, Detective," Keane said. "You are a key witness yourself, in dozens of cases. You have been undercover with the Mob for months. Your testimony will be vital to securing convictions against Evan O'Malley and his associates. If it comes out that you have been acting in an extra-legal capacity, it could poison all those cases. Every one of those gangsters you've worked so hard to put away could skate."

"Sir, I don't know what Vitelli told you—" Erin began.

"Vitelli told me the truth!" Keane interrupted.

There was a moment of silence. Then, speaking slowly, Erin said, "You're right, sir. Valentino Vitelli isn't a member of the O'Malleys."

"Your point being?"

"He's not a member of the NYPD, either."

One of Keane's eyebrows went up ever so slightly. "So?"

"I'm just wondering why he was speaking to you, sir," she said. "Why would a Mafia captain have a line to an Internal Affairs Lieutenant?"

"He contacted me because this is an issue bearing on an officer in this Department," Keane said. "I need hardly remind you that the Mob has eyes and ears everywhere in this city, including in this building. You're worrying about the wrong things, Detective. You should be thinking about your future. If this comes out, and Vitelli has evidence to back it up, you're looking at serious felony charges. Forget your cases and your career; you'll spend the rest of your life, such as it is, behind bars. And you'll do hard time. Even in a women's correctional facility, former police officers don't fare well."

"Why did Vitelli tell you this?" Erin asked. "What does he want? If I go down for it, so does he."

"He's already going down," Keane said coldly. "Maybe he doesn't want to see an accomplice walking around free."

"What about *omerta*?" she retorted. "That Sicilian code of silence? Vitelli's an old-school Mafioso. He'd never rat out anybody else in the Life, not without a damn good reason."

"Again, you're worrying about the wrong thing," Keane said. "We're not talking about Vitelli's motivations. We're talking about you. How could you be so stupid? Did you really think this would never come back on you? A car bomb? You're sleeping with the best bomb-maker in Manhattan!"

"I'd advise you not to pursue this any further, sir," Erin said stiffly.

"Oh?" Keane's voice was softer now. Softer, and more dangerous. "And just why is that? I hope you're not threatening me, Detective. Now *that* would be stupid."

"It won't go anywhere," Erin said. "Because like I told you, I didn't kill Teresa Tommasino. Neither did Carlyle."

"How do you know that?"

She took the plunge. "Because Teresa isn't dead."

Chapter 11

It was very rare to see genuine surprise on Andrew Keane's face. Erin savored the moment; the way his eyes widened, the way his mouth dropped slightly open. For a few seconds he looked like an ordinary human being. It was incredibly gratifying.

He recovered quickly, his analytical mind kicking into action. "You orchestrated a switch," he said. "At the last minute. It was raining heavily that night. Visibility was bad. Did you make the switch in the hotel room?"

"Outside," Erin said. "Teresa got in the car, slid across the seat, and got out again before the bomb went off."

Keane nodded. "But there was a body in the wreckage," he observed. "Who *did* you kill?"

"Nobody, sir."

"Bodies don't simply appear out of thin air," he said. "As a homicide investigator, you know that better than most."

"A Jane Doe from the city morgue," Erin said. "I have no idea who she was, but she was dead long before we loaded her into that car."

For the second time in as many minutes, a real human expression crossed Keane's face. This one was a smile. It made an amazing improvement to his appearance. He chuckled. It sounded real and unfeigned.

"An anonymous corpse," he said. "Ingenious. I'm surprised the Medical Examiner didn't notice."

"She was in on it," Erin said. "Dr. Levine filed an inaccurate report, but she wrote up a genuine one, too. She's as straight an arrow as they come."

"And the Bomb Squad?" Keane asked.

"Their investigator was also informed," Erin said. "He advised how to construct the device to avoid any casualties and minimize collateral damage."

"And who gave permission for this little escapade?"

"Captain Holliday."

"It seems the only person uninformed was me." Keane was no longer smiling. "Why wasn't I consulted?"

Because I didn't trust you and I still don't, Erin thought. "As you said earlier in this conversation, sir, the Mob has informants in the Department," she said. "There'd already been an attempt on Miss Tommasino's life while under the Marshals' protection. We told only those people with an absolute need to know."

"Which did not include this office?"

"It was a tactical decision, sir. It was under Captain Holliday's jurisdiction."

"Oh, I'll be talking to the Captain, have no doubt about that," Keane said. "Where is Miss Tommasino now?"

"I don't know, sir."

"You don't know, or you won't tell me?" Keane demanded. Now he was getting pissed off. The man must be really off his game tonight. His self-control was much less in evidence than usual.

"I don't know, sir," she repeated. "She's not in New York City."

"Who does know where she is?"

"Why is that relevant, sir?"

"Because we need to establish that she is alive," Keane said. "To refute the allegations against you."

"That's not necessary," she said. "Captain Holliday, Dr. Levine, and Lieutenant Taylor will all confirm what I said. Levine's report, her corrected report, will verify that the body in the car was not Teresa Tommasino, and she will testify how the body was obtained. There was no murder, sir."

"Only the detonation of a destructive device in front of a busy New York hotel," Keane said. "This isn't Baghdad, O'Reilly. We can't just set off bombs for shits and giggles."

"If you'd like to file a formal reprimand, that's your right, sir," Erin said. She was suddenly tired of the conversation. She just wanted to get out of this room and get back to doing real police work, or maybe get some damn sleep.

"I may just do that," Keane said. "I really thought you had better judgment than this, Detective. I thought you had ambitions for promotion, for going places."

"Will there be anything else, sir?" she asked stonily.

"Not at present," Keane said. "But we're going to talk again. Soon. Dismissed."

Erin had learned from Vic how to convey sarcasm through body language. She threw a subtle hint of it into the salute she snapped off, before turning and getting the hell out of there.

* * *

Halfway down the stairs, Erin felt the sandwich and Diet Coke trying to climb back out of her stomach. Head swimming, she hurried the rest of the way down to Major Crimes, shoved open the restroom door, stumbled into the nearest stall, and dropped to her knees, feeling the jarring shock in her kneecaps. She barely made it.

Rolf had stayed beside her the whole way. He poked her cheek with his cold, wet snout and wagged his tail worriedly. Throwing up wasn't a big deal for dogs; it was a sort of trial run for their digestion, after which the questionable item could be either discarded or re-ingested. But humans had more of a problem with it. He could tell his partner wasn't feeling good, and wanted her to know he was there if she needed him.

"Shit," Erin said. "Not now, God damn it." A headache was hammering at the weak spot in her skull where she'd been recently shot, and it didn't seem to care that the timing was inconvenient.

She needed to think. Valentino Vitelli had contacted Keane. What did that mean? And why had she spilled the secret of Teresa's survival to that cold-blooded bastard? It had gotten him temporarily off her back, but was it worth it?

Erin became aware another woman was in the bathroom, standing behind her. "I'll be done in a minute," she said thickly and spat into the toilet bowl, trying to clear the sour aftertaste from her mouth.

"Take your time," Piekarski said. "Believe me, I know all about puking. You've never been knocked up, so you don't know how much fun morning sickness can be. I thought you might want someone to hold your hair back, and Rolf hasn't got hands."

"Thanks," Erin said. She got shakily to her feet. "Shit," she said again.

"That bad, huh?" Piekarski said.

"It's pretty bad," Erin said.

"What'd Internal Affairs want? Or aren't you allowed to say?"

"Oh, the usual. He threatened to throw me off the Force and into prison."

"He *what?*" Piekarski exclaimed. "What the hell for?"

"The usual," Erin said. "Corruption and murder."

"That son of a bitch!" Piekarski said. "I ought to go up there and plant my foot in his ass!"

Erin gave her a wan smile. "You really are a lot like Vic, you know that? Forget about it. I straightened it out."

"Who're you supposed to have killed?" Piekarski asked.

"Teresa Tommasino."

Piekarski had to think for a second. Then she got it. "The witness who got blown up at the hotel?"

"That's the one."

"But you didn't kill her."

"I know that."

"Why's he think you did?"

"Because Valentino Vitelli says I did."

"Why does Keane give a shit what some perp says?"

"Because he's ninety percent right. The cat's out of the bag, I guess, but don't go spreading this all over the place, okay?"

"Okay," Piekarski said doubtfully.

"Carlyle built the device and planted it in the car," Erin said. "He set it off by remote control."

"Holy shit," Piekarski said. "You mean your boyfriend's a murderer?"

Well, actually, yes, Erin thought. *He beat a guy to death with a barstool about twenty years ago in MacKenzie's Bar near La Guardia Airport, since you ask.* "That's not what I mean," she said. "It was a setup. We faked it. Teresa got out before the bomb went off. It was the only way we could think to protect her."

Piekarski whistled. "So that's why Vic's always been weird about that night," she said. "He gets funny whenever it comes up. He knows, doesn't he?"

"Yeah. It's the main reason the Mob trusted me as much as they did. By now they all know I'm really playing for the good guys, but they may not have figured out the Teresa angle just yet."

"If they do, won't she be in danger again?"

"Yeah, but she ought to be okay. She's not even in New York, and there's only one guy on Earth who knows where she is."

"Who's that?" Piekarski blurted. Then, before Erin could say anything, she shook her head. "Right. You can't tell me, and you shouldn't. Sorry. This secret-agent stuff is new to me. Just as long as she's safe, that's the main thing."

"Yeah," Erin said. "We need her to testify against Vitelli's son. It'll be a little ticklish getting her back to New York, but we'll figure something out in time for the trial."

"Wasn't Keane happy?" Piekarski asked. "That you weren't a murderer, I mean?"

"He was pissed that I hid it from him."

"Wait a second," Piekarski said. "Shouldn't he have known about this whole thing from the beginning? I mean, a cop pretending to murder someone, that's a big deal. There's gotta be people in the underworld who know about it, right?"

"It's part of my street rep," Erin said. "I'm Junkyard O'Reilly, remember?"

"And if that got back to IAB, Keane would have to investigate it, wouldn't he?"

"He wouldn't be doing his job otherwise."

"Then why didn't he already know?"

"I'm starting to wonder if maybe he did," Erin said quietly.

"Erin? What on Earth are you talking about?"

"One thing at a time," Erin said. "We've got to put the O'Malley thing to bed first. Then we can worry about the rest of this crap."

"Oh, that reminds me," Piekarski said. "While you were upstairs, Webb and Vic got back with Evan O'Malley. They're downstairs right now, getting him booked."

"Really?" Erin felt a surge of fresh energy, temporarily dispelling her fatigue and headache. "I better get down there. Can you watch Rolf for a little while?"

"Copy that," Piekarski said. She wrinkled her nose. "He smells a little charbroiled."

"You're not the first person to say that," Erin said. "I haven't had time to give him a bath."

"That's okay," Piekarski said. "We've all smelled worse."

"How do I look?" Erin asked.

Piekarski pointed at the mirror over the sink. "Like you walked away from a plane crash. See for yourself."

Erin took a look. A hollow-eyed, pale-faced woman stared back at her. Soot was smudged on her cheeks and forehead. Sleet and sweat had smeared it and left channels on her filthy face. She had blood on her right cheek, just below the eye, and had no idea how it had gotten there. Her hair was a mess. Traces of bile lingered at the corners of her mouth.

"Yikes," she said. "I better wash up."

"Maybe you should stay the way you are," Piekarski offered. "You can play bad cop and scare the hell out of O'Malley."

Erin actually considered it longer than she should have. Then she turned on the hot water and reached for the soap dispenser.

* * *

When she got down to the interrogation rooms, Webb was just stepping out of Room One. For a middle-aged guy who'd been up all night, he seemed positively energetic. He closed the door and paused to adjust his necktie. His bulletproof vest had left the clothes underneath a little rumpled. Then he saw her.

"O'Reilly," he said. "Good. I was just going to see if you were upstairs, in case you—"

He stopped short. His eyes narrowed and his gaze traveled over her face. The almost cheerful expression on his own face dissolved.

"What?" Erin asked.

"You look awful," he said.

Erin fought down a half-hysterical laugh. *You should've seen me five minutes ago*, she thought. "I'm fine," she said. "Is he in there?"

"That's right," Webb said. "But don't worry about that right now. Shouldn't you go to the hospital and get cleared?"

"I said I'm fine," she said sharply. "The building caught fire. I didn't."

"It's been a night," he said. "I'm glad you're not hurt. What about Carlyle? He was brought in a little while ago, but I haven't seen him."

"He's okay," she said. "Except for being under arrest after watching his home and his place of business burn."

"The Barley Corner was a money-laundering operation for the O'Malleys," he reminded her. "And a center of gambling and arms smuggling."

"And a damn fine bar," she said.

Webb's shoulders moved in a fractional shrug. "That, too. Carlyle's in Room Three. Not because we're asking him any questions, but to keep him out of Holding. That place is packed to the bars with O'Malley associates and we really don't want him mingling with them right now. Is he blown?"

"We have to assume so," she said. "Me, too. I don't know who Pritchard might have told before coming to the Corner. Carlyle's going to need protection."

"You mean besides that ex-Marine who's always following him around?"

"Ian can't come into a police station," she said. "Not packing a pistol, at any rate. And he's good, but do you really want to farm out our witness protection to a vigilante?"

"No, we certainly wouldn't want to do that," Webb said, more dryly than usual. He cleared his throat. "I haven't questioned O'Malley yet. I guarantee he'll lawyer up the moment I ask him anything. The only thing I can think of that might shake him is you. Are you game to go in there with me? It might not be pleasant."

As opposed to what I've been doing? Erin thought. She squared her shoulders. "Absolutely, sir."

Chapter 12

Evan O'Malley hadn't been expecting ESU to knock on his door. He'd been smart enough to cooperate when they'd pulled him out of bed, offering no resistance whatsoever, so the cops had let him change out of his pajamas into actual clothing. He still looked more disheveled than Erin had ever seen him. He was in his shirtsleeves, unshaven, hair uncombed. His cuffs lacked their usual diamond-studded cufflinks. The jewelry he wore instead was a pair of steel bracelets. holding his wrists together on the stainless-steel tabletop.

For all that, he retained an impressive, scary presence. When Erin and Webb walked into the room, he looked steadily at them with eyes colder than the December morning. He regarded Erin as if she was a complete stranger.

"I understand you might be feeling a little confused right now, Mr. O'Malley," Webb said. "I apologize for waking you so abruptly. You have a reputation as a consummate businessman, a reasonable man. You've had a little while to consider your situation, so I'm hoping you're willing to be reasonable."

Evan said nothing. He was studying Erin intently, paying no attention whatsoever to the Lieutenant. She felt like he was stripping away not only her clothing, but her skin and bones. He was drilling down to her brain and heart. He was reevaluating everything he knew about her, figuring out her angle.

"What you should be thinking," Webb went on, "is how to minimize damage to yourself. You know how we dismantle organizations like yours, of course. We start at the bottom and get your underlings to flip on their bosses. Then we get the bosses and lean on them until *they* flip, and so on up the chain until we get to you. Your problem, Mr. O'Malley, is that you're the man at the top. There's nowhere to go from you. Unless you can implicate the Governor, or the President, or maybe the Pope, the buck stops with you. That makes your options for striking a deal somewhat limited."

"I'm a businessman," Evan said quietly, without taking his eyes from Erin. "I deal primarily in real estate and construction. You're free to audit my companies' books. My income is completely legitimate, as the IRS has repeatedly determined."

"You mean we can't get you like the Feds got Capone," Webb said, smiling thinly.

"Which books do you mean?" Erin interjected. "Are you talking about the fake ones, or Maggie Callahan's ledger?"

To Evan's credit, he didn't twitch a muscle. The man's self-control was incredible. "Maggie Callahan?" he repeated. "Miss Callahan is not employed by any organization to which I belong, as you know perfectly well. She is a talented young woman in whose education and improvement I took a charitable interest, nothing more. If you are insinuating our relationship is somehow improper, I'm offended by the implication."

"We've got her books," Erin said bluntly. "It's over. We have everything and everyone."

"You're making a terrible mistake," Evan said, boring icy holes in her with his eyes. "I hope you're considering the consequences."

"Don't you dare threaten me," she snapped, returning his cold glare with a hot one of her own. "You can't do a goddamn thing to me!"

"You think you're invulnerable because of your badge and your connections," Evan said. "I assure you, that protection will vanish instantly once they know what you've done. You have blood on your hands, Miss O'Reilly, and it's a stain that doesn't wash out."

"That's where you're wrong," Erin said. "It was all a setup, from the very beginning. I've been playing you from the start. Half the talks I've had with you, I was wearing a wire. We've got recordings to go with the ledger. Remember Phil Stachowski?"

"The failed policeman?" Evan retorted. "The cripple who'd shit himself if he didn't have his pathetic wife to haul his useless ass to the toilet?"

It was Erin who flinched. She'd never heard words like that come out of Evan's mouth before. The pure arctic hatred pouring off him was something new to her. If his hands hadn't been secured, she believed he might well have tried to strangle her on the spot.

"You knew he had an informant inside your crew," she said, keeping her voice as steady as she could. "That was me, Evan. I was Phil's guy. Everything I heard, everything your people did around me, I fed it all back to him. You say whatever you want. Yeah, Phil may be in a wheelchair, but he can roll that chair wherever he wants. You may be able to walk, but you'll be making laps in the exercise yard at Sing Sing for the rest of your life."

For just a second, Erin thought Evan really would come over the table at her, handcuffs notwithstanding. She tensed, getting ready to fight. But the moment passed. The mask fell back over Evan's face. His control was back, leaving no trace of the rage he'd shown a few seconds before.

"Well played, Detective," he said softly. "You played an excellent hand for very high stakes. You'll soon see, I imagine, whether or not your winnings were worth what you've lost. I'd like my telephone call now, Lieutenant Webb. And my lawyer."

* * *

"Good work," Webb said. They were in the observation room next door, looking at Evan through the one-way glass.

"I didn't get much," Erin said. She picked up her Glock and backup revolver from the table where she'd left them and replaced them on her belt and ankle. You never brought guns into interrogation rooms.

"You got more than I expected," he said. "Besides, I was telling the truth. We don't need his testimony, and there's nothing he can offer us. The only deal he'll get will be from the DA, and Markham isn't in a mood to go easy on him. Evan O'Malley's going to die in prison."

Erin nodded.

"He's a murderer, O'Reilly," Webb said. "He's directly responsible for the death of Veronica Blackburn, plus God only knows how many others."

"I know that," she said.

"He can't hurt you," Webb said. "Not anymore."

"I know," she repeated, less convincingly.

"This was always the endgame," Webb said. "And I have one piece of good news for you."

"What's that?"

"He didn't say a thing about Carlyle."

"So?"

"So he may not know you turned him," Webb said. "Not yet."

"It doesn't matter," Erin said. "Carlyle's the one who let me in. Even if Carlyle didn't know what I was doing, Evan would still kill him for screwing up."

"Erin," Webb said.

He hardly ever used her first name. She turned to face him. "Yeah?"

"You've done a good job," he said. "An exceptional job."

"Then why do I feel like shit?"

It sounded cheaply pitiful as she said it. For an embarrassing few seconds, she thought she might break down and cry in front of her commanding officer.

"You've been in a fire," Webb said. "Someone tried to kill you. Don't try to shrug that off. These are scary people, so it's natural to be a little scared of them. It's a human reaction. But trust me. Evan O'Malley is done. The O'Malleys are finished."

She nodded again.

"I'd tell you to go home and get some rest," he said.

"Except my home is a smoking ruin," she said.

"Do you have a place to stay?"

"I could crash at my brother's," she said doubtfully.

"But...?"

"But I don't want to bring my family into this until I'm sure it's safe," she said. "They've been through enough. How long are we keeping Carlyle in custody?"

"It's for his own protection," he reminded her. "The FBI is cleaning house pretty thoroughly. O'Malley doesn't have anyone in the Marshals. They're arranging a WitSec detail for him as we speak. He'll be in a safe house by the time the sun comes up."

"Then I'd just as soon stay here until then," she said.

"All right," Webb said. "I suppose it's useless to suggest you get some sleep."

"How much stuff still needs to be done?"

"We've got mountains of arrest reports."

"Then I might as well pitch in on those," she said. "I don't think I can sleep right now. All that paperwork may help the adrenaline wear off."

"We'll go on up to Major Crimes, as soon as we stash O'Malley in Holding," Webb said.

"Copy that, sir."

Erin stepped out of the observation room and ran directly into Vic, who was walking the other way. Erin was five-foot-six and weighed about one-forty. Vic was six-three and well over two hundred pounds. She bounced off him like a pinball.

"Watch where you're going, asshole!" Vic snapped.

"Glad to see you too, Vic," she said.

He blinked. "Erin! Shit, I'm sorry. I didn't mean that. I wasn't looking."

"Good thing you don't drive the way you walk," she said. "What's going on?"

"I heard they got Finnegan in Holding," he said. "I was gonna take a quick look. Jesus, Erin, you look—"

"—like crap," she finished for him. "Yeah, I know. You should see the other guy."

Webb came through the doorway with a little more caution. "Did you get everything filed, Neshenko?" he asked.

"Just about," Vic said, his eyes going slightly shifty. "I mean, I've got sixty, maybe seventy percent of it done."

He fell in step with Webb. Erin followed them. They collected Evan from Interrogation. Vic guided him to the station's lockup with a big, meaty hand on the mobster's upper arm.

"You ever notice in the movies, a guy grabs a girl here, she's suddenly helpless?" Vic said. "It's gotta be the easiest hold in the world to break out of, unless you're wearing cuffs like our boy here. Just duck and twist. Anyone ever try to grab you on the bicep, Erin?"

"Bad guys try to grab every part of me," she replied. "It doesn't end well for them."

Evan pretended not to hear. He walked in stolid silence, lost in his own thoughts.

Erin took off her guns again and secured them in a locker outside the holding cells. Vic and Webb had been handling prisoners and weren't armed. The three detectives marched Evan through a steel door into the Eightball's holding facility.

They didn't keep perps at the station longer than absolutely necessary. It was loud, messy, chaotic, and dangerous. A fleet of prisoner transport vans should have been waiting to ferry the bad guys to Riker's Island, where they'd await arraignment. But the accelerated timetable of the arrests had thrown the schedule into chaos. They were still waiting on the vans. In the meantime, the cells were filled to capacity with O'Malleys.

A chorus of jeers and catcalls met the cops and their prisoner. It was the usual stuff: speculation as to their parentage and ethnicity, crude sexual suggestions, and thinly-veiled threats. Then, as recognition trickled through the room, the comments became sharper and more personal, aimed at Erin in particular.

"Hey, Junkyard! Trailer-trash bitch!"

"Traitor!"

"Goddamn rat!"

"You feel proud, slinging your ass for the City?"

"Somebody call the Vice squad, there's a hooker working the neighborhood!"

"How much did they pay you to screw your way into the gang? I bet you earned every dollar!"

"Bitch!"

"Cow!"

"Slut!"

"Whore!"

Erin had heard it all before. A female cop had to learn to let the language slide off her, or she wouldn't last a week on the street. But she knew a lot of these guys, had been friendly with many of them. They'd trusted her. They had every right to be angry.

She wasn't usually a blusher, but she felt an unfamiliar burning in her cheeks. She didn't look any prisoners in the eye, didn't engage with their taunts. She wished she hadn't come in here. She should have gone upstairs, where she was a hero. It was cowardly, but it was the truth.

A trucker, one of Wayne McClernand's buddies, thrust his face against the bars as close to her as he could get. "How'd it taste?" he snarled. "Sucking off our guys?"

"Why don't you ask your mom?" Vic suggested. "I hear she's into it."

The trucker spat at Erin. Saliva spattered her shoulder. She kept walking down the middle of the corridor. Jail hallways were extra wide, so officers could stay out of arm's reach of the cells. She, Webb, and Evan were in the center of the concrete. So was Vic, but when the trucker spat, he sidestepped.

Vic was such a big guy, it was easy to forget how fast he could move when he wanted to. He let go of Evan and darted toward the holding cell. The guy tried to pull back, but Vic's arm snaked through the bars. He grabbed a handful of the trucker's shirt, just under the collar, and yanked him forward. The man's face met the hardened steel of the bars with a surprisingly loud clang.

"Neshenko!" Webb snapped.

Vic let go of the trucker, who groaned and slid down the inside of the bars to his knees. "What?" he asked with false innocence. "He slipped. I tried to catch him."

Webb shook his head and rubbed the fingers of his right hand together, wishing he was holding a cigarette. Vic glared at the other gangsters, daring someone to say something, but they suddenly found other things to look at than the belligerent Russian.

The detectives deposited Evan in the least crowded holding cell. It might've been better to keep the O'Malley leadership separate from their underlings, but there just wasn't room. Erin supposed it might do Evan some good to mingle with the rank-and-file. She wondered whether he'd appreciate it.

"There's the guy," Vic said, nodding toward the adjacent cell.

Kyle Finnegan was sitting on the bench against the wall. Two more guys could have fit, one on either side of him, but in spite of the crowded conditions he had the bench to himself. He was wearing a tweed sport coat over a tank top. His hair stuck out at odd angles. His watery, vacant eyes wandered around the room. His skull showed the dent where a Detroit Teamster had caved it in with a tire iron a decade ago. He looked like a homeless bum, but Erin knew better.

"I gotta apologize, buddy," Vic said to him. "I was supposed to be there to bust your ass, but I got a little sidetracked. I didn't want you to think I forgot about you. How do you like it in there? You nice and comfy?"

Finnegan blinked and more or less focused on Vic. "The mind is its own place and, in itself can make a heaven of hell or a hell of heaven," he said.

"Your mind is a place I wouldn't even want to visit," Vic said. "You oughta have warning labels on your face, you crazy son of a bitch."

"Men have called me mad," Finnegan said. "But the question is not yet settled, whether madness is or is not the loftiest intelligence—whether much that is glorious—whether all that is profound—does not spring from disease of thought—from moods of mind exalted at the expense of the general intellect."

"I friggin' love this guy," Vic said. "We should set up a booth and sell tickets, like those old carnival freak shows."

Erin wasn't listening to Vic. She was staring at Finnegan, trying to puzzle him out. She'd suspected for a long time that he wasn't nearly as crazy as he seemed. What did he know? What was he thinking right now? As if sensing her attention, he turned toward her and smiled vaguely.

"If all you've got to say is the words of other, better men, I think we're done with you," Webb said. "See you in court, Mr. Finnegan."

"Fear is the real prison," Finnegan said, still looking at Erin. "A man with nothing to lose is the freest man alive, for he has nothing to fear. By that argument, you're in prison and I'm flying free."

"You think I'm scared?" Erin said. "Of *you?*"

"I know you're scared," Finnegan said. "Fear has a smell, you know. It's the scent of rainy nights, old blood, maggots... and smoke. Little girls shouldn't play with fire. Your hair might catch fire. How would that feel, do you suppose? Would you feel each strand burning, or would it all be one blazing pain?"

Erin needed to get out of that room, away from the jeering crowd of angry criminals. Finnegan was right in at least one thing. Fear did have a smell. The Precinct 8 lockup was thick and heavy with it. These men were angry because they were scared. It should have made her happy. Instead, she wanted to throw up again.

She hurried down the hall outside Holding. As she passed the interrogation rooms, she slowed to a stop. Carlyle was sitting in there with only his thoughts for company. He was probably desperately worried, though he'd be doing his best to conceal it. She ought to at least check on him.

He wasn't alone. She should have anticipated that. The Eightball was full to bursting with cops and bad guys. Some of the cops might *be* the bad guys. Webb and Holliday weren't taking any chances on somebody popping Carlyle. An ESU officer in full tactical gear was standing in a corner of the room. He'd broken the rule against firearms in interrogation rooms, and he'd broken it hard. He was holding an AR-15 assault rifle.

Carlyle himself sat quietly at the table. He looked up when the door opened. At the sight of Erin, an expression of mixed relief and worry flashed across his face.

"Corky's in surgery," she told him. "Critical condition, but he's still breathing. I would've heard if... if anything had gotten worse."

He smiled thinly. "This is where you tell me no news is good news, aye?"

"Yeah. I'll get to the hospital when I can. Are you okay here?"

"I'll keep. Officer Rowlands and I were just discussing the finer points of literature."

Erin glanced at the ESU guy. "Really?"

"I'm a Tom Clancy guy," Rowlands said. "*Rainbow Six*, that's what I'm talking about. Special Forces blowing away terrorists. This guy, he don't appreciate a good book."

"Do you need anything?" Erin asked Carlyle.

"A shower, a shave, and a change of clothing," he said. "But one can't be choosy. Matters might, on the whole, be a great deal worse."

"Yeah," she said. "The building could be on fire."

"Precisely."

Chapter 13

Back upstairs, Erin and the others plunged into the ocean of paperwork. It would have been nice to prepare it ahead of time, but that might have compromised the operation's security. Piekarski had been doing what she could, but had mostly needed to handle the phones and coordinate the various branches of the op. So there was nothing for it but to fill out the endless DD-5s, arrest reports, preliminary evidence reports, and so on and on and on.

Webb drank cup after cup of black coffee, clearly wishing he could smoke in the office. Vic, unwilling to trust his wakefulness to the Eightball's vending machines, made a run to the nearest convenience store and came back with thirty-six cans of Mountain Dew and a twelve-pack of Diet Coke. He gave the Diet Coke to Erin, opened a can of Dew, and started typing and drinking. He stacked the empties at the end of his desk and soon had a small aluminum stockpile.

Erin caffeinated herself only slightly less than Vic. She resolutely avoided looking at the clock, concentrating on one official form after another. Officers came and went, most of them with urgent business for Webb or Holliday. Rolf finally managed to curl up and fall asleep beside her desk in spite of the constant activity. Gradually, order emerged from chaos. Words blurred together on the pages in front of her. She kept going, trying not to notice the names of the suspects on the forms. Most of them were assholes, sure, but not all. Some basically decent guys were going to prison because of her.

A big, muscular hand fell on her shoulder. She was so tired that she didn't even twitch in her usual defensive reaction. She blinked and looked groggily up into Vic's face.

"Huh?" she said, or a sound to that effect.

"The Marshals are here," he said in an undertone.

"What Marshals?" she asked stupidly.

"The US Marshals," he said. "You know, the guys who chase down fugitives and handle Witness Protection?"

Worn-out neurons fired in what was left of Erin's brain. "Oh," she said. "Right. Where are they?"

"Captain's office," Vic said cocking his head toward Holliday's door. "They walked right past you. Look, Erin, if you want to catch some Zs, I can lend you my key and you can crash at our place."

"Thanks, but I'm good," she lied. She got to her feet, bracing herself on her desk. Rolf sat up, yawned, stretched, and tilted his ears toward her, wondering what was going on. She and the dog crossed the room, trying not to stumble on tired legs.

A moment after she knocked, a man in a black suit opened the door. He had a dark red tie around his neck, an automatic pistol in his shoulder holster, and a silver star on his belt.

"O'Reilly," he said, nodding. "Good to see you again."

"Marshal Calley," she said, recognizing one of the men who'd guarded Teresa Tommasino. He'd also been on Alfredo Madonna's ill-fated protection detail.

"Come in, Detective," Captain Holliday said.

Erin and Rolf stepped inside. Calley closed the door behind them. Another Marshal, a broad-shouldered hulk with no visible neck, took up space next to the window. Outside, the sky had turned a dull gray. The sun had come up, but the sleet was still falling.

"Glad to have you with us," Holliday said. "You know Marshals Calley and Hodges, I think?"

"Yes, sir," she said.

"They'll be taking charge of the protection detail for our primary subject," Holliday said.

"Excellent," Erin said, and she meant it. She'd seen Calley in action. The man was rock solid under pressure. Hodges had helped with the Teresa situation, too. She trusted both of them much more than she would a pair of strangers.

Calley grimaced. "Detective," he said. "I didn't get the chance to apologize."

"For what?" she asked.

"I've only ever lost one protectee," he said. "I should've been more on the ball at the Hilton."

"Forget about it," she said. "No harm done."

"No harm…" he echoed incredulously, and in his eyes she could see the memory of an SUV turning into a fireball.

"Seriously," she said. "It's fine. Anyway, I'm not the one you should apologize to. You ought to be talking to Teresa Tommasino."

"That might be a little difficult," Calley said. His jaw was tight.

"Not as hard as you might think," she replied.

His eyes went wide, then narrowed. "Are you saying what I think you're saying?" he asked quietly.

"That's neither here nor there," Holliday said. "The important thing is, from the point of view of Major Crimes, you and your partner have an unblemished reputation. I trust you will maintain the excellent work you have thus far performed."

"We'll do everything we can, Captain," Calley said. "Who's the protectee?"

"Morton Carlyle," Holliday said.

"Wait a second," Hodges said. "I've heard of him. Isn't he that IRA terrorist guy? The bomb-maker?"

"Retired," Erin interjected.

"Didn't we look at him for the Hilton bombing?" Hodges pressed. "We talked to your Bomb Squad and everything."

"That's beside the point," Holliday said. "He's in WitSec now, and his safety is your responsibility. Is that a problem?"

"Of course not, sir," Calley said crisply, before Hodges could say anything else. "Every protectee receives the same protection."

"I would expect nothing less," Holliday said. "O'Reilly will be accompanying you to the safe house. Your subject is in Interrogation Room Three, downstairs. She'll show you."

"Gentlemen," Erin said, leading the way.

As they passed through Major Crimes, Erin noticed someone had set up a TV at one end of the room. The Commissioner was on, the words NYPD PRESS CONFERENCE marching across the bottom of the screen. All activity in the outer office had ceased, cops pausing in their duties to watch.

Erin ignored it. She already knew what had happened and wasn't interested in the PC's spin. He was a politician, not a cop, and he'd say what he thought would make the Department look good. Anything he left out or distorted would only piss her off, and she had places to go. He probably wouldn't name her anyway, not until the dust had settled. This was his victory lap, and she'd just finished a marathon. She was too tired to make another trip around the track.

They took the stairs down, Hodges bringing up the rear. The Marshals seemed wide awake and alert. Erin was glad *somebody* was. She felt oddly disconnected from what was going on, like her feet were floating about two inches off the floor. She wondered whether that was another symptom of a traumatic brain injury, or just the cumulative effect of stress and residual adrenaline.

Carlyle was sitting quietly in Interrogation Room 3, hands clasped in front of him. He was sooty and dirty, the borrowed NYPD raincoat still draped over his shoulders, but his face was calm. When he saw Erin, he smiled and stood up.

"A fine morning to you," he said.

"It's some kind of morning," Hodges said. "We're rolling. You ready?"

"I've no baggage, if that's what you're asking," Carlyle said.

They moved out, Calley on point now, Hodges still trailing. Erin, Rolf, and Carlyle walked in the middle, like VIPs being escorted by the Secret Service.

"We'll go out through the basement," Calley said. "No goddamn TV cameras down there. I guess they're all thinking about that press conference anyway. A car's waiting."

"I won't be needing to ride in the boot, will I?" Carlyle asked with a slight smile.

"Boot?" Hodges asked, glancing down at his feet.

"Trunk," Erin translated.

"Do you want to?" Calley asked.

"It wouldn't be my first choice," Carlyle said.

"Windows are bulletproof," Hodges said. "Tinted, too. You ought to be fine in the back seat unless somebody shows up with a rocket launcher. But you can lie down if it makes you feel better."

When they got to the garage, Calley held up a hand. "O'Reilly, with me," he said.

The two of them approached the Marshals' car, a black Lincoln Town Car. Calley nodded to Erin.

"You want Rolf to check it?" she asked.

"We wouldn't want there to be a bomb under it, would we?" he replied dryly.

"Very funny," she muttered. "Rolf, *such!*"

Rolf obediently circled the car with her, snuffling at the wheel wells and undercarriage. Smelling no trace of explosives, he finished his search and looked up at her, wagging his tail.

"Good boy," she said, rubbing his ears. "Okay, we're clear."

Calley waved the others over. He slid behind the wheel. Hodges waited while Erin, Rolf, and Carlyle piled into the back seat. Then he got into the shotgun seat and they drove away into the wet, gray Manhattan dawn.

* * *

"Clear," Hodges said over the radio.

"Let's move," Calley said. He'd stayed with the car while Hodges went ahead to make sure nobody was lurking inside the safe house.

Erin, Carlyle, and Rolf quickly crossed the few yards of asphalt between them and the building. Erin's eyes darted around the skyline, looking for silhouettes on rooftops or shapes behind windows. She thought of Ian again, imagining riflemen taking aim at them.

It was all nonsense, of course. Even if Evan had known Carlyle was a traitor, and where they were going, and was able to set up a contract on such short notice, the O'Malleys had no professional-quality marksmen. Ian himself, and maybe one or two of his Marine buddies, were the only guys who might qualify, and they didn't work for Evan; they weren't even technically criminals.

But paranoia had an insistent voice. Once awoken, it never entirely shut up. So Erin kept her wits and eyes as sharp as she could, in spite of her worn-down condition, until they were not only inside the building but inside the apartment unit. Then, as Calley slid the deadbolt home with a reassuring click, she sagged against the wall.

"You've got nothing to worry about," Calley assured her. "We're fine. This was completely routine."

"Maybe I should have Rolf do a sweep," she suggested.

"If it'll make you feel better," he said. "But nobody knew we were coming here until yesterday evening, and we didn't know who our subject was until we got to your Captain's office."

"Pritchard blew up the gas line into the Corner," she argued, wondering even as she said it why she was bothering. Pritchard was dead, damn it, and he'd known where Carlyle was. This was a completely different situation.

"Like I said, feel free," Calley said. "Hodges, did you see anything out of place?"

"That's a negative," Hodges said, emerging from the bedroom.

"Rolf, *such*," Erin said wearily.

Rolf paused, one paw raised, and looked at her. He thought he'd heard her correctly, but she hadn't given the command in her usual firm tone.

"*Such!*" she repeated, more emphatically.

His tail started wagging and he forged ahead, quickly searching the apartment. He found nothing of interest, but that was okay. Erin told him what a good boy he was, and though he already knew it, he never got tired of hearing it. She gave him his rubber ball, and that made everything good.

"There's food in the fridge," Calley said. "The stove's electric, so don't worry about another gas explosion. You're going to need some fresh clothes. If you can get me a list with your sizes,

I'll have Hodges run out and get some stuff. The TV's hooked up, and so is the phone line, but stay off the Internet and social media. No outgoing calls unless it's an emergency. You screw up, it won't be me you're answering to. We clear?"

"Crystal, Marshal," Carlyle said.

"I can stay in here with you, or I can hang out next door," Calley continued, producing a slip of paper from his pocket and handing it to him. "Whatever you're more comfortable with. Here's the numbers for Hodges and me, along with the main office. Let me repeat, do *not* contact anyone else directly. Do you have family?"

"My mum's in Belfast," Carlyle said. "And my brother's in Kenya."

"Kenya? Really?" Calley was surprised. "What's he doing there?"

"Missionary work," Carlyle said. "You needn't fret, I've not spoken to either of them going on twenty years. I'm hardly likely to ring them up now. I've no idea how to reach Norbert, come to that. Chances are he doesn't have a telephone."

"Don't call anyone local, either," Calley said. "I'm not joking about this."

Carlyle nodded. "You can stay next door for the present," he said. "I'm thinking that's close enough. I'll have Detective O'Reilly and her dog looking after me here."

"Okay," Calley said. "Just write down your measurements and we'll get those clothes. It's a good day for it."

"How do you mean?" Erin asked.

"Boxing Day," Calley said, smiling. "Second-biggest shopping day of the year. Everything's on sale."

Once Hodges had departed on his errands and Calley had left, Erin and Carlyle considered the apartment. It was a one-bedroom unit, furnished to about the same level as an inexpensive motel. The plaster on the walls showed some cracks, and the carpet was scuffed and stained, but it was clean and apparently vermin-free.

"It's kind of a shit-hole," Erin commented.

"Ah, it's not so bad," Carlyle said. "It rather reminds me of the flat Rose and I had when we were married. A fresh coat of paint and a few pictures on the wall would make this feel like home. Though I doubt I'll be hanging my coat here long enough."

"We'll be hanging our coats, you mean," she said.

"Erin, darling, I'd not ask you to share my exile and confinement," he said.

She laced her fingers through his and leaned her head against his shoulder. "It's only for a little while, like you said. Besides, it's not like I've got somewhere else to live."

"I've plenty of money," he said. "You can stay wherever you want."

"Then I'm going to save you some of that money," she said. "I want to stay here with you. What, you think I've been hanging out with you because you have a fancy downtown apartment, a nice bar, and some flashy suits?"

"It's always been something of a mystery to me why you're spending time with a lad like myself," he replied.

"Bullshit," she said, stepping back and looking up into his face. "You know exactly what you're doing, you charming son of a bitch. You're the only guy I've ever been with who really understands me, what I do, and what I want. You took a bullet for me, for Christ's sake! Even my dad gets it, and he used to hate you."

Carlyle nodded. "I do love you, darling," he said.

Ignoring the smell of smoke and sweat, their dirty clothes and the dampness that still clung to them, Erin put her arms around him and drew him close. As she tilted her lips up to kiss him, she felt something bump against her hip, a small lump in the front pocket of Carlyle's trousers.

"What've you got in there?" she murmured. "I know you don't carry a gun..."

"Nothing like that," he said. "It's naught but a wee keepsake I rescued on my way out of our flat."

"Oh?" she asked. "What is it?"

"It's something I'd just as soon discuss later," he said. "We've had a difficult night. Perhaps you're wanting a shower and a bit of sleep now."

"God, yes," she said. "But I'll wait for Hodges to get here with some more clothes. I'm not putting this underwear back on. I think maybe I should burn it."

"Waste of good undergarments, darling."

"It's not my good stuff anyway," she said. "Should I have sent Hodges to Victoria's Secret, do you think? Asked him to pick out something black and lacy? Imagine the look on his face."

Carlyle chuckled. "Now there's a thought," he said. "But you're lovely enough, whatever you're wearing."

"Careful there," she said. "I'm a woman whose house was just set on fire. I'm tired and I'm vulnerable, but don't think that means I'm easy."

"I've never thought you were easy, Erin," he said. "In fact, you're possibly the most difficult lass I've ever known. But that merely makes you more rewarding in the end."

She pulled back to arm's length and wrinkled her brow at him. "Is that a compliment? I'm too tired to tell."

"It is," he said. "Nothing, and nobody, who's easy is worth having. This conversation reminds me. When do you think I'll be able to visit poor Corky in hospital?"

"Not right away," she said. "We'll need to confirm we've got all the O'Malleys, and give things a day or two to settle. I can check on him if you like."

"Grand," he said.

"But first, like you said, shower and sleep," she said. "God, I hope Hodges gets back soon. I guess I can bathe Rolf while we wait."

Rolf gave her a mournful look. He'd been afraid of this.

Chapter 14

When she woke up, Erin had no idea where she was. Her head was pounding. She was lying in an unfamiliar bed in a strange room. She didn't even recognize the smell of the place: a combination of cheap tobacco, bleach, and pine-scented air freshener. And she wasn't alone in the bed. A man lay beside her, his back toward her. Had she been drunk? How drunk?

Memories flooded into her as her brain rebooted itself. She was in the Marshals' safe house. Carlyle was sleeping beside her. Rolf lay curled at the foot of the bed, tail wrapped around his snout. She could hear Carlyle's slow, steady breathing and the whistle of air in and out of Rolf's nostrils.

She sat up and saw her phone and guns on the nightstand, within easy reach. She picked up the phone and checked it. The clock read 11:32AM. She'd been asleep for a few hours, but couldn't remember when she'd tumbled into bed. The phone showed a handful of messages, nothing urgent. Webb requested that she come to the office when it was convenient. A text from Vic applauded her for being a celebrity, which Erin didn't take as a good sign. She also had congratulations from three other cops, one of whom was her dad's old friend Sergeant Malcolm.

The lack of emergency messages was good news as far as it went, but she'd been out of circulation too long. She rolled out of bed and had to take a moment remembering where the bathroom was. The floor was cold and hard under her bare feet; the apartment's heating system left something to be desired.

Her reflection looked better than it had in the last mirror she'd stared into. Her face wasn't as pale and the shadows under her eyes weren't as dark. She was clean and not too battered. Her hair was a tangled mess, since she'd gone to bed with it still wet from her shower, but one of the Marshals, bless him, had left a little bundle of toiletries next to the sink. This included a comb and hairbrush, as well as a pair of toothbrushes, soap, shampoo, shaving cream, a disposable razor, and even a package of black hairbands.

After she'd brushed her hair and tied it back in a ponytail, she returned to the bedroom and started sorting through the clothes Hodges had bought. His taste wasn't as bad as she'd feared. He'd opted for conservative clothing that would blend into the background, befitting people who were hiding under the radar. She selected a royal blue turtleneck and a pair of black jeans. As she pulled the turtleneck over her head, she saw Carlyle and Rolf watching her.

"Sorry," she said. "I didn't mean to wake you."

"It's no trouble, darling," Carlyle said. "I'll likely go back to sleep once you're gone. Stern call of duty, is it?"

"Yeah. I'd better get back and see how we're doing," she said. "Don't worry, you'll be fine here. Calley and Hodges are good guys."

"I'm not worried about myself," he said. "It's you I'm fretting over. Oughtn't you to be staying hidden, too?"

"Relax," she said. "It's probably all over by now."

"Ian told me once complacency was the enemy of security," Carlyle said.

"That sounds like the sort of thing he'd say," Erin said. "But I can't hide here. There's work to be done. Do you need anything?"

"A bit of reading material wouldn't come amiss," he said. "Perhaps a bottle of whiskey. And I'd appreciate learning how Corky's faring."

"I'll see what I can do," she said. She leaned over and kissed him. "Sorry you got uprooted like this."

"An Irishman grows accustomed to being torn from his home," Carlyle said. "That's why we've gone and colonized the whole world. Remember, we've more Irishmen in New York than there are in Ireland."

"You're saying New York is an Irish colony?"

"Isn't it?"

* * *

Two news vans were parked in front of the Eightball. Erin, anticipating this, had asked the cabbie to drop her off at the end of the block. She and Rolf slipped into the basement garage on foot and infiltrated the building from below. They evaded notice, even going so far as to use the elevator instead of the stairs.

Then the doors slid back to reveal Major Crimes. Vic, Webb, and Piekarski were at their desks, but a bunch of other officers were there, too. Most of the work seemed to consist of sorting and filing documents. The chaos of the previous night had subsided, replaced by the low-level hum of competent activity. Erin walked her K-9 through the middle of it, angling toward her own desk.

She was about halfway when Vic noticed her. He stood up and started clapping. Piekarski and Webb joined him, and soon everyone was applauding. Someone gave a piercing two-fingered whistle. Erin feigned grumpiness, waving a hand to dismiss the noise, but she felt something give a little leap inside her. It felt good to be cheered instead of jeered.

On her desk lay the morning copy of the *Times*. The top headline on the front page read NYPD TARGETS ORGANIZED CRIME. Under the headline was a large photograph of Erin O'Reilly. The picture was from four years ago, a portrait taken when Erin had first been partnered with Rolf. She was wearing her Patrol uniform and was kneeling beside Rolf. The K-9 sat alert and energetic, bright-eyed, tongue hanging out.

"Jesus," she murmured. "We look like babies."

"You've got a meeting at two," Webb said.

"Where?" she asked. "With whom?"

"One PP," he said. "With our esteemed and fearless leader."

"He's talking about the PC," Vic said. "Not the Mayor. At least, I hope not."

"The Commissioner," Webb confirmed. "He wants to meet you in person."

"My name isn't even supposed to be out there," Erin said. "Sir, this was an undercover operation!"

"'Was' being the operative word," Webb said. "As you may have noticed, the Department leaks like an underbid plumbing job. I can't even guess how many sources leaked your ID to the press, but you're all over the news."

"Don't worry," Vic said. "It's, like, ninety percent good press. And that tabloid bullshit doesn't count for jack."

"What tabloid bullshit?" Erin demanded.

Vic blinked and clamped his mouth shut, clearly wishing he'd done so a moment sooner.

"Vic..." she growled, stepping toward him.

"I don't read that crap!" he protested. "It was Zofia. She reads those rags at the grocery checkout!"

"Real classy," Piekarski said. "Throwing your girlfriend under the bus. And I thought you were brave!"

"What's he talking about?" Erin asked.

It was Piekarski's turn to look uncomfortable. "Erin, you know how those writers are," she said. "They're like soap operas. They're always sexing stuff up, making it more dramatic. They gotta sell papers."

"You've got a copy, don't you," Erin said.

"Well... yeah," Piekarski said. "I made another drink run about an hour ago and the new issue of the *Inquirer* was on the stands."

"Another drink run?" Erin echoed. "Good God, Vic. How much Dew have you drunk? Your kidneys are going to melt!"

"It wasn't just me," he muttered sulkily.

Erin advanced on Piekarski and held out her hand. Reluctantly, the other woman produced a copy of a scandal sheet and handed it over.

NYPD in Bed with Irish Mob
Hero Detective "Goes to the Mattresses"
By Andy Carver

According to anonymous sources within the NYPD, in a twist straight out of a Mario Puzo novel, Detective Erin O'Reilly, the decorated officer who foiled last year's attempted terrorist bombing of the New York Civic Center, has been conducting an explosive clandestine affair with alleged mob boss and accused IRA bomb-maker Morton "Cars" Carlyle. The attractive, thirty-six-year-old O'Reilly, daughter of retired NYPD officer Sean O'Reilly, has been cohabiting with Mr. Carlyle in his apartment above the Mob hangout known as the Barley Corner.

This bar was at the center of a catastrophic blast in the early hours of December 26, as fire engines and ambulances responded to what the FDNY claims was a gas explosion. At least one mobster was reportedly slain in the resulting fire, which was contained before it could spread to adjacent buildings. This is only one of a series of dramatic events connected to the Irish Mob, as the NYPD has launched a major operation apparently aimed at decapitating that organization by arresting all its major figures. Dozens of alleged gangsters have been dragged from their beds in handcuffs, while their families looked on in horror. These men are expected to be charged within the next forty-eight hours with a wide variety of crimes.

However, one man is conspicuously absent from the NYPD's holding cells this morning. Where is Cars Carlyle? He was arrested and taken to the Eighth Precinct, but is no longer there. Has he been transferred to another location? Or has his influence with New York's Major Crimes squad secured his release?

Neither Detective O'Reilly nor her commanding officer has replied to requests for comment. Precinct 8's Captain Fenton Holliday dismissed speculation regarding O'Reilly and Carlyle's alleged relationship as "unfounded, hyperbolic flights of fantasy."

Erin gradually realized she was clutching the newspaper so tightly it was ripping in her hands. She relaxed her grip and saw cheap newsprint staining her fingers.

"Who the hell is Andy Carver?" she asked no one in particular. "He didn't damned well ask for my comment."

"Doesn't matter," Vic said. "These tabloid jerks are like roaches. Stomp on one and five more come out of the woodwork. All you end up with is messy shoes."

"What I want to know is how this Carver punk knew about you and Carlyle," Piekarski said.

"It's not exactly a state secret," Webb said. "Especially after the fire at the Barley Corner."

"Have we heard anything from there?" Erin asked.

Webb shook his head. "The Bomb Squad's still sifting ashes. It'll take hours, maybe days."

"Listen, Erin," Vic said. "I was serious. You can stay at our place as long as you need to."

"Absolutely," Piekarski said. "The baby's not due until March. We've got a spare bedroom. Rent-free."

"Thanks," Erin said. "But I'm good. Didn't a guy get murdered in your apartment?"

Vic shrugged. "That's the Manhattan real-estate market. When they say it's cutthroat, they're not exaggerating."

"You ought to be able to get your stuff from your apartment," Webb said. "I'll give Taylor's boys a call and see how they're coming."

"Thanks," Erin said again. "So, what needs doing?"

In answer, Vic pointed to a pile of forms.

Erin groaned quietly. But she didn't voice any complaints. Maybe a little quiet paperwork would be good for her. At least nobody shot at you while you were filing DD-5s. But she took a detour to the break room first. She'd need coffee.

Her cup was just about full when her phone buzzed. She thumbed the screen with one hand and rescued her coffee from overflowing with the other.

"O'Reilly," she said.

"This is Dispatch," came the familiar tones in her ear. "I have Officer Beaufort for you. He's at Bellevue, on the Corcoran detail."

Erin's heart lurched. "Copy that," she said. "What's—never mind. Put him through."

There was a short pause. Then a man's voice came on the line.

"O'Reilly?" he said.

"Go ahead," Erin said.

"This is Beaufort, at Bellevue. Got a woman wants to talk to our guy. Says her name's Lopez, but I dunno... looks more Italian than Mexican to me. I'm getting' a kinda shady vibe off her."

More Italian than Mexican, Erin thought. It couldn't be. Not a chance. Nobody would be that reckless, that stupid.

"What's she look like?" she asked.

"About five-four," Beaufort said. "Medium build, mid-thirties, black hair. Looks kinda like a schoolteacher, not a wiseguy, you ask me. But she's up to something, I'd bet my shield on it."

The description was a dead ringer for a certain woman from Brooklyn, a witness to a Mob killing. A certain woman who'd called Corky's phone the previous night. Erin had tried to reassure her, but apparently all she'd managed to do was set Teresa Tommasino on course straight back to New York.

"You want me to take her in?" Beaufort asked. "Bring her downtown, run a check?"

"No!" Erin snapped.

"Copy that," Beaufort said. He sounded baffled. "What do you want me to do with her, then?"

"Ask her something," she said. "What car was Corcoran driving the first time she met him?"

There was a short pause. Then Erin heard the woman's answer, faintly through the phone.

"A gray Toyota Corolla."

"She's okay," Erin sighed. "Let her in." The main thing was to keep Teresa's presence quiet. If she ordered Beaufort to block her, Teresa might raise a commotion, and that could get her noticed, which could get her killed.

"Copy that. Beaufort out." The cop hung up.

"Shit," Erin said, staring at her phone. "That crazy *bitch!*"

She was halfway to the stairs, coffee abandoned in the break room, Rolf trotting eagerly beside her, by the time Webb noticed.

"O'Reilly!" he called. "Where are you going?"

"Bellevue," she tossed over her shoulder. "I have to check on Corcoran. It's important."

"If you say so," he replied. "But remember: two o'clock, One PP. The PC won't want to be kept waiting."

"Screw the PC," Erin said under her breath. She had bigger things than departmental politics to worry about.

Vic caught up with her before she got to the garage. "I'll ride with you," he said.

"I don't need any help," she said.

"Bullshit," he said cheerfully. "You got blown up last time you wandered off alone."

"You don't even know what's going on," she said.

"That's never stopped me," he said. "You're worried. That'd be obvious even if I wasn't a big-shot detective. Hell, maybe you're even scared. And if you're scared, then I'm right there beside you, no matter what."

"No matter what, huh?" she said, opening the door to the basement level of the garage and angling toward her Charger.

"Ride or die," he said.

"I'm scared of nuclear bombs," she said.

"Wait a second. Do you mean there's a *nuke* involved?" Vic blinked.

"Of course not! I'm just saying fear exists for a reason, Vic. You don't want to just blindly barrel into it."

"If you say so," he said. "It's always worked out okay for me." He got in the passenger seat and pulled a packet of pork rinds from his jacket pocket. Rolf had already smelled them. The K-9 poked his head through the hatch between the seats and snagged one from Vic's hand.

"I wish you wouldn't give him those," Erin said, putting the car in gear.

"How come?"

"They make his breath smell terrible."

"He's a dog. His breath always smells terrible. I just want him to like me."

"Rolf likes you fine. He'll only bite you if I tell him to."

"Now that's what I call true friendship. What's up with Corcoran? Did he die or something?"

"Not yet."

"Is he awake and talking?"

"He had a bullet in his lung," she reminded him. "He's going to be on a tube. He won't be talking for days, even if he lives."

"Then why are we wasting time watching a comatose gangster?"

"Nobody asked you to come."

"It beats paperwork. Come on, Erin, spill. What's up?"

"He's got a visitor."

"Who?"

"I'd better not say."

Vic pursed his lips. "Ooh, mysterious. Is it anybody I know?"

"You've met."

"Let's play Twenty Questions. That was my first one, so nineteen left. Is it a man?"

"Vic..."

"I'm gonna know in a few minutes anyway. Why the big secret?"

She frowned and concentrated on the road. There were patches of ice in unexpected places and she didn't want to skid into another car. "Because she's dead," she finally said.

"We're gonna kill her?" Vic sounded surprised, but not completely opposed to the idea.

"No!"

"Somebody else is gonna kill her?"

"I hope not. I meant, she's already dead. Legally speaking."

He got it then. "It's that chick from Brooklyn. Teresa what's-her-name. I was wondering why she called Corcoran's phone last night, but we were busy chasing the shooter. What the hell? I assumed he was in on the fake hit along with your boyfriend, but there's more to it, isn't there?"

"Yeah. They're in love."

Vic snorted. "Of course they are. When did they find time to do that?"

"When Corky was looking after her," Erin said. "When they were on the run."

"Wait just a goddamn minute," he said. "You faked her death and dumped her out of WitSec so she could run around with *Corcoran*? That was your big friggin' plan? Shit, Erin, I thought you were smart!"

"We had to get her out of town. Corky's not one of the bad guys, Vic."

"Oh, my mistake. He's not really a gangster. He's not a career criminal. He's not a two-timing, womanizing son of a bitch who tried to *screw your brother's wife!*"

"It's complicated."

"It always is."

"And it worked!" she protested. "She was perfectly safe."

"Then why's she back in town?"

"Like I said, they're in love."

Vic rolled his eyes. "And love makes people stupid," he said. "Ain't that the truth. What is it about you chicks and bad boys? Can't any of you keep it in your pants?"

Erin bristled. "Just what do you mean by that?"

"Look at the scoreboard," he said. "If I was a mobster, girls would be all over me."

"Quit bitching," she said. "You've got one girlfriend. Isn't that enough?"

Vic smiled ruefully. "Some days, one feels like too much for me."

Chapter 15

The officers who volunteered, or were selected, for protection details tended to either be burned-out, middle-aged Patrolmen with big guts and small imaginations, or screw-ups who'd pissed off their commanding officers enough to get pulled off street duty.

Maybe Beaufort was a screw-up, but Erin didn't think so. He was young, but his eyes had a wariness that spoke of good street instincts. He'd recognized Corky's visitor wasn't what she seemed, and that was a point in his favor. He was keeping one eye on the hospital room and the other on the corridor, and that was another. Erin noted the safety strap on his sidearm was unfastened. He wasn't just ready for trouble; he was expecting it.

"Easy there, Officer," she said, flipping back her jacket to show her gold shield. "I'm Detective O'Reilly. This is Detective Neshenko."

"Copy that," Beaufort said, relaxing a little. "Dispatch didn't tell me you were coming."

"They didn't know," Erin said. "Where's Ms. Lopez?"

"Still inside," Beaufort said, cocking his head toward the door. "Can you tell me what this is about?"

"Major Crimes case," she replied. "We need to keep things under wraps. Sorry."

"Copy that," Beaufort said. "What do you need me to do?"

"Just keep doing what you've been doing," she said. "Excellent work, Officer."

His face didn't change, but he seemed to gain about an inch of height. "Thank you, ma'am," he said.

"That kid's gonna go places," Erin muttered in Vic's ear as they went through the door. "Five bucks says he'll wear a gold shield one of these days."

"No bet," Vic answered.

The woman sitting next to Corky's bed looked different than Erin remembered. She was slimmer, more darkly tanned, and dressed less conservatively. But there was something else; Teresa Tommasino the schoolteacher had been a deeply frightened woman, nervous and twitchy. Teresa the survivor gave off an entirely different impression.

When the door opened, Teresa's head came around. Her eyes jumped from Vic to Erin, sizing them up with quick calculation. She half-rose and her hand dropped to the call button on the side of the bed. Then recognition dawned when she locked on to Erin's face.

"Detective," she said. The audible relief in her voice showed she hadn't been quite as calm and confident as she'd appeared.

"Ms. Lopez," Erin said, swinging the door shut behind her. "We need to talk. Vic, can you watch the hallway?"

He rolled his eyes. "Sure, boss. Whatever you say."

"Rolf, *sitz*," she ordered. "*Bleib.*" The K-9 settled onto his haunches next to Vic.

"How's Corky?" Erin asked, walking to the bedside.

"He was awake a little while ago," Teresa said. Her left hand was curled into a fist around a scrap of paper. She opened her fingers to show a single sentence, scrawled by a guy without much control over his penmanship.

"We've a long way to go, and plenty of time for talking," Erin read aloud. "He wrote that?"

Teresa nodded. Now that Erin was up close, she saw bloodshot eyes and shadows under them.

James Corcoran took no notice of the new arrivals. He was ashen pale, a tube taped to his mouth, more tubes running into his good arm, which was handcuffed to the bed. His other arm was in a sling. His eyes were closed. The only way Erin could tell he was breathing was by looking at the readouts on the machines hooked up to various parts of him. The rise and fall of his chest was imperceptible.

"Jesus," she murmured. "That bastard really did a number on him."

"Did you find the man who did this?" Teresa asked.

"More or less," Erin said. "He found me. Ms... *Lopez*, what are you doing here?"

Teresa looked at her like she was crazy. "I came to take care of James," she said. "He needs me."

"What he needs is six weeks of hospital care and a lot of rest," Erin retorted. "You can't be here. You're in danger."

"Teresa Tommasino is in danger," Teresa said, setting her jaw. "Elena Lopez is perfectly safe."

Erin shook her head. "Listen to me," she said. "I took care of Gordon Pritchard, but there may be others."

"Who is Gordon Pritchard?" Teresa asked.

"He's the guy who shot Corky," Erin said.

"Why did he shoot him?"

"Corky slipped up," Erin said. "He was acting a little weird and this other guy got suspicious. He followed Corky home and confronted him at gunpoint. Corky got the drop on him and threw a couple of knives, but got shot."

"Yes," Teresa said. "James is very fast with a knife."

"How do you know that?" Erin demanded.

Teresa's mouth clamped shut and a stubborn, defiant look came into her eyes. Erin knew that look; she'd seen it in plenty of interrogation rooms. Breaking through that defiance would take time and effort, if it was even possible. She sighed and tried a different tack.

"We arrested Valentino Vitelli this morning," she said. "Gabriel's dad."

"For what?" Teresa asked.

"Conspiracy to commit murder."

"Whose murder?"

It was Erin's turn to look at Teresa like she was nuts. "Yours."

"Oh. Of course." Teresa's cheeks flushed slightly. "He's the one who told you to... to kill me."

"Yeah."

"But if he's in jail now, what's the danger?"

"Don't you understand?" Erin asked. "You haven't testified yet. We don't have all Vitelli's guys locked up. He's already tried to finger me for blowing you up. When that doesn't stick, he may figure out the truth. The moment he does, he'll have three dozen goons combing the streets for you. While you were in Mexico or wherever the hell you were, he couldn't touch you. But now you're here! What were you thinking? You can't be here!"

"I'll take my chances here," Teresa said stubbornly. "James saved my life."

"I get it," Erin said more gently. "He's a charmer all right. He's my friend too. But this is really dangerous. You have to get out of town again."

"I'm not going anywhere. If you want me to leave, you'd better bring two more guys like your big friend there, because you're going to need them."

Erin stared at her. "What happened to you?" she couldn't help asking. "You were a mouse the last time I saw you."

"It was a very educational vacation," Teresa said.

"I can see that," Erin said. "We've plugged the leak in the FBI. If you want to go back into WitSec, I can make it happen."

"No. I'm staying with James."

"You're planning to just crash in his apartment? Is that it?"

"I've been worse places with him," Teresa said quietly. "Do you really want to help me, Detective?"

"If you'll let me," Erin said through gritted teeth.

"Then get me a revolver."

"A what?!"

"A revolver. A pistol. With bullets."

"I can't do that. You're a civilian. You're not licensed to carry a gun, and you've got no training. It wouldn't be legal and it wouldn't be safe."

"Then you can get me a nursing certificate," Teresa said.

"A which?" Erin had completely lost the thread of the conversation.

"So Elena Lopez can work as a stay-at-home nurse," Teresa explained. "That way my papers will be in order, in case anyone looks. I can stay with James without attracting attention."

"I don't believe this," Erin said. "You do understand, the Mafia will be looking for you. If they find you, they will kill you."

"They'll try," Teresa said.

Erin studied her. Teresa's façade might be bravado, but she thought it was something much stronger. It was the sort of love and devotion that had made Carlyle once take a bullet for her.

"The Lucarellis may have the NYPD infiltrated," she said, speaking slowly. "Here's my card. It's got my phone number. If anything happens, or if anything looks weird, you call me. I don't care what time it is. I'll get help to you as fast as I possibly can. Got it?"

Teresa's lips tightened in a grim smile. "Yes," she said.

"It'll be a while before Corky can be moved," Erin went on. "You'll need somewhere to stay. They won't let you sleep in the hospital. And it'll be dangerous to visit too often."

"I understand," Teresa said. "I'll find a place."

"Do you need money?"

"I'll manage."

"Then I'll see what I can do about your paperwork," Erin said. "Are you a citizen?"

"Of course I am."

"I mean, is Elena Lopez? Do you have a passport? US credentials? Valid ID?"

"Oh. Yes." Teresa produced an American passport under her false name.

"Okay. It may take a few days. I'll get you some protection, reliable guys."

Teresa was already shaking her head, before Erin had finished her sentence. "No," she said. "I'll be better on my own."

"I have to ask," Erin said. "You've changed. Is it because of Corky?"

"We changed each other," Teresa said. "We made one another better."

"Let's just make sure you don't get one another killed," Erin said. "Corky's a dangerous guy to stand next to."

"I don't care," Teresa said. "I've made up my mind."

"I guess you have. Stay safe, ma'am."

"You too, Detective," Teresa said. "I think maybe you're in more danger than I am right now."

* * *

"That go about like you thought it would?" Vic asked.

Erin just shook her head and turned the key in the Charger's ignition. She twisted it so hard that the engine made an indignant noise before growling sullenly to life.

"Like I said," he continued. "Love makes you stupid."

"I thought you loved Zofia," Erin said, putting the car in gear and pulling out of the hospital lot.

"I never said I was smart," he said. "In fact, I remember saying the exact opposite more than once. And you never disagree."

"That's a good point," she said.

"What're we gonna do about her?"

"What *can* we do?" Erin replied. "She's come back to a city she's not supposed to be in. She's refused protection. What, exactly, am I supposed to do?"

"You could've given her a gun, like she asked."

"You weren't supposed to be listening."

"You told me to watch the door. You didn't tell me to shove cotton in my ears. I was in the same friggin' room, Erin, and you weren't exactly whispering."

"I'm not giving her a gun!"

"She seemed like she knew what she was doing," Vic said. "I guess she's a grownup. But God only knows what she sees in that punk."

"Corky's a better guy than you give him credit for," she said. "He helped you take down Mickey Connor's goons, remember?"

"Broken clocks are right twice a day," he retorted. "That mope pulls enough shit, he's gonna do something right every now and then by accident. It's a probability thing. Where are we going now?"

"Police Headquarters. I've got a meeting with the PC, remember?"

"Ah, shit. I don't want to go there! It's full of brass! I hate those waffle-butts!"

Erin smiled nastily, some of her bad mood dissolving. "What I'm hearing is, you failed to consider the possible consequences of your earlier actions and now you're stuck. How, exactly, is this my problem?"

"It's your problem because you have to work with me," he said. "If I'm miserable, I'm gonna make damn sure I'm not the only one."

"We should put that on our motivational posters," she said. "We could post them in the locker room, right next to the ones about serving the public trust."

"I didn't make up that slogan," he said. "I heard it somewhere, only they said it different. 'Misery loves company,' that's how it goes. That's a damn good line. Who said that, anyway?"

"I think it was the Devil," Erin said, dredging up memories from a long-ago high school literature class. "Explaining why he wants more souls in Hell."

"Oh. Well, he may be an asshole, but nobody ever said the Devil wasn't smart."

* * *

The Police Commissioner was a big man: big shoulders, big chest, big stomach, big smile. His teeth were way too white and gleaming. Erin suspected they were artificial, like the smile itself. But his eyes held genuine warmth and his handshake was firm and friendly.

"The famous Erin O'Reilly!" he said, clapping her on the shoulder with his left hand and giving her right another squeeze.

"I've been hearing a lot about you since our last meeting. Only good things, of course."

"I guess you've been talking to the right people, sir," she said. She was trying not to be overawed by his office. It was as big as the whole Major Crimes unit at the Eightball, and much better furnished. The PC's walls were lined with expensive wood paneling; Major Crimes had bare brick. The PC's chair looked to be real leather; Erin wasn't sure what hers was made of, but it had never been part of a cow. Portraits of previous Commissioners, including Theodore Roosevelt himself, stared solemnly down at her. A framed issue of the New Yorker hung behind the PC's desk. At first glance it was pure black, but Erin knew better. If you angled your head, you could see different shades of black on black, an outline of the World Trade Center. The PC had been there, back when he'd been a Captain with the NYPD.

The PC laughed, flashing those pearly whites at her again. "And this would be your K-9?" he asked.

"Yes, sir."

"He's very well trained."

Rolf was sitting at Erin's side, his snout moving slightly as he tracked her every movement.

"He's the best dog in the NYPD," Erin said in tones of absolute certainty.

"I wish my staff had his discipline," the PC said. "Maybe you can give me some tips."

"Do you have a dog, sir?" she asked, genuinely curious. She knew she wasn't here for small talk, but she was nervous. That didn't make sense. She'd met with much more alarming guys than the PC. However this conversation went, she rated it unlikely he'd have her shot and dumped in the East River.

"I have cats," he replied. "When I need practice for CompStat meetings, I herd them."

Erin mustered up a dutiful laugh.

"Would you like something to drink?" he asked.

"Coffee would be great, sir," she said.

He raised an eyebrow. "I'd heard you were a whiskey girl."

"I'm on duty, sir."

"And during Prohibition, buying liquor was illegal," he said. "But half the NYPD were Irish, so what could you do? Your father was an officer, wasn't he?"

"Yes, sir. Sean O'Reilly. He worked the One-One-Six in Queens."

"He must be proud of you."

"I hope so."

A coffeepot sat on a side table, percolating away. The PC poured a cup and handed it to her. It smelled fantastic.

"I suppose you're wondering why I've called you in," he said, motioning her to a leather couch which commanded an amazing view of Manhattan. The vista was somewhat spoiled by the persistent freezing rain, which continued to spatter the glass.

You probably want a photo op with the hero of the hour, Erin thought. It was an uncharitable notion. She reminded herself he'd been a hero on 9/11, and at other times in his own long career. He'd shifted rubble with his own hands, digging for dead friends and comrades for two solid days. He wasn't the enemy.

"Yes, sir," she said.

"I don't know whether you caught the press conference this morning," he said.

"Some of it," she lied. "I've been pretty busy the past twenty-four hours."

"And for quite some time before that," he said. "From what I understand, you more or less single-handedly dismantled a major criminal organization."

"That's not really accurate, sir," she said. "I had a lot of help."

"Of course," he said. "Teamwork is essential to our job."

"Lieutenant Philip Stachowski, for one," she said, pressing the point. "I couldn't have done it without him. And he paid for it."

"I'm familiar with Lieutenant Stachowski's situation," the PC said, his smile fading. "Terrible, terrible business. A very fine officer."

"And Lieutenant Harold Webb," she went on. "Detective Viktor Neshenko. Doctor Sarah Levine, with the Coroner's Office. Lieutenant Taylor with the Bomb Squad. There's more."

"Why don't you write up the commendations in a letter for me?" he suggested. "I guarantee I'll read it, and it will end up in each officer's file."

"I'll be happy to, sir."

"But what about you, Detective?"

"What about me, sir?"

His smile came back again, undimmed. "How do you feel?"

A number of answers flitted through her brain, but she settled on the simplest. "Tired, sir."

He laughed. "I'd imagine so. I'd like to perk you up, if I can. You've already received the Medal for Valor for that business last year. You stopped this very building from being destroyed by terrorists. It's entirely possible you saved my life."

"I remember it, sir."

"When I pinned that medal on you, I thought you were marked for even bigger and better things," he said. "I'm glad to see I was right. You'll be receiving a gold leaf for the medal, obviously."

"Thank you, sir." He meant she'd be getting a second Medal for Valor. It was a big deal, but Erin was having a hard time caring too much about it right now. She kept thinking about Teresa and Corky in that hospital room, and about Carlyle in his seedy safe house. Maybe this was how Ian had felt when they'd given him the Silver Star. A piece of metal and a scrap of ribbon, however well-intentioned, were a pretty sorry reminder of a terrible experience.

"The Precinct 8 Major Crimes squad will receive a Unit Citation as well," the PC said. "And, of course, you're due for the Purple Shield for the head wound you sustained earlier this month. You'll have quite the salad bar to hang on your dress blues."

"Yes, sir." It was an inadequate response, but all she could manage.

"Are you happy as a detective, O'Reilly?"

"It's what I was born for," she said, startled into telling the straight truth.

"Are you sure I couldn't tempt you with a position on my staff?" he asked. His eyes twinkled. "I happen to have an opening for a supervisor for the Organized Crime Task Force. It would be a significant bump in your salary. It would be somewhat less physically and emotionally taxing than the work you've been doing, but you'd have major responsibilities and the opportunity to do a lot of good for our community."

"A supervisor, sir? I don't understand. I'm a Detective Second Grade. Wouldn't that be a Captain's position?"

"Normally, yes. But in light of your proven expertise, a promotion to Lieutenant would serve admirably, don't you think?"

Erin said nothing. Getting bumped up to Lieutenant would be an enormous leap in prestige, not to mention an increase in her pay and pension.

The PC stepped closer. "What do you say, Detective?" he said. "Are you ready to hit the big time?"

"That's a very generous offer, sir," she said slowly.

"Nonsense," he said. "You've earned it."

"It's a big change from what I'm used to. Can I have a little time to think it over?"

His eyes became wary. He'd clearly expected her to leap at the chance. But he kept smiling. "Of course," he said. "But this sort of opportunity doesn't come around often, and it doesn't wait forever. You have to strike while the iron is hot, you know. I'll need your final answer in forty-eight hours."

"What would happen to Rolf?" she asked.

"Who's Rolf?" the PC asked. Then, before she could speak, he answered his own question. "Oh yes, your K-9. He'd undergo a medical examination, I imagine. If he's still fit for service, you could help transition him to a new handler. He's a valuable piece of field equipment, after all. We can't have him shelved."

You have no idea how valuable he is, she thought. "I guess I don't need to think it over, sir," she said.

Chapter 16

"What'd he want?" Vic asked. He'd been kicking his heels in the PC's outer office, eating shortbread cookies and drinking bottled water.

"To make me a Lieutenant and kick me upstairs," Erin said. "He wanted me to run the Organized Crime Task Force."

"Hot damn!" Vic said. He clicked his heels together and threw her a salute that managed to be both respectful and sarcastic at the same time; no easy feat.

"Knock it off," she said.

"You're not happy?" he said. "Oh shit. Don't tell me you turned him down."

She nodded. "I said thanks, but no thanks."

"No wonder the Irish get shit on by everybody. Jesus Christ! You're so used to losing, you don't know how to take the win! What's wrong with you?"

They were passing through a cubicle farm full of desk jockeys. Several heads turned to stare at Vic. He didn't notice, or if he did he didn't care.

"They would've given Rolf to a new handler," she explained.

Vic swallowed whatever else he'd been about to say. "Oh," he said instead. "Shit."

"What would you have said if you were me?" she asked.

"I would've told him to shove his job offer up his very substantial ass," he said. "But respectfully."

"That's what I thought."

"So what do you get out of all this?" he asked, pushing the call button for the elevator. They were on the thirteenth floor of the Civic Center, which would have meant a lot of stairs.

"A couple ribbons and a pat on the back," she said.

"Ooh," he said. "Maybe they'll name a park bench after you."

"I'll end up riding a desk someday," Erin went on. "Rolf's eight years old. A working K-9 only has nine or ten in him, and that's assuming nothing too bad happens."

"Like getting shot," Vic agreed. "Or lit on fire, or Tased..."

"Or knocked out," Erin added. "Or had ribs broken. Or been shot again. Rolf's been through the wringer."

"He's one tough puppy," Vic said in admiring tones.

Rolf gave Vic the look one tough guy gives another.

"But he's not a puppy anymore," Erin said. "That's the point. Another year, tops, and he's through. Hell, maybe he'll flunk his medical exam and they'll force him into retirement the next time he goes for a checkup."

"You're saying you turned the PC down, and it might be for no reason? Seriously, you weren't tempted?"

"Of course I was tempted! But if you'd heard the way he was talking about Rolf... like he was a spare flashlight! He's my partner! I know, I know, legally he's departmental equipment, but that's bullshit and you know it."

"Hell yeah," Vic said. He reached down and ruffled Rolf's ears. Rolf gave him a dubious look but submitted with dignity.

"The way I see it," she said, "I have to stay in the field while Rolf's still got what it takes. He's saved my life more times than

I can count. After that, they'll let me adopt him. By then, maybe I'll be ready to take it a little easier."

"What about the rest of us?" Vic asked.

"What about you? Webb's only got a few years left, and that's assuming a heart attack doesn't get him. And I hope you don't think I'm going to hang around just to keep you company."

He smiled ruefully. "Yeah, I know. I'm un-promotable, and you're on the fast track. Or at least you were. You didn't piss the PC off too bad, did you?"

"I don't think so, but it's hard to tell with politicians. Those bastards keep smiling no matter what you say. I think I hurt his feelings a little."

"Boo hoo," Vic said. "What about my feelings? I'm a sensitive guy now, didn't you know? It's all Zofia's fault. I'm in touch with my feelings."

"Rage and hate, mostly?" Erin guessed.

"Yeah, but I'm making progress with my self-awareness," he said. "I'm growing as a person. Where to now?"

"I'm thinking a late lunch."

"Suits me. What're you hungry for?"

"How about Italian? I feel like we ought to celebrate. I need something to cheer me up."

"Good plan," Vic said. "Zofia showed me this little mom-and-pop joint in Little Italy. It's pretty good."

"It's not a Mafia front, is it?" Erin asked, only half joking.

"No! Her old squad eats there all the time. Geez, Erin, all that undercover work made you paranoid."

"Okay, fine. But just so you know, it's not paranoia. I've personally seen a Mafia don get his throat slit in a restaurant. On a Sunday morning. Right after church!"

"You live over a gangster bar. You can't tell me you don't like it just a little."

* * *

The restaurant was a tiny piece of real estate on Mulberry Street, sandwiched between a dry cleaner and a shoe repair place. The paint on the door was peeling and it was almost impossible to see through the small, stained front window. The sign over the door was essentially illegible.

"You sure about this place?" Erin asked.

"Absolutely," Vic said. "You won't be sorry."

"Okay," she said doubtfully. She'd been in seedier places, but they'd been meth labs and sketchy nightclubs.

Inside, the restaurant was cleaner than it looked from the street, but just as old and dark. A tiny plaque over the counter proclaimed it had been family-owned since 1947, which made Erin feel a little better.

A stout waitress with a round, good-natured face gave them a cheery smile. "Vic, isn't it?" she said. "Been a couple weeks since we saw you, but I'd never forget that face."

"It's memorable," Erin agreed. It was kind of nice to have someone recognize Vic instead of her for a change.

"Follow me," the waitress said, leading them to a booth. In spite of its small size, the restaurant wasn't crowded. It was too late for most people to have lunch and too early for supper. The waitress laid down a couple of menus and took their drink orders; Diet Coke for Erin, Mountain Dew for Vic.

"I tell you, this place has got the best veal scallopini you've ever tasted," Vic said. "Beats the hell out of me what they put in it, but it's fantastic. Zofia likes the eggplant parmigiana, but I've never tried it. I mean, friggin' eggplant? I don't feel right eating anything that looks that much like a body part."

Erin studied the menu, trying to make out the words in the dim lighting. She was usually a spaghetti girl, but maybe she ought to expand her horizons. After all, they were celebrating.

When the waitress returned with their drinks, Erin ordered chicken parmigiana. Like Vic, she distrusted eggplant. Vic ordered the veal.

"Y'know," he said, "veal's what that police captain, McCluskey, orders in *The Godfather*."

"Yeah," Erin said. "Right before Michael Corleone shoots him in the face."

"That's not the veal's fault," he said.

"Real classy, Vic. You bring me to a little mom-and-pop restaurant in Little Italy and immediately start talking about an Irish cop with Mob ties getting whacked. I have to ask, is this a setup? Is Pacino about to come out of the bathroom with a gun in his hand?"

Vic snickered. "Nah, my salary's not high enough to hire Pacino. But I'm buying."

"Like hell you are."

"Erin, your apartment got set on fire. You're wearing somebody else's clothes and sleeping God knows where. I'm buying you lunch."

"I'm not broke," she said. "Carlyle's got plenty of money."

"Oh yeah? How much?"

Erin wished she hadn't said anything. "Enough," she said evasively.

"Mob cash? Dirty money?"

"The Barley Corner's a successful bar," she said. "It makes legitimate money. Well, it made legitimate money."

"So he really is your sugar daddy, huh?" Vic grinned. "C'mon, tell me. What's he worth? You must've run his financials."

"Four or five," she sighed.

He waited, tapping his fingers on the edge of the table.

"Million," she finally added, just as Vic took a sip of his Mountain Dew.

He spit soda across the table, narrowly missing her. "Jesus!" he choked. "And the Department's not taking it away from him?"

"It's clean," she said. "At least, as far as anyone can tell."

"That's because he's a *money launderer* for the Mob!" Vic said, too loudly. "Of course it's clean! That's his goddamn job! Erin!"

"I'm not the IRS," she said. "I'm not auditing my boyfriend. The DA's office looked at him. If they say he's clean, then that's what he is."

A man cleared his throat politely. He was standing a few steps from their booth. Erin and Vic's heads snapped around, both of them dropping hands to their sidearms, more out of reflex than genuine fear. The man was wearing an expensive suit, immaculately tailored. His hair was neatly combed. He would have looked like any well-to-do Italian-American, except that his skin was way too dark.

"Please forgive my intrusion," he said. His voice, cultured and educated, had a strong flavor of Jamaica.

"King!" Erin blurted.

"It is a great pleasure, and a surprise, to find you here, Miss O'Reilly," Kingston Schultz said. "I hope I am not interrupting important police business."

"You're interrupting an important police lunch break," Vic growled.

"Detective Neshenko," Schultz said. "I am glad to find you unchanged, both in appearance and manners."

Vic scowled, trying to decide whether he'd just been insulted.

"We're just catching a late lunch," Erin explained. "As you probably know, it's been a busy couple of days."

"Indeed," Schultz said. "And I am glad of this chance meeting, Miss O'Reilly, as it gives me the opportunity to repay some small part of the debt I owe you."

"You don't owe me anything," she said.

"I disagree. You did everything in your power for my client and friend."

"That reminds me," Vic said. "How's your buddy Alfie adjusting to prison life? Is it everything he hoped for?"

Alfie Madonna was in prison for nearly decapitating the infamous mobster Vincenzo Moreno in the middle of a Manhattan courtroom. Vic and Erin had watched it happen from only a few feet away as Vinnie the Oil Man had finally found himself in a situation he wasn't slippery enough to slither out of.

"Mr. Madonna is content with his circumstances," Schultz said.

"Glad to hear it," Vic said, his voice dripping insincerity. "I bet he's a big man in there for whacking the Oil Man."

"He was determined to avenge his father's death," Schultz replied. "This is an important thing to an Italian boy. Perhaps you do not understand such a motivation."

"Payback? Yeah, I think I understand it pretty well," Vic said.

"Is there something I can do for you, King?" Erin asked, trying to divert the conversation before Vic turned it into a fistfight. He despised lawyers and mobsters more or less equally, so a mob lawyer merited a double dose of hatred.

"I have heard Rudy is in a bit of trouble," Schultz said.

For a moment, Erin had no idea who he was talking about. Then she recalled Valentino Vitelli's Mob nickname was Rudy, after the famous silent-movie star Rudolph Valentino. "Yeah," she said. "Looks like he's taking a hard fall."

"Indeed," Schultz said. "Word on the street is that he is to be charged with the death of an unfortunate woman outside an airport hotel."

"Is that so?" Erin said, keeping her voice neutral.

"Anyone associated with that business would be well advised to tread carefully," Schultz said.

"I appreciate your concern," Erin said, fighting down the urge to laugh. She was in no legal danger whatsoever.

Schultz didn't like what he saw in her eyes. He leaned forward, resting his hands on the tabletop. He spoke in a near whisper. "This is no laughing matter, Miss O'Reilly. Rudy is very angry."

"Rudy's in no position to hurt anybody," Erin replied.

"He is not without resources," Schultz countered. "I have heard, from reliable people, that he is seeking a particular woman."

"What woman would that be?" Erin asked.

"This I think you already know," Schultz said.

"And what's he gonna do if he finds her?" Vic asked.

"This, also, you know," Schultz said. "If you were to be aware of the whereabouts of that woman, you would be well advised to spirit her to safety. I will let you enjoy your meal now in peace. Good day."

He turned and walked out the front door of the restaurant.

"Now I've seen everything," Vic snorted. "Just a friendly neighborhood gangster. You believe that happy crap? If he's doing this out of the goodness of his heart, I'm the Ghost of friggin' Christmas Past."

"Of course he isn't," Erin said absently. She was thinking, and thinking hard.

"Then what was the point of all that?" Vic demanded.

"King Schultz is a very smart guy," she said. "He's the reason Vinnie Moreno is dead."

"Alfie Madonna's piano-wire garrote is the reason Vinnie's dead," Vic said.

"It was Schultz's plan," Erin said. "I'm sure of it. He orchestrated the whole thing."

"To put his client in jail for the rest of the kid's dumbass life? Real smart move. You sure this guy's as clever as you think?"

"He took Vinnie off the table," Erin said. "Now Valentino Vitelli's gone, too. Who do you think that leaves to take charge of the Lucarellis?"

"There aren't that many Lucarellis still standing," Vic said.

"The Oil Man got rid of most of the old guard," Erin said. "Now, with him and Vitelli out of the picture, what's to keep a guy like Schultz from taking over?"

Vic blinked. "Erin, I dunno if you noticed, but Schultz is a black guy."

"So?"

"So the Mafia are pretty notorious racists," he said. "There's no way Vitelli's buddies would let him come in and boss them around."

"That's true," she agreed. "So if he wanted to take control…"

"He'd have to get rid of the last of Vitelli's hardcore supporters," Vic said.

"Exactly the people Vitelli would send after Teresa Tommasino," Erin said. "By warning us, he makes it more likely we'll stop them. He doesn't give a damn about her. He wants to get rid of his own internal competition."

Vic whistled. "What a son of a bitch," he said.

"The really clever thing is, it's just like he did with Alfie Madonna," Erin said. "He gets people to do what they already want to do. He just sets things up so he's the one who benefits in the end."

"Let's arrest that bastard," Vic said. He tensed, as if he was getting ready to jump to his feet and do just that.

"On what charge?" Erin retorted. "Aiding and abetting the New York Police Department? Protecting a Mob witness?"

"When you say it that way, it sounds stupid," Vic said, sagging back in his seat.

"Yeah," she said. "Probably because it's a stupid idea."

"So what do we do about this?"

"We figure out a way to get Teresa the hell away," Erin said, speaking very quietly now. "Before Vitelli's people find her and kill her."

Chapter 17

Erin called Dispatch and asked them to patch her through to Beaufort at Bellevue Hospital. Rolf, sensing her nervous energy, poked his head through the hatch and tilted his ears at her.

"Beaufort," the officer said.

"This is Detective O'Reilly," Erin said. "Is Elena Lopez still there?"

"That's a negative, Detective," Beaufort said.

Erin's heart sank. "Where did she go?"

"Beats me," he said. "Corcoran had some fluid in his lung. The docs took him to get it drained, and they made Lopez leave. Could be she's still in the building, or she might've left."

"Copy that," Erin said. She hesitated, thinking hard.

"I can contact security," Beaufort suggested. "They can sweep the building."

Normally, that would have been a good idea. But if she had Beaufort bring hospital security in on the search, word would get round that Corky had a female visitor. The description would be of an olive-skinned woman in her mid-thirties, black hair, exactly the person they didn't want the Lucarellis to know about.

"Negative," she said. "We need to keep this quiet."

"I copy," Beaufort said. "What do you need?"

"When did she leave?"

"More than five minutes, less than ten. She was carrying a suitcase. I didn't look inside. Should I have checked it?"

"Forget about it," she said absently. "It just would've been clothes."

"Clothes?" Beaufort's confusion was obvious. He was probably expecting it to be full of guns, or maybe cocaine.

"Where are you now?"

"Operating room gallery," he said. "My job is to stick with Corcoran. I've got visual on him through the window. Docs wouldn't let me in."

"Okay, stay there," she said. "Bellevue's too big for you to search, and she's probably long gone. Stand by. I'll let you know if I need anything else."

"Copy that, Detective. Beaufort out."

"Damn," Erin murmured. Where would Teresa have gone? It didn't really matter whether she could find the woman; what mattered was whether the Mafia could. She briefly considered calling Carlyle and asking if he could put the word out, then remembered that the members of Carlyle's network were pretty much all locked in holding cells. Corky would still have some friends on the street, but without Corky to contact them, that didn't matter.

New York had over eight million people, packed into a million buildings. That was way too much ground to cover. Teresa could have gone almost anywhere. Their food had arrived while she was talking to Beaufort. Vic was already diving enthusiastically into his veal.

"Don't wait for me or anything," she said.

"Hey, I didn't know how long you'd be," he said through a mouthful of food. "I didn't want it getting cold."

Erin shrugged and picked up her fork. She took a bite of the chicken, chewed, and swallowed. She wasn't really thinking about eating, and didn't have much appetite, but the dish caught her attention.

"Wow," she said. "You weren't kidding. This is fantastic."

"Told you so," he said. "Did you find her?"

"No. She's in the wind."

"Any idea where?"

"Nope."

"Good."

"Why is that good?"

"You're a detective. From what I hear, you're a pretty good one. If you can't find her, that means the bad guys probably can't either."

"That's a good point." She took a piece of bread from the basket in the middle of the table and dipped it in her sauce.

"You wanna know what I'm wondering?" he went on.

"I expect you'll tell me."

"It's about our buddy Schultz."

"What about him?"

"Nobody knew we were coming here. Hell, I didn't know until we were on our way, and it was my idea!"

"You're wondering if his being here was a coincidence," she said.

"Yeah."

Erin had been pondering that same question. "I'd say yes and no," she said.

"That's just about the least helpful answer there is," Vic said.

"He's not psychic," she said. "And I don't think he was camped out at this particular restaurant, on the off-chance I'd drop in. I think he was in Little Italy, trying to sort out the mess we left when we hauled Vitelli off to jail. You've been coming here often enough that the waitress knows your name."

"Yeah," he said. "Like the bar in *Cheers*."

"Either she or someone else recognized us. That person called Schultz. He must've been pretty close by."

"Why would they do that?" he asked.

"Because he wanted to talk to me and people knew that."

"Jesus!" Vic said, rubbing his forehead. "You've got a phone! And e-mail! If he wanted to reach you so bad, it's not hard."

"Phones leave call records," she said. "And e-mail leaves an electronic trail. He'd rather see me face to face, off the record."

"To give his cryptic, creepy message," Vic said. "You know what I hate?"

"Mob lawyers?" Erin guessed.

"Mob lawyers," he agreed.

A dog started barking somewhere outside. This wasn't some little yappy lapdog. It was a full-throated, deep-chested bark, ferocious and aggressive.

"That sounds a little like—" Vic began.

"It's Rolf," Erin interrupted. She was already on her feet and on her way, leaving a half-finished meal and a startled Russian behind. There was no doubt in her mind. She knew her K-9's bark as well as a mom knew her kid's voice. She also understood the emotion behind the barking. Rolf felt threatened. By the time she got to the restaurant's front door, she was running.

Vic, to his credit, was only a few strides behind her when she hit the street. She sprinted to the police parking space. There was the Charger. Rolf wasn't barking anymore, and she didn't see anyone nearby, but she whipped out her Glock anyway and scanned for targets. All she saw was a handful of pedestrians watching her and Vic with varying degrees of curiosity and alarm.

"NYPD," she told them, flashing her shield with her free hand. "Did anybody see anyone near this car?"

None of the bystanders stepped forward.

Vic caught up with her. He'd also drawn his Sig-Sauer. "What gives?" he asked.

"I don't know," she said. She approached the Charger. Rolf was visible through the tinted back windows. His ears were fully perked, tail sticking out stiffly, hackles bristling.

"He looks pissed off," Vic said. "You think somebody tried to jack your car?"

"Not likely," she said.

"Yeah." He snickered. "It takes a special kind of stupid to try to swipe a police car with a K-9 in the backseat. The Auto Crime Unit would need to hose the dumb bastard's guts out of the driver's seat."

Erin only half-heard him. She was still paying attention to the dog. A lot of K-9s were reactive and would go berserk if anyone broke the invisible bubble around their car. Rolf was more aloof and restrained. An intruder would have to actually touch the car to set him off like that.

"Vic," she said quietly. "Back away."

"Huh?" He didn't understand, but he knew her well enough to recognize her tone, which was dead serious. He retreated about ten yards, back onto the sidewalk.

Erin reached for the release button for Rolf's compartment. Then she hesitated as paranoia whispered into the back of her brain. If her fears were accurate, the last thing she wanted to do was send an electric signal toward her car.

Rolf stared at her. The hair on his back was beginning to settle as he calmed down. Now he was baffled. His partner left him in the car a lot, but she never just watched him from outside. She ought to be in there with him or, better yet, he ought to be out there with her, chasing bad guys. He snorted, fogging the glass.

"Erin?" Vic said. "What's going on?"

"Just stay right there," she said, not taking her eyes from her dog. "Rolf! *Such!*"

They'd practiced their search drill hundreds of times. Rolf could do it with his eyes closed. Eyes weren't the point; nostrils were what mattered. But this was all wrong. How was he supposed to search from inside the car? Was Erin all right? Rolf was confused and he didn't like being confused. He liked everything to be straightforward and clear. He whined anxiously.

"*Such!*" she repeated, more loudly.

Rolf was a good boy, so he gave it his best shot. He started in his compartment, sniffing along the edges and corners, turning a tight circle in the small space. Then, finding nothing, he squeezed himself into the hatch between the seats. It was a very snug fit. His shoulders got momentarily jammed and he glanced at Erin. He knew he wasn't supposed to be in the front seat. His tail, trapped in his compartment, wagged hesitantly.

"Good boy!" she called. "*Such!*"

He bunched himself and forced his way forward. With an almost audible pop he was through, squirming into the passenger seat. He got his paws back under himself and snuffled at the upholstery. He found one of Vic's discarded pork rinds on the floor, but he'd been taught to ignore food if he was in the middle of a search, so he left it where it was. After a moment, he scrambled into the driver's seat and sniffed at Erin's door from the inside.

He stopped short and sat back on his haunches, staring straight down.

"Shit," Erin said. She ought to be praising Rolf. Searches were a game for him, almost as much fun as bite work. When he found the scent packets Erin left for him, she'd always tell him what a good boy he was and give him a few minutes with his Kong ball. It was one of the highlights of his day. She varied the game to keep it interesting. Sometimes the packets were in the trunk, sometimes the wheel well, once even tucked behind the gas cap.

But this was no game. Some K-9s were trained to sniff out narcotics, but that wasn't Rolf's area of expertise. He could track people and he could locate explosives.

"Hold on," Vic said. "Do you seriously mean..."

Erin ignored him. She holstered her gun and pulled out her phone with the same motion. "Dispatch," she said. "This is O'Reilly, shield four-six-four-oh. I need the Bomb Squad in Little Italy, forthwith. Possible device attached to my car."

* * *

"Either somebody's trying pretty hard to kill you, or they're sending you one hell of a message."

Skip Taylor smiled as he said it, but Erin didn't think he was joking. The bomb tech took the binoculars from his face and shook his head. He was filthy. His Bomb Squad uniform was black with soot and he had blood on his knuckles. His eyes were red-rimmed and he looked like he'd been up all night. Come to think of it, he probably had.

"You can tell that from way back here?" she asked. They were a good hundred fifty feet from Erin's Charger; half a football field. The car looked tiny.

"I don't need to," he said. "Somebody blew up your home last night. Now your dog sniffed a bomb under your car. Whether it's the same guy or not, the pattern is what matters."

"What do you mean?" she asked sharply. "Gordon Pritchard's dead, isn't he?"

"We haven't finished checking your basement," he said. "We got interrupted by something about a bomb in Little Italy, not that you'd know anything about that. But we haven't found any human remains yet. I've still got a couple guys checking, working with FDNY search-and-rescue. I was actually hoping to borrow your K-9 to sniff around. SAR's cadaver dog got loaned out to a bunch of hicks upstate. Apparently a couple idiots went hiking in the snow and got lost. You know how it is."

"So maybe Pritchard's running around planting bombs," she said.

He shrugged. "That's a detective question."

"Do we really need to stand this far back?"

"I'm assuming a briefcase bomb," he said. "That means a charge up to fifty pounds. That's mandatory distance of fifty yards. I don't make the rules."

"My dog's still in there," she reminded him in dangerous tones.

"And civilians are in those buildings," he said, pointing to either side of the street. Patrol officers were going through them at that very moment, knocking on doors and emptying the structures. "Once we've got a perimeter, I'll send the robot in for a closer look."

"I should've just gone under the car myself," Erin grumbled.

"What if it's motion-detonated?" he countered. "Or set off by remote control? The bomber could be sitting on the roof watching, with a cell-phone detonator. You get nice and close and boom! No open casket for your departmental funeral. Hell, no casket, period. We'd be burying you in a lunchbox."

Erin grimaced. "Thanks for that thought," she said. "But whoever it was, they didn't have much time. I ran outside as soon as Rolf started barking. This isn't anything fancy."

"Assumptions get you killed anywhere," Skip said. "They just kill you quicker and messier in the Bomb Squad. We wait."

Half an endless hour passed before a couple of Patrol sergeants reported the surrounding buildings empty. Vic paced the perimeter, scowling. Erin fretted impotently. Skip spent the time checking the robot. It was a weird little machine that would be right at home on the set of *Star Wars*. It moved on toy-truck wheels and looked like it had been assembled out of a kid's Erector set. A camera was mounted on a vertical pole, and it had a grabbing claw that extended forward. One of Skip's guys was in the Bomb Squad van with a monitor and a set of controls.

Finally, Skip gave the okay and the robot started rolling down the street. It was eerily solitary. The usual bustle of Mulberry Street had been shunted aside by a set of NYPD barricades at either end of the evacuation zone, manned by grim-faced officers. Skip and Erin leaned over the shoulders of the operator, watching the TV screen.

"Get closer," Skip said. "Nice and easy. That's it. Okay, six more inches. Stop."

"What's that?" Erin asked, pointing.

"Metal, about a foot long, maybe less. Looks like a can. Plain, ordinary tin can, if you believe it. Not very sophisticated. I don't see how it's detonated... hold on. Zoom in on the left front wheel. See that?"

"No," Erin admitted. The monitor didn't have the best resolution and it was at a high angle.

"It's a wire," Skip said. "Looped to the axle. Cute."

"What is it?" she asked.

"Grenade trap, I think," Skip said. He was smiling more broadly now. "Classic booby trap. Just like that one we ran into in that basement last year. Usually you use a tripwire to pull the grenade out of the can. The lever pops off and the grenade arms.

This one has the wire attached to the car. When you put the car in gear and start driving, the wire tightens. Then either the grenade jumps out of the can or it pulls the pin out of the grenade. Either way, about five seconds later it blows."

"You can disarm it, right?" Erin was thinking about Rolf.

"Absolutely," Skip said. "And the shrapnel won't penetrate exterior walls. It might not even get through the floor of your car."

"You're saying it wouldn't have killed me even if I'd set it off?" Erin asked.

"Depends on what else is in that can," Skip said. "I need to get a closer look and this robot isn't worth crap. The camera's mounted too high. I'm going in to take care of it by hand."

He hopped down from the van and started up the street, a toolbag in his hand. Erin was right beside him. He paused.

"Erin, this is my job," he said. "Not yours."

"And it's my car and my dog," she retorted. "I won't get in your way."

"Then what, exactly, were you planning on doing?" he asked.

"Helping."

"How? By absorbing some of the shrapnel?"

Erin didn't laugh. "Rolf's in there," she insisted.

"Okay," Skip said. "But if I say 'go,' don't hesitate, don't think it over, *move*. We have to assume there's extra explosives packed around that thing, and probably a fragmentation sleeve or some ball bearings, so the lethal radius on that bastard is impossible to figure. You'll have five seconds to save your own life. If I say to run, you run like hell and don't stop for anything."

"Copy that," she said.

"Don't distract me."

"Understood."

"And do exactly what I tell you."

"Gotcha."

Then Skip did smile. "You know what we called this, back in the Sandbox?"

"What?"

"The long walk. You get inside the evac zone and you walk up on the bomb. Could be half a damn klick, could be just round the corner. Doesn't matter. It's the longest walk of your life. You've got plenty of time to think things over. Like, why become an EOD guy? Why not go into, say, life insurance? Or data entry? Some job where you don't get blown up."

"Why did you become a bomb guy, Skip?"

"Too much time with a junior chemistry set," he said. "Your cell phone's turned off, right?"

Erin put a hand in her pocket and turned off the phone. "I thought you had jammers up."

"We do. But we don't like taking chances and we don't trust technology. That shit will let you down at the worst possible moment."

They were only a few yards shy of the Charger now. Skip still seemed calm on the surface, but his eyes had taken on the tight, focused quality Erin had seen in Ian's more than once. It was the look of a combat veteran right before the bullets started flying. He'd shifted his weight to the balls of his feet and was keeping himself balanced, ready to move in any direction the instant anything happened.

Rolf was watching them from inside the car, wondering what the humans were up to now. He'd been in this car a long time and was getting a little impatient. Erin could see his silhouette behind the glass, tail waving slowly. Just in front of them, the bomb squad robot crouched on its wheels, unmoving.

"Okay," Skip said. "You stay back. Don't say anything and don't touch anything, especially me or the car, unless I say so or you've got a really, really good reason. Now take this."

He handed her a flashlight from his toolkit. Then he dropped to his belly on the pavement. Erin did likewise.

"Give me some light," he said.

Erin obediently shone the light under the car. She saw the booby trap immediately. It was just like it had appeared on the robot's video feed: a metal can with a wire trailing out of it to the car's left front wheel.

"I'd like to jack the car up," Skip said. "But it's better not to move it, in case there's nitro or some other unstable compound in there. I'm only guessing it's a grenade. But it looks like a pretty simple device. No remote detonator in sight, no anti-tampering features. Your average bomb-maker isn't a genius, you know. None of this cut-the-blue-wire bullshit like you see on TV. If there's no electric current, I can cut wires all day and the bomb won't go off. There's wire cutters in my bag, black rubber grips. Hand them to me, right hand."

Erin complied. Skip's upper body was under the car, only barely fitting into the narrow space. He moved slowly but smoothly, careful not to brush against anything.

"You haven't pissed off your boyfriend lately, have you?" he asked.

"What? No!"

"Good. A Carlyle special isn't something I'd want to mess with barehanded. Now *that's* a guy who knows what he's doing. Okay, I can see the can. It's a grenade all right, standard M67, military-issue. Looks like it's surrounded by Semtex. That's your garden-variety plastic explosive. They just packed it in nice and tight. Simple but effective. No secondary detonator. Interesting. The wire's wrapped around the lever. No pin in sight. That means the grenade's armed, but the fuse won't light until the lever pops loose. That'll happen once the wire pulls taut."

Erin swallowed hard at the word "armed," but kept the light steady, bracing her wrist against the street. Skip knew what he was doing.

"Easy-peasy," he said. "Snip, snip, and that's it for the wire. Can's attached with a magnet. That's a neat trick. Easy to install that way, no mucking around with packing tape or baling wire. I just pull hard and twist and... ta-da! I'm going to hand it to you. Don't worry, it won't blow up. Just make absolutely sure you don't hold it upside-down. Slow and easy, here it comes. Got it?"

"Got it." Erin took the can very carefully. She knew Semtex was a stable explosive and wouldn't go off from anything as innocuous as a light jostling, but she also knew she was holding an awful lot of bang. She set it gingerly down on the asphalt beside her.

Skip scooted out from under the car. "Clear," he announced. "But there might be a backup device. I'd recommend having your dog double-check the vehicle."

Erin opened Rolf's compartment. The K-9 jumped down to greet her. They went over the Charger inch by inch, finding nothing unusual. Then Rolf paused and angled toward Skip, who was studying the bomb. The Shepherd stopped in front of him and sat, staring at the can.

"Good boy," Erin said. "*Sei brav.*" She reached into her pocket and came out with the greatest of treasures: the Maltese Falcon, the Hope Diamond, and the Holy Grail all rolled into one.

Rolf caught the rubber Kong ball before it could get anywhere near the ground. His eyes went soft and his jaws started working, making the familiar wet squeaky sounds. Life was good.

"I'm going to get this back to the lab," Skip announced. "Maybe I can find out who's trying to kill you."

"These days, the shorter list is who's *not* trying to kill me," Erin sighed. It was time to start thinking what she was going to tell Lieutenant Webb.

See, it's like this, sir. Vic and I were hungry, and he wanted veal scallopini, so we went to Little Italy. Sure, the Mafia hangs out there, but Vic had this restaurant he wanted to show me. The food's to die for. Almost literally...

Chapter 18

"Protection detail," Webb said. "And that's an order, not a suggestion."

"Sir, this really isn't that big a deal," Erin said, but she'd fought enough losing battles against commanders to recognize one when she started fighting one.

"We shouldn't even be here," Webb said, gesturing to the Major Crimes office.

"It's a police station," she said.

"It's a place people know you work," he replied. "You've worked security gigs before, when the President of West Who-Gives-A-Crap comes to town. What's the worst thing you can be?"

She sighed inwardly. "Predictable," she said.

"I knew you'd say that," Vic said, grinning. At least somebody was having fun with this, Erin thought sourly.

"Neshenko, shut up," Webb said, not even bothering to look at him.

"I have a job to do," Erin insisted. "I'm not going to let these bastards intimidate me."

"Since I'm the one giving the orders, I'm the one who'd be hypothetically intimidated," Webb said. "Your detail's going to consist of an ESU team, plus Neshenko."

"What?" Vic said. "Why me?"

Webb held up four fingers and ticked the reasons off. "One: you're an experienced detective and ESU operator, so you're uniquely suited to liaise between O'Reilly and ESU. Two: you've shown a remarkable ability to keep one another alive in the past. Three: I don't like you very much and I'll take any opportunity to shunt you out of this office, even if it's only for a couple of days. And four: I have the feeling you'd volunteer for this job if I didn't hand it to you."

Vic opened his mouth to argue. No words came out, for once.

"You're welcome," Webb said.

"What about our cases?" Erin asked.

"We'll be filing paperwork on the O'Malleys for days," Webb said. "You won't miss much. Piekarski and I can handle it. But until we confirm who's targeting you, and why, you're on modified assignment."

"You didn't even have to shoot anybody this time," Vic said, recovering the use of his tongue.

"I know who it was," Erin said. "Gordon Pritchard."

"Assuming he's not dead," Webb said, "Pritchard is seriously injured. He's been stabbed, bitten by your K-9, and almost certainly suffers from burns and smoke inhalation. I doubt he's even able to stand upright, let alone run around New York assassinating detectives. I've got a BOLO out to all New York hospitals. If he's alive, which I doubt, and he walks into the ER, that's where we're likeliest to pick him up."

"You don't know this guy, sir," she said. "He's been burned before. He's as tough as they come. If he's after me, he'll keep coming until we put him in jail or in the ground."

"That sounds like a very compelling argument for having a protection detail on you," Webb said. "Fortunately, I've already decided to assign one to you."

"What is it with you and these Irish hitmen?" Vic wondered aloud.

"Siobhan wasn't a man," Erin reminded him.

"Yeah," he said. "She was a babe. A smokin' hot one, if you could get past the crazy."

Piekarski was cleaning one of the whiteboards. She threw an eraser at Vic. It ricocheted off his shoulder.

"It's just for a day or two," Webb said. "You'll be back to making my life miserable before you know it."

"It might not be Pritchard," Vic said. "It could be the Italians. I mean, we were in Little Italy and we'd just talked to a Mob guy."

"Schultz would never get his hands dirty like this," Erin said. "I don't think he even has the skills."

"But he's got people," Vic said. "Didn't you say he was taking over the Lucarellis?"

"Better and better," Webb said. "Here's the drill. You're going to go to ground while we wait on ESU. Once they get here, you'll go somewhere safe with them. Then the rest of us will sort this mess out. I'm not having one of my detectives blown up."

"I understand how inconvenient it would be for you if that happened," Erin said with a straight face.

"We need to put you someplace secure," Webb said. He snapped his fingers. "Go down to Taylor's lab. It's as well protected as anywhere in the building. You can find out what he's learned about the bomb while you're there. But you are not to leave that room without an escort. Understood?"

"Yes, sir." There was nothing else to say.

* * *

Skip hadn't even bothered to change out of his dirty clothes. Erin, Vic, and Rolf found him at his workbench. He'd already taken the bomb partially apart. Erin saw a nasty-looking olive-green sphere next to a metal canister.

"M67," Vic said. "Army-issue grenade."

"Bingo," Skip said. "Wrapped in Semtex. Ball bearings pressed into the explosives. It's a poor man's Claymore mine. Don't worry, it's safe enough now. I'm running the chemical ID on the explosive now."

"That'll tell us where it came from, right?" Erin said.

"You got it. The manufacturer's added a tagging agent since 1991. It's manufactured in the Czech Republic."

"Those Czechs know their weapons," Vic said. "The Skoda Works was the biggest weapons factory in Austria-Hungary during World War I."

"You know your history," Skip said.

"I know my guns," Vic replied.

"I've traced this batch," Skip went on. "Looks like it was sold to a construction company in Belfast about three years ago."

"You don't say," Vic said, shooting Erin a look.

"My thoughts exactly," Skip said. "They'd discontinued sales to Northern Ireland during the Troubles, but they've recently resumed. This lot was reported destroyed in a warehouse fire last March."

"Sounds like you've got an insurance fraud case against the owners," Vic said.

"Or thieves torched the place to cover the theft," Erin said.

"Where was your pal Pritchard in March of last year?" Vic asked.

"I have no idea," she said. "I didn't even know who he was then. We didn't have surveillance on him until recently. Besides, he might not have personally stolen it."

"I bet he did," Vic said. "This guy's a goddamn firebug. You think he'd miss the chance to burn down a building?"

"Do you know Gordon Pritchard's work?" Erin asked Skip.

He shook his head. "Only by reputation. I've seen his jacket. I try to keep tabs on all the bomb guys in the area. I know the guy was a suspect in some arson jobs in Jersey a few years back, but that's outside our jurisdiction. Anyway, I was still in the Army then, so he wasn't my problem yet."

"Did anything jump out at you about him?" she asked.

"He's got paramilitary training," Skip said. "He was with the Brigades in Northern Ireland, but you know that already. He's no artist. He's a technician. Very bare bones and practical."

Erin pointed to the bomb. "Could this be one of his?"

"Absolutely. The explosive and the grenade indicate military proficiency, and the design points to asymmetric warfare experience. It's exactly what I'd expect from a former IRA soldier. But it could just as easily be a guy from any of a dozen paramilitary groups. Al Qaeda gives its guys that training too."

"Do they get their explosives from Belfast?" Vic asked, voice dripping with sarcasm.

"No, we gave the Taliban a lot of their gear back when they were fighting the Russians," Skip answered. "I dusted the casing and the grenade for prints, but didn't get anything usable."

"Pritchard always wears a glove on one hand," Erin said. "And his other one was hurt."

"If he assembled this thing one-handed, he's kind of a badass," Skip said. "But lots of bomb-makers are missing fingers. They make do."

"You dealt with homemade explosives in Iraq," Erin said. "What else does this one tell you?"

"He doesn't give a shit about collateral damage," Skip said. "This isn't a shaped charge. If it'd gone off, it wouldn't have been focused up into the car. It would've taken out the car, sure, and everyone in it, but there would've been significant blast in all directions. If the street had been crowded, it would've been like the Boston Marathon bomb. I think it was thrown together pretty fast. This guy's improvising. He's in a hurry, which means he'll make mistakes. We'll catch him."

"That's comforting," she said. "Before or after he blows me up?"

He shrugged. "Depends."

"On what?"

"Tactical variables."

"Hey, Taylor?" Vic said.

"Yeah?"

Vic showed him a single finger on each hand. "I got your tactical variables right here."

Skip grinned. "I love the NYPD. Some days, it feels like I never left the Army."

Vic leaned against the wall. "So, Erin, how come this jerkoff wants to kill you so bad?"

"Besides the fact that I arrested all his buddies after pretending to be on his team for months?"

"Yeah, besides that. Killing cops is a big deal. I mean, I get trying to pop Carlyle. No offense, but he's part of the Life, right? It's in the job description."

"None taken," Erin said wearily. "Pritchard's former Irish Republican Army. They've got a thing about moles and traitors. Anyway, like you said, it might not be him."

"Do you really believe that?" Vic asked.

"No," she admitted. "Damn it, where *is* he?"

"More to the point, how'd he know we'd be in Little Italy?" Vic wondered. "How come every lowlife in Manhattan knew where we were eating lunch?"

"He didn't," Erin said. "The only thing that makes sense is he was following us."

"From One PP?" Vic raised an eyebrow.

She shook her head. "Before that. He's been on our tail from the Eightball. Think about it. That's one place he knew I'd be. He must've been camped out there, waiting. He knows my car. There aren't many black Chargers in the motor pool, and mine's got K-9 plates. He'd been waiting for his opportunity ever since we left the station."

"How come he didn't make a move sooner?" Vic asked.

"Maybe he wasn't ready to move when I was at the hospital," she said. "Or he didn't see a good opportunity. The garage at One PP is guarded. Ever since the bombing last year, they've doubled the surveillance. And when I've been outside the car, I've had you with me."

"You think Pritchard's scared of me?" Vic was pleased with the possibility.

"I think he'd rather take me alone," she said. "And he's hurt. He might chance it if he was healthy and it was just me, but with only one good hand against the two of us, plus Rolf? Forget about it. Those are shitty odds."

"Yeah," Vic said. "Even if he got the first shot off and got lucky, there's no way he's walking away from that."

"The bomb was him trying to kill me and get away clean," she said. "What worries me is what he'll do if he decides he doesn't care if he lives or dies."

"You're right to worry about that," Skip interjected. He'd been working on the bomb, but listening with half an ear. "Suicide bombers are the worst. Even if you shoot them, it doesn't always stop them."

"Is Pritchard a fanatic?" Vic asked.

"I hope not," Erin said. "But I don't know how angry he is. You don't want to piss off an Irishman, Vic. We get nasty."

"And that's why you're going to have a bunch of big, strong ESU guys around you," he said. "Anybody wants you, they'll have to get through all them. And I'll be there, too."

* * *

"Sorry you missed our last party, Detective," Lieutenant Lewis said.

"Forget about it," Erin said. "This time I get to be the guest of honor."

"Just like at a funeral," Vic said.

"Where are we going?" Erin asked, ignoring him.

"You can't go home," Lewis said. "For obvious reasons."

"Yeah," Vic said. "It's a smoking pile of rubble, for one."

Lewis coughed. "I meant it's a place people know you'd be," he said. "I was thinking we'd go to a safe house."

"New York must be running short of those," Erin muttered. "At the rate I'm going through them, we'll be out by the end of the week. Why don't we go to the WitSec house the Marshals already set up?"

"I don't think we should know about that," Twig said. "I'm not cleared for WitSec. I'm not even supposed to know you're in it."

Lewis looked around at his detail, which consisted of ESU officers Twig, Parker, and Carnes. "If any of these guys are working for the Mob, I'll eat that man's dirty jockey shorts," he said. "No salt."

"Mine are salty enough already, boss," Parker said. "They're my lucky shorts. Can't risk the luck getting washed out of them."

"Okay, we'll play it your way," Lewis told Erin, ignoring Parker and his undergarments. "But we'll have to be careful not to compromise your situation. Team, we're going dark. I'm talking full radio silence, turn off your phones, the works."

There was a brief pause while the squad deactivated their various electronic devices.

"We have a van in the garage," Lewis continued. "Unmarked, no rear windows. O'Reilly, you'll be in back with your K-9. Parker, Neshenko, you're on either side of her."

"How come?" Parker asked.

"We're the biggest," Vic said, grinning.

"What's that got to do with anything?"

"We make the best bullet sponges."

"Good thing I'm wearing my vest," Parker said. "How likely is it someone takes a shot at us?"

"Unlikely, but we won't hang around to find out," Lewis said. "Carnes, you're wheelman. I'm shotgun. Twig, you're in the middle with your AR-15 locked and loaded. If we hit a roadblock, we divert if possible and shoot our way through if not. O'Reilly, I'll need the route."

Erin brought up a map of Manhattan on her phone and showed it to Lewis. The Lieutenant studied it for a couple of minutes, memorizing the address.

"Got it," he said. "Now turn your phone off, too. Remember, everyone, your job is to protect the principal, but I want us all to go home at the end of the shift. That means no dumbass heroics. You copy?"

The others gave variations on "We copy, sir."

"All right," Lewis said. "Let's roll."

Erin had been on plenty of protection details in her Patrol days. It was very strange to be the one in the middle of the tight diamond of armed men. The whole thing felt ridiculous, in spite of the bomb they'd found under her car. She was a cop, damn it. Her job was to protect others, not be protected.

The ESU team moved with the smooth coordination to be expected from a squad of hardcore professionals. Carnes led the way, clearing each corridor and doorway before motioning the others to follow. Two of the team, Parker and Twig, carried assault rifles at their shoulders. Everyone, Erin and Rolf included, was wearing body armor.

"This must be how Presidents and Senators feel," she murmured to Vic as they paused in the stairwell, waiting for Carnes to give the go-ahead from the parking garage.

"Nah," he said. "You've got no idea what it's like to be them."

"Why not?"

"You're not an asshole."

Three minutes later, Erin was crammed into the back seat of a beat-up old van between two of the biggest men in the NYPD, headed away from the Eightball.

"That was anticlimactic," she said.

"That's what we want on protection duty," Parker said. "If it's exciting, we're doing it wrong."

Rolf, on the floor at Erin's feet, sniffed the air and snorted.

"What's that smell?" Erin asked, wrinkling her nostrils. "It's like an old gym bag."

"Oh, that?" Parker said. "This van's a seizure. The LT grabbed it from Impounds. It belonged to a drug dealer who got capped by one of his competitors. He had something like a dozen garbage bags full of weed in the back. Unfortunately, moisture got into the bags and it got moldy. The whole crop got ruined. All that skanky grass sat around in here for a week and a half."

"Now I know what moldy pot smells like," Vic said. "That's something I could've lived without. Any odors I ought to know about where we're going?"

"It's a WitSec safe house," Erin said. "It smells like old cigarettes, cheap aftershave, and remorse."

Vic brightened. "Like the car I drove in high school," he said.

Chapter 19

Erin, remembering a request Carlyle had made, convinced a reluctant Lewis to allow a quick stop at a store along the way. Once that was done, the team made their way to the WitSec apartment. Erin had called ahead from a payphone, not wanting Calley and Hodges to get the wrong impression from a group of heavily-armed men popping up on their doorstep. The Marshals weren't overly pleased at playing host to a squad of New York's Finest, but they welcomed the ESU team with the best grace they could.

Carlyle was even less happy. He'd gotten up to greet Erin, then sat down again on the living room couch. When Erin explained what had happened, the Irishman sprang to his feet once more.

"Good Christ, darling!" he exclaimed. "A car bomb?"

"It's not a big deal," she said. "Rolf warned me in plenty of time."

"That's not the point," Carlyle said. "I should have blown that scunner to bits."

"We'll all pretend we didn't hear that," Lewis said mildly.

"It's okay," Erin insisted. "I'm fine. Everybody's fine! Anyway, I brought you this."

She produced a brown paper bag which she handed to Carlyle. He pulled out a bottle of Glenlivet Scotch.

"I know it's not Glen Docherty-Kinlochewe," she said. "But it's the best I can do. I'm afraid most of the Glen D in Manhattan got torched."

"Aye, that's so," he said. "This is grand, darling. I don't suppose your colleagues would care for a wee nip?"

"We'd love to," Lewis said. "Unfortunately, we're on duty."

"I'm not," Vic said. "Well, not precisely."

"That's not true," Erin said. "You're the liaison, remember?"

"So this is where they put you when you're in Witness Protection," Vic said. "Looks boring as shit."

"It is that," Carlyle agreed.

"You know, just because you're playing for our team now doesn't mean I like you," Vic said.

"Of course not."

"The whiskey doesn't mean anything either."

"Nor that."

"And the fact you're my partner's boyfriend makes me like you even less."

Carlyle smiled thinly. "I'd never think otherwise."

"You break her heart, I break your arms," Vic said. "Just so we're clear."

"Vic always wanted a little sister," Erin explained. "It's kind of sweet, in a thuggish way."

"We'll discuss the topic of possible heartbreak later," Carlyle said to her. "Together with possible arm breakage, come to that. When there aren't quite so many other ears."

"It'll be a lot later, I'm afraid," Lewis said. "We're setting up camp here. Until this Pritchard punk gets nailed, we're on you two like a cheap suit."

"And I'm stuck here?" Erin said.

"No," Lewis said. "You can go places. You can't announce your schedule, and you'll have bodyguards. You know the drill. It won't be so bad."

"Just boring," Vic said. "Anybody got a deck of cards?"

Hodges raised a hand. "Gotcha covered," he said. "And a Gideon's Bible. This isn't my first rodeo. Between that and the whiskey, we've got us a nice WitSec care package. What's your game?"

"Texas hold 'em," Erin said.

"Penny ante?" Parker suggested.

"The O'Malleys had a thousand-dollar buy-in for their poker nights," Erin said. "Sometimes two thousand."

"Jesus," Parker said. "I'm on a cop salary. Remind me, boss, how come we gotta be the good guys?"

"It has intangible rewards," Lewis said.

"My wife would like some tangible ones," Twig said.

"Don't worry," Parker said. "I've been giving her plenty of tangible rewards on my off days."

"Watch your mouth," Twig said. "When we're deployed, I'm the guy with the sniper scope and a clear field of fire."

* * *

Several hours, and dozens of hands of poker later, Erin was three dollars and fifty-seven cents richer. Vic had run out of cash and was muttering about stacked decks and marked cards. Carlyle, usually a canny and clever card player, was also broke.

"You're not hustling these guys, are you?" Erin asked him.

"Nay, darling," he said. "I've found it's wise not to have the lads protecting you owing you money. It creates a conflict of interest."

"Is he saying we'd let him get killed to get out of paying five bucks?" Parker demanded in mock outrage.

"I'm saying it's best if you enjoyed our game and would look forward to another at some point in our mutual future," Carlyle said, smiling.

"It's getting late," Lewis said. "Two hours on watch, two men awake at all times. I've drawn up a schedule. Everyone else, sack out. You've all got your overnight bags."

"Yes, sir," the ESU guys chorused.

"I call top bunk," Vic said.

"No bunks here," Calley said. "Some lucky bastard gets the couch. The rest of us can find a nice comfy piece of floor."

"I won't fit on the couch," Vic said. "Can I use Parker for a pillow?"

"Not if you want to wake up in the morning," Parker replied.

"He snores," Erin told Parker.

"And just how would you know that?" Parker asked, winking.

"Boring stakeouts," Vic said, before Erin could think of a comeback.

Erin, Carlyle, and Rolf had the bedroom to themselves, but the interior walls were thin and they could hear cops and Marshals moving around in the living room. Counting everyone, protectees and guards, they had nine people and one dog squeezed into a fairly small one-bedroom apartment.

"This reminds me of my college days," Erin whispered.

"How's that?" Carlyle asked.

"Making out with my boyfriend as quietly as possible," she explained. "Because my roommates were having a party right outside."

"I'd no notion that was on your mind," he said. "But since you brought it up..."

"We'd better not," she said. "With our luck, a Mob hit squad would kick down the door right as we were getting to the good part. What was it you wanted to talk to me about?"

"It'll keep," he said. "Now isn't the proper moment."

She wrapped her arms around him under the covers. "Now you're just being mysterious," she said. "Trying to get me interested."

He bent his head toward her and kissed her. "Is it working?"

"I don't understand you," she said. "One minute you're mad as hell about that stupid bomb, the next you're all over me."

"Corky told me once there's nothing like riding the feeling you get from cheating the Reaper," Carlyle said. "Are you feeling anything of the sort?"

"Mostly I'm tired," she sighed. "Damn it, I thought we'd be celebrating by now. Maybe sharing drinks at the Corner, looking forward to what comes next. But this never ends. The Corner's toast and people are still trying to kill us."

"Hush, darling," he murmured. "Everything's darkest at night."

"That's the dumbest thing I've ever heard," she said.

"I mean it," he said. "You oughtn't to make important decisions after dark, especially after midnight. Once the twilight fades, you'd best go to sleep. Things will look brighter in the sunlight."

"If you say so," she said. "I'm glad you're okay. Rolf still smells like smoke. I gave him one bath, but he needs another."

"We'll do that in the morning," he said. "Unless you'd rather a damp dog be sharing your blankets."

He had a point. Erin tried to put her worries away for tomorrow. But maybe because of the slightly pungent K-9 at her feet, her dreams were full of smoke and flames.

* * *

"Rise and shine, lovebirds!"

Someone was pounding on the door. Erin jolted awake. She'd rolled out of bed, grabbed her Glock, and had taken cover behind the mattress by the time she recognized Vic's voice. She stood up and walked to the door, muttering darkly to herself. Rolf trotted beside her, curious to see what was going on.

"Everything all right, darling?" Carlyle asked. He'd also been awakened, but hadn't reacted quite so violently. When something startled him, he tended to hold very still while he analyzed his environment. When Erin got surprised, she *moved*.

"No," she said shortly. "I'm about to kill Vic."

She unlocked the door and yanked it open. Vic stood outside, one hand frozen in the act of knocking again, the other behind his back.

"Nice look," he said.

Erin rolled her eyes. She was wearing an extra-large T-shirt Hodges had loaned her. It was tight on him; on her, it reached almost to her knees. Her hair was uncombed, she had dark shadows under her eyes, and she was still holding her pistol in her right hand.

"Sleep well?" he went on.

"Right up until a dumb Russian started banging on my door," she said. "What do you want at this ungodly hour?"

His brow wrinkled. "What's ungodly about it? Do you have any idea what time it is?"

"Too damn early. Do you know what it feels like to get shot? Because I kind of want to shoot you right now."

"Yeah, actually, I do. So do you. We actually get shot a lot, in case you hadn't noticed. Boy, you're cranky when you oversleep."

"Oversleep?" she echoed. "Vic, what time is it?"

"Two o'clock. In the afternoon. 1400 hours, they'd call that in the military."

Erin ran a hand through her hair. "Sheesh," she said. "I don't believe it."

"You must've been tired," he said. He brought his left hand from behind his back. He was holding a brown paper bag. "Carnes made a food run. I've got bagels. Nice fresh ones, from a kosher bakery just down the way. I got the variety pack, with cream cheese! We got coffee in the kitchen."

"Okay," Erin said. "I guess you get to live."

"That's a relief," Vic said.

"What did you want, anyway?" she asked. "You must've had a reason to come knocking."

"I wanted to make sure you weren't dead," he said. "Or wearing out that poor old guy sharing the bedroom. You can't expect me to believe you were sleeping that whole time."

"Believe what you want," she growled. "And mind your own damn business."

"Oh, and I heard from the Lieutenant," he added, holding up a cheap cell phone. "Burner phone, don't worry. Nobody's tracing it. Your Irish gangster pal is awake."

"I think we're all aware of that, lad," Carlyle said from behind Erin. "Small thanks to you."

"Your other Irish gangster pal," Vic said. "The redheaded smartass. Corcoran."

Carlyle liked to think before he moved, but he was faster than he looked. He was on his feet and beside Erin in moments. "How is he?" he asked with unfeigned eagerness.

"They pulled his tube," Vic said. "So Webb said he ought to be able to talk. The Lieutenant thinks somebody ought to interview him."

"That's a good idea," Erin said. "He can tell us exactly what went down with Pritchard."

"And how much the Snake knows," Carlyle said.

"Yeah, Webb's on his way to Bellevue now," Vic said.

"Great," Erin said. "We'll meet him there." She spun on her heel and started sorting through the meager available clothing.

"Erin, I'm not sure you understand how this whole witness-protection thing works," Vic said. "It means you're supposed to stay—Jesus Christ, warn me when you do that!"

Erin wasn't thinking about modesty. She'd stripped off Hodges' shirt and was fastening her bra. Her back was toward Vic, so it wasn't like he was getting a view of anything too important. She was wearing her work underwear, very functional and not too sexy. All the same, Vic cranked his head around so fast and so hard, she heard his vertebrae crackle. She glanced over her shoulder and saw him concentrating very hard on something in the living room.

Carlyle, watching the whole thing, put a hand to his mouth to hide his smile.

"You heard what Lewis said," Erin said, pulling on her pants. "I can go places, just not predictable ones."

"And you don't think the bad guys will predict you'll be at Bellevue?" Vic demanded. He was still keeping his eyes fixed the opposite direction.

"Of course not," she said. "That'd be a crazy place for me to be. You can turn around now, I'm decent."

"You're never decent," he said. "And we agree, it's crazy, which is why you shouldn't do it!"

"It's a hospital," she said. "I'll have ESU guys all over me. And I want to hear what Corky's got to say. It could be important. Maybe he knows where Pritchard hides out."

"That's a good point," Vic said. "I've got an idea. How about I go talk to the smartass, and you stay here and play some more cards with the Marshals and your silver fox?"

"You think he's a fox?" Erin asked, giving Vic a sly grin.

"It doesn't matter what I think. I'm not the one sleeping with him. I'm sorry I got you bagels."

"Don't be." Erin snatched the paper bag from Vic's hand. "I'll eat in the car."

* * *

"Sorry about this," she told Lewis. They were back in the dead pot dealer's van, on the way to Bellevue. Erin was in the back seat once more, sandwiched between Parker and Vic.

"Forget about it," Lewis said. "We've had plenty of worse requests from protectees."

"Yeah," Parker said. "Remember that one diplomat? The guy from Tajikistan?"

"Kyrgyzstan," Carnes corrected.

"I think it was Uzbekistan," Twig said.

"Whatever," Parker said. "This guy, let's call him Stan, he spoke, like, ten words of English. And what's the first thing out of his mouth when he gets in our car? 'Take me to whores. Good American whores.' Practically his whole vocabulary."

"What'd you do?" Vic asked.

"We dropped him at his consulate," Lewis said.

"We figured there were plenty of whores there," Parker said. "Just of the political variety, not the sexual kind."

"And there was that other guy who tried to score some coke," Carnes said. "Right in front of us. We had this whole debate over whether we were allowed to arrest a guy we were supposed to be guarding."

"I still say we should've," Parker grumbled.

"He would've been safe in lockup," Vic said.

"That's what I thought," Parker said.

"Okay, knock off the grab-ass," Lewis said. "We can talk about the good old days later. Eyes open, people. I know

Bellevue's got metal detectors and uniforms on duty, but don't get lazy. It's still a big place with a few hundred people in it and that makes it hard to secure. Everybody check your weapons?"

"Sure did, dad," Parker said.

"Dad?" Lewis repeated in a soft voice that promised mortal danger.

"He means 'yes, sir,'" Vic said. "I can translate. That's what the liaison is supposed to do, right? Make sure everybody's communicating?"

"You know where this Corcoran's being kept?" Lewis asked.

"Yeah," Erin said. "ICU."

"They won't want all of us clogging up that space," Lewis said. "Bringing in germs and all that crap. Parker, Twig, Carnes, you'll be on perimeter duty. Remember, bad guys might be disguised as docs or nurses. Just because some mope's got a white coat and an ID badge doesn't mean he's okay. You can buy that shit online these days. Carnes, you're in charge of these two troublemakers."

"Copy that, sir," Carnes said.

"Neshenko and I will be on you, O'Reilly," Lewis went on. "They may not want you bringing your dog in, depending on the patient's condition."

"I can leave Rolf with the others," Erin said. "He'll stay where I put him. Don't worry, this whole thing won't take more than half an hour, tops."

"Thirty minutes?" Lewis said. "Is that supposed to comfort me? You can get killed in thirty seconds."

"Are these guys always like this?" Erin asked Vic in an undertone.

"Hell yeah," Vic said. "I loved working ESU. It's like being on a TV show. You get to hang out with a bunch of badasses, kick down doors, and take names. I miss it."

"You can come back anytime," Parker said.

"Tell that to my old Lieutenant," Vic sighed. "He hates me."

"Any particular reason?" Lewis asked.

"Insubordination, mostly. Attitude problems. Too many excessive force complaints. And there was that time I showed up for my shift hung over. The Union wouldn't let him fire me, so he transferred my ass to Major Crimes."

"Lucky us," Erin said.

Chapter 20

"I hate winter," Vic said.

"How can you hate winter?" Carnes said. "It's the most magical time of the year."

"Because it's black friggin' magic, that's why," Vic said. "It's cold, it's wet, and the sun goes down as soon as it's up. It's miserable."

The sky was clear, for a change, but Erin had to admit Vic was right. Twilight came early to the concrete canyons of Manhattan. The parking lot was already in shadow as the security detail hustled into Bellevue Hospital. Lewis flashed his ID to the officers at the door and the ESU team moved into the building.

"Corcoran's in ICU," Vic reminded them. They walked briskly down the hall, weapons in hand but aimed at the floor or ceiling. There was no point scaring the doctors, nurses, and civilians more than necessary. Erin didn't like being the center of all this attention one bit.

"I'm smothering in here," she muttered.

"That's just Parker's deodorant," Twig said. "Try not to breathe through your nose."

"I'd be fine on my own," Erin grumbled. "I'd attract less attention."

"You do know your picture was on the front page of the *Times*, right?" Vic shot back. "Half the bad boys in Riker's probably have it on the ceiling over their bunks by now."

Erin made a face. "It was an official portrait," she said. "With Rolf in it. I was wearing my Patrol gear, for Christ's sake! You're talking like I was a goddamn centerfold!"

He grinned. "Doesn't matter. A chick in uniform is hot."

Parker started quietly singing the annoyingly-catchy chorus of "Centerfold." Carnes joined in.

"Na, na, na na na na, na na na na, na na na na na..."

"Neshenko's point is that you're not exactly inconspicuous," Lewis said without looking at her. "Keeping a low profile is pretty much out of the question."

Erin rolled her eyes. "I've got a gun. Two of them. I've killed men."

"And our job is to make sure you don't have to kill any more today," Lewis replied, unperturbed. "Next right, gentlemen. Slow is smooth..."

"...and smooth is fast," Twig, Carnes, and Erin finished in unison.

They reached the doors to the Intensive Care Unit a couple minutes later. As Lewis had ordered, Carnes, Twig, and Parker peeled off and took up position covering the hallway. Carnes and Parker stood in front, Twig a few yards back with his rifle.

"Rolf, *sitz*," Erin said, pointing to the wall next to Carnes. She handed her end of the leash to the ESU guy and made sure Rolf saw her do it. "*Wache.*"

Rolf settled morosely but obediently to his haunches and watched Erin walk away. Then he turned his snout back the way they'd come. "*Wache*" meant "guard." The K-9 knew he was on sentry duty until Erin got back, and that he was supposed to do what Carnes told him. That was all well and good, Rolf decided, but Carnes wasn't Erin. If things got serious, the Shepherd intended to take Carnes's instructions under advisement and follow his own counsel.

"Busy this afternoon," Vic observed. A squad of nurses was in the process of rolling a gurney into a nearby room. Erin caught only a quick glimpse of its occupant, but the patient didn't look like they were having a good day. Another was on its way down the hall.

"What's going on?" Lewis asked one of the nurses as their paths crossed.

"Apartment fire," the nurse hurriedly replied. "Multiple casualties. Goddamn gas lines again."

"Shit," Vic murmured. "That was a little kid on that stretcher. Two days after Christmas. Unbelievable."

A uniformed officer was standing guard outside one of the rooms. He was young, but sharp-eyed. He had his hand on his Glock as they approached.

"Beaufort," Erin said.

"That's right," Officer Beaufort said. "Who're these guys?"

"Lieutenant Lewis," Lewis said, holding up his shield. "I've got Detectives Neshenko and O'Reilly here. We need to see Corcoran."

"Copy that," Beaufort said, relaxing. "Lieutenant Webb just got here a minute ago. He's inside. So is that lady. The one I talked to you about yesterday, O'Reilly."

"Really?" Erin said. "Miss Lopez?"

"That's her," Beaufort said.

"Who's she?" Lewis asked sharply.

"Friend of Corcoran's," Erin said. "It's okay, she's clean. Civilian."

Lewis nodded, but he had his gun ready as he pushed through the door. He was clearly prepared for anything.

However, all they found was Corky lying there with a man and woman standing at his bedside. Teresa Tommasino was holding Corky's hand. Webb had his own hands in his trench coat's pockets, looking tired and in need of tobacco.

"Cheer up, sir," Vic said. "Your favorite detectives are here."

"That's good," Webb said dryly. "Where are they?"

"Now, lieutenant, that's no way to talk," Corky said. His voice was raspy from his recent intubation, and weak due to his damaged lung, but there was no suppressing the Irishman's cheerfulness.

"How're you feeling?" Erin asked, walking quickly to join Teresa beside the bed.

"Like I've been to an Irish wedding," Corky replied. "But you should see the other lad."

"That's what we need to talk about," Erin said.

"Lieutenant, if you could take Ms. Lopez outside?" Webb said to Lewis.

"I'd rather stay," Teresa said.

"No fear," Corky said. "These fine officers just need a few words in private. It'll be grand, love. You do know, you oughtn't to be here at all."

Teresa's jaw set and her eyes hardened in a way Erin would never have expected from the mousy schoolteacher. "But I am," she said.

"With me, please, ma'am," Lewis said, taking her lightly by the arm and guiding her to the door. "We'll wait right outside."

"You do know she's not one to be running to the Mob with our secrets, aye?" Corky said as the door swung shut behind Lewis and Teresa.

"You really don't understand operational security, do you, Mr. Corcoran?" Webb asked wearily.

"I understand it at least as well as yourself, you puffed-up gobshite," Corky snapped. Then he coughed weakly and sagged back against his pillow.

"Take it easy," Erin said. "You've been shot."

"I'm well aware of it," Corky said. "I've rarely been more aware of anything in my life. But if this scunner's suggesting I've spilled any secrets, I've half a notion to drag my sorry bones out of this bed and teach him a lesson about an Irishman's honor."

"Are you okay to talk?" Erin asked. She really didn't like his color. Corky had always been pale-skinned, but his complexion was almost as white as his sheets.

"Oh, aye, it's nothing," he said, waving a hand weakly. "As I said, you should see the other lad. Did I get him, by the by? I know I marked him, but is he breathing?"

"He got out of your apartment," Erin said. "That's what we need to talk about. Who was it?"

"Snake Pritchard, obviously," Corky said. He tried to snort derisively, but only managed another coughing fit. It doubled him up with pain.

"Can you tell us what happened?" Erin asked gently, once he'd recovered.

"I went to the Teamster's Christmas party," Corky said. "I saw the Snake there, but didn't think much of it. I'd a few drinks and some pleasant conversation."

"With a blonde?" Erin prompted.

"You know about her?" Corky was surprised. "Why's everyone so hung up on that colleen? She was nothing to me. I scarce knew her. She's some manner of secretary at an office in Yonkers. Her name's Melinda, I think, though I couldn't swear to it."

"Pritchard told me about her," Erin said. "He also said you didn't give her the time of day."

"He's right. If I'd known I could get in such trouble *not* bedding a lass, I'd have spent even more of my time between the sheets. But you said he slipped off. You've spoken with him?"

"We'll get to that," Erin said. "What happened next?"

"I'd promised a call to my lovely lass," Corky said. "So I made off home. I should've marked Pritchard, but he's a wily one. I went into the bath to draw some water, then came out to the kitchen for a bit of red wine."

"I thought you were a whiskey man," Erin said.

"Terry likes red wine," he said, like that explained everything. Erin supposed, in a way, it did.

"Damn it," she said, rubbing the bridge of her nose in a gesture she'd picked up from Webb. "You weren't supposed to do anything different. You made him suspicious."

"I know that now, aye," Corky said. "Pritchard was already suspicious, though, on account of that business with your Lieutenant Stachowski. He was on the lookout for anything out of the ordinary, and what with my friendship with Maggie Callahan and my reformed behavior, he reckoned he'd found his traitor. When I turned around, the lad was standing right there in my flat, revolver pointed at my heart, and there's me in naught but my robe, my fighting knives clear on the other side of my flat. He said he just wanted to talk, but the both of us knew better."

"What did you tell him?" Erin asked.

"That he was a daft bugger and Evan would have his bollocks for paperweights," Corky said. "But he wasn't having any of it. You'll laugh at this, Erin, but he'd a notion you'd turned me with your not insignificant charms."

Erin did laugh. It just popped out of her mouth, a choking burst of unplanned, half-hysterical hilarity.

"Pritchard was of the opinion Carlyle was a victim of your feminine wiles as well," Corky went on. "I found myself wondering how a lad could be so nearly right, but so totally wrong. But the main thing was, he'd tumbled to the truth about you, Erin. While we weren't lovers, he'd hardly believe that, and it was wide of the point in any case. I wasn't about to tell him about Terry, and he'd no intention of letting me live out the night whatever I said."

"That's true enough," Erin said.

"So I waited my chance," Corky said. "Then I let my eyes drift to one side, like I was looking at something just over his shoulder. The lad turned his head to see what it was, and that gave me my opening. I snatched a couple of knives from the block and threw them. He's a quick one, that blighter, and he got off a shot while the steel was spinning. The first pass was even honors. He tagged me once, I caught him in return and knocked his revolver from his hand. But he got it up again in his off-hand and gave it me proper. Then he ran. I'm thinking I hurt him badly enough he thought he'd best tend to himself, and he believed he'd done for me."

"And there were the gunshots," Vic interjected. "He probably figured somebody would have heard them and called us."

"Which they did," Webb added.

"That stands to reason," Corky said. "I don't really remember much beyond that, until I found myself here. Now tell me, Erin, how do you know what Pritchard was saying?"

"I had a talk with him later on," Erin said grimly. "At the Corner. At gunpoint."

"Whose gun?" Corky asked.

"His."

"Then how is it you're still standing, love?"

"Things got a little out of hand. Pritchard blew up a gas main and torched the joint."

"Cars!" Corky exclaimed, trying to sit up. He coughed again and flinched, but took no notice of it. "Is he all right?"

"Carlyle's fine," Erin assured him. "Everybody got out. We thought Pritchard died there, but now it looks like he might've gotten away. He got knocked into the basement but…"

"The old smuggler's entrance," Corky said.

"You know about that?" Erin asked.

"Know about it?" Corky retorted. "I've *used* it! Cars used to move guns through the cellar, didn't you know?"

"Whatever," Erin said. "That's how he got in, and it must be how he got out. The fire wasn't intended to kill us. It was a diversion, so we didn't know he was sneaking…"

She trailed off. Vic, Webb, and Corky all looked quizzically at her.

"What is it?" Webb asked.

Erin shook her head. She had a headache. Overdosing on sleep after going on too little for too long wasn't always good. She felt sluggish, almost drunk. She'd had a thought, and it had seemed important, but now she wasn't sure.

"Sorry, sir," she said. "I guess it's nothing."

"Bullshit," Vic said. "I saw your face. Something's there. Spill."

"Pritchard likes fire," she said slowly. "He uses it to attract attention and to move people where he needs them to be."

"Like the Barley Corner," Webb said. "Of course. I don't see what—"

"The nurse outside," Erin interrupted. "Didn't she say something about an apartment fire?"

"Yeah," Vic said. Then he blinked. "And a gas line."

"Talk faster, O'Reilly," Webb said. He was suddenly very alert and attentive.

"Pritchard struck out with me," she said. "He knows after I found the bomb under my car, I'd be a hard target. But I'm not his only target."

She drew her Glock and crossed the room in five quick strides. She shouldered the door open, startling Lewis.

"Pritchard's here," she snapped.

To Lewis's credit, he didn't ask for an explanation. He was a man of action. "We need to get you out," he said. "Come on."

"No!" she said. "He's not here for me. We need to lock down this whole wing. Get Hospital Security and report an active shooter in ICU."

Lewis's face clouded. "Nobody's shooting," he said.

"They will be," she said grimly. "Then call Dispatch. We need everybody they can spare. More ESU if you can get them. Bomb Squad, too. Forthwith."

"What about you?"

"I'm staying here with Corcoran."

Lewis nodded. He gestured to Teresa. "Get inside, ma'am. Stick close to the detectives, do what they say."

Teresa returned the nod, tight-lipped. Erin held the door for her and whistled to Rolf.

"*Komm!*" she called.

The Shepherd sprang up and loped to meet her, trailing his leash. He hopped once on his hind legs, then stood at attention, ears perked.

"Keep your team outside," Erin said to Lewis. "This is the only door. Pritchard's about average height, scars on his face and right side. Dark hair, raspy voice. He'll probably be in disguise."

"Copy that," Lewis said. "Now get inside and hunker down."

Erin and Rolf retreated into Corky's room. Vic and Webb had their guns out now. Vic, understanding the general gist of Erin's thought processes, had taken up position in a corner, covering the door. Teresa was once more beside Corky, gripping his hand.

"O'Reilly," Webb said. "You're not in command here. Tell me what the hell is going on."

"I don't know, sir," she said. "But Pritchard's got three targets: Carlyle, Corky, and me. Carlyle's in WitSec, and the Marshals don't have a mole anymore, so Pritchard doesn't even know where Carlyle is. If he did, he would've made a move by now. He knows I know he's after me, and he missed me with the car bomb, so he'll expect me to go to ground. That just leaves Corky. By now he must know Corky survived the shooting. He's stuck here and can't be moved. That makes him the best possible target. Now we hear about a gas fire that's sending people to ICU? Isn't that a little convenient?"

"It is," Webb said. "You think he's infiltrating the hospital? How? He's got a pretty distinctive face."

"I'd better call Carlyle," Erin said. "Just in case."

"He's got Marshals all over him," Vic said. "I'm sure he's fine. We've got plenty of problems right here."

At that moment an alarm began hooting. It was a loud, insistent, penetrating noise that grated on Erin's ears. A recorded voice came over the PA system.

"Attention, patients and staff. An active shooter has been reported in the hospital. Please remain calm and in your rooms. Lock and barricade your doors. Do not panic. The police have been notified and are on their way."

"Jesus Christ," Vic muttered. "That door doesn't lock, does it?"

Erin glanced at it. "No," she said. It was double-hinged, designed to swing either direction. She supposed that made sense if you were a nurse and needed to push a gurney through, but it also made it almost impossible to barricade.

"Do you think he stole a firefighter's uniform?" Webb suggested. "He might be able to get in wearing an oxygen mask."

"Not a chance," Vic said. "FDNY may be jerks, but they're not idiots. They know their own guys and they'd sure as shit know if some random schmuck latched onto their crew."

"He got in as a patient," Erin said. "Think about it. He has visible injuries. What better way to get brought into Intensive Care than to need medical attention?"

"We put out a BOLO for him," Vic reminded her. "The hospital must know that."

"They were expecting him to walk into the ER," Erin said bitterly. "Not be brought here in an ambulance. The EMTs wouldn't have even thought about it, especially if there were other victims."

"You're saying Pritchard started a whole other fire and burned a bunch of innocent bystanders as camouflage?" Webb asked. He appeared both horrified and impressed by the idea.

"It's worse than that," Erin said. "He would've needed fresh injuries for the EMTs to bring him here."

"Hold on," Vic said. "You're telling us he *set himself on fire?* Like one of those goddamn Buddhist monk protesters from the Sixties?"

"His nerves were already pretty well shot on one side of his body," she said. "It might not hurt so much to burn himself again."

"Holy shit." It was Vic's turn to look impressed in spite of himself.

"Interesting theory, O'Reilly," Webb said. "And I can see how he'd get into ICU that way. But how would he come at us? He'd be even more injured than before, and unarmed. And he doesn't even know where Corcoran is."

"Of course he does," Erin said. "His room's the only one with cops outside the damn door! We'd lead him straight to Corky!"

The alarm was still hooting monotonously away. The recorded voice was looped into a repetitive cycle. It was really starting to get on her nerves.

"All right," Webb said. "Let's suppose, for the sake of argument, you're right. We've still got three armed officers in this room, plus five more outside. He's one man, wounded and unarmed."

"We can't assume he's unarmed," she said.

Webb rolled his eyes. "Medics always check victims for weapons."

"He could've crammed something up his ass," Vic suggested. "A shiv, maybe."

"He wouldn't bother," Erin said. "There's plenty of sharp objects in hospitals."

"This is paranoia," Webb said. "One wounded man with a knife and one good arm can't get in here. I hope you're right, because if you are, he's stuck in this wing. We'll sit tight until the cavalry arrives. Then ESU can do a room-by-room sweep. We'll find him if he's here."

Erin tried to believe him. But what she was thinking of was the way Pritchard had snuck up behind her in the Barley Corner, and how he'd gotten the drop on Corky in his own home. The man was uncanny. They were covering the obvious possibilities, but Pritchard knew what was obvious too. If she was right, and he'd been willing to mutilate himself just to gain access to the hospital, he wouldn't have just hoped to get lucky once he was in the ICU. He had a plan.

Vic and Webb were watching the door. If Pritchard somehow stabbed and slashed his way past an entire ESU squad, plus Officer Beaufort, they'd perforate him the moment he stepped through. Erin turned her attention away from the door and scanned the room.

Teresa met her gaze. The other woman was obviously frightened, terrified even, but she was standing firm next to her man.

Corky lay in the bed, surrounded by all sorts of gadgets and machinery, his right wrist still cuffed to the railing. He couldn't have been a more inviting target. He relied on his speed and reflexes to keep out of trouble, and now he was quite literally shackled to the spot. He had IV lines in his good arm and an oxygen tube with its prongs up his nose. He was breathing nearly a hundred percent oxygen, so his damaged lungs could get enough of the stuff into his bloodstream.

It was a good thing Pritchard couldn't get a gas line into this room, Erin thought. The oxygen-saturated air around Corky would go up like a goddamn firecracker.

That thought hung in her aching, overworked brain, repeating itself like that God-awful recorded announcement. If fire got into this room somehow, that would be the end.

Then she stopped looking at the room and looked at the ceiling.

It was a very nondescript ceiling, composed of square tiles of some sort of artificial material. Every tile had an irregular pattern of holes. She'd never understood the purpose of those holes. Maybe, when you were flat on your back in a hospital, counting them would give you something to do.

The tiles rested on a metal framework. But above that was... what?

Suddenly Erin understood everything. Her headache was gone, swept clean out of her skull on a tidal wave of adrenaline and raw terror.

"Teresa!" she snapped, completely forgetting the woman's fake identity. She pointed at the machine that was hooked up to Corky's nose-tube. "Turn that off! Right now!"

The old Teresa Tommasino, the Brooklyn schoolteacher, might not have understood. She would have hesitated, frightened by the sharp note in Erin's voice. She might have argued. After all, that machine was helping keep the man she loved alive. But this was a different Teresa. This Teresa had traveled clear across the country with James Corcoran and fought for her life. She had looked death in the face, more than once, and death had been the one to blink.

Teresa lunged for the oxygen machine, fumbled with the unfamiliar controls, and found the power button. The machine beeped and its indicator light went dark.

Erin was already turning to Vic and Webb. She pointed up at the false ceiling, and at the crawlspace she knew was above it. Even as she did so, she saw one of the tiles sliding away, revealing a black void beyond.

A firm rule of the NYPD was that you did not fire your gun at something you couldn't see, particularly if you were in a hospital full of civilians. You could hit an important piece of medical equipment or, if you were really unlucky, an innocent bystander. Bullets didn't care who they killed.

That wasn't why Erin held her fire. What made her finger pause on the Glock's trigger was the knowledge that the room was still full of oxygen. She didn't know what the chances were that the air would ignite from the muzzle flash, but they were more than zero. If she fired, she might kill everyone in the room.

In that moment of awful uncertainty, a metal cylinder tumbled through the hole. It glowed an eerie, lurid red. A sputtering road flare was strapped to its side.

The cylinder struck the floor end-on. Its opposite end was open, hissing as the pressurized gas inside sought freedom. Erin distinctly heard the heavy clank of metal on tile. She saw the flash as the gas ignited.

She barely had time to fling her arms in front of her face and turn halfway away from the blast before it rolled over her. The heat was immense, much worse than in the Barley Corner's cellar. There was a roar of formless noise, like a subway train rushing straight overhead.

The tile was blessedly cool against her cheek. Erin was on the floor, though she had no memory of falling. Alarms were going off somewhere, but they sounded very far away. The obnoxious recording had been overridden by the high-pitched beeping of a smoke detector. Oddly, she felt cold and wet. It was raining.

Had the explosion torn the roof clean off the hospital? No, that didn't make any sense. They hadn't been on the top floor. Any bomb strong enough to rip several floors off the building would have blown her apart. It must be the sprinkler system.

It was really important to get up. Erin couldn't remember why, but she knew it was true, so she planted her hands against the floor and did a half push-up. That got her to her knees. The dizziness wasn't too bad. In a moment, she decided, she'd stand up.

The overhead lights had shattered. The only illumination was from the flames. Everything seemed to be on fire, in spite of the sprinklers, but the air was full of smoke and she could hardly see a thing.

A dark silhouette dropped to the floor, fell to one knee, caught itself on one hand, and drew itself upright. Its other arm hung limp. In its good hand was something that glinted red in the firelight; a blade. For just a moment the smoke drifted aside and Erin recognized Gordon Pritchard.

"NYPD!" Erin croaked, but the man paid no attention. He began walking toward the corner of the room where Corky had been lying.

Where was her gun? She'd been holding her Glock a moment ago, but must have dropped it. She tried to collect her scattered thoughts and looked for the pistol. Debris was scattered across the floor. Her eye caught a dark, furry lump only a few feet away.

"Rolf!" She forced the words through her burning throat. "*Fass!*"

The K-9 rolled onto his belly and came up. His snout wrinkled, lips writhing back from his fangs in a snarl of pure rage. He coiled and lunged at Pritchard.

His left foreleg collapsed under him and he went down, rolling clean over with a yelp of surprised pain. He tried to get up again. His leg buckled.

Erin stared at her dog in horror. Rolf forced himself up once more, dragging his paw and hobbling toward Pritchard. His partner had given him an order and he was damned well going to obey it.

Erin saw the Glock then, half-buried under a fallen ceiling tile. She hurled herself at it. A snarl of her own was rumbling in her chest. Where were Vic and Webb? What about Teresa? She scrabbled at the rubble, clawing the gun free, knowing she and Rolf were too slow. Pritchard was already there. Corky was helpless, if he was even alive. Pritchard raised the blade, clutching it clumsily.

Teresa rolled off the bed and came at Pritchard with a scream that would've done a banshee proud. Her sweater and hair were smoldering, but she held tight to something Erin vaguely recognized as a bedpan.

Teresa slammed it into Pritchard's shoulder. The O'Malley enforcer lurched sideways. He didn't drop the knife, but the blow spoiled his strike and the blade clanged off the railing on the side of the bed.

Erin's fingers closed around the Glock's grip. "Drop it!" she shouted, bringing the pistol in line, but she already knew he wasn't going to do it. Gordon Pritchard wasn't a man to be reasoned with.

Pritchard ignored her completely, if he heard her at all. He made an awkward backhand slash at Teresa, who fell back with a cry. Then Erin's finger curled around the trigger and she pulled it again and again.

She fired five shots from her knees, gripping the Glock in both hands to steady it. The first went wide and punched a hole in the plaster over Corky's bed. The other four slammed into Pritchard's center of mass. He shuddered under the impacts and fell forward across Corky's blanket. His hand unclenched and the knife hit the floor. Pritchard followed it down, sliding in a boneless sprawl to land in a huddled heap.

Rolf was there a moment later. He ducked his head and grabbed Pritchard's arm, exactly as Erin had told him to. The K-9 was still growling.

The door flew open. Lieutenant Lewis came into the room at a stumbling run. Carnes and Parker were right behind him. The ESU Lieutenant's nose was streaming blood. He seemed entirely unaware of it.

Erin shoved the Glock back into its holster. She crawled on hands and knees across the few yards of floor to her dog. Rolf was standing on three legs, the fur on his back bristling. But when she got to him, he wagged his tail.

"Good boy," she choked out. "Good, good boy."

Chapter 21

"Take it easy, O'Reilly," Carnes said. "You're going to be okay. Hell, we don't even have to call you a bus. We're already in the hospital."

"Vic," Erin said. "Take care of Vic. I'm fine."

"Of course you are," Carnes said soothingly. "You just lie there. Neshenko's getting all the care he needs."

"And Webb," she went on. "What about him? And Rolf and Corky and... and..."

Carnes had dragged Erin, feebly protesting, out of the room. It usually wasn't a good idea to move an injured person before diagnosing their wounds, but getting her away from the fire had been the top priority. Now she was sitting against the wall in the hallway. Rolf was lying with his head in her lap. The dog was stubbornly refusing to admit the existence of such a thing as pain, but his ears were laid flat against his skull and he was panting.

She'd checked the K-9 as well as she could while her fellow officers tended the other victims. Uniforms had flooded the place. Now FDNY was on the scene too, putting out the flames that hadn't been extinguished by the sprinklers. Erin looked around, turning her head carefully. Her headache had roared back full force, coupled with a very stiff neck. She knew she'd have bruises all over. Her clothing had partially protected her from the fire, but her hands were scorched where she'd thrown them up to shield her face.

Vic was sitting on a gurney a few yards away, pressing an icepack to his head and looking even grumpier than usual. His face was streaked with soot and blood. Further down the hall, a nurse was helping Webb into another room in the ICU. Yet another nurse was examining Teresa's face. The woman's right cheek sported a gash that had missed her eye by about an inch. Corky had already been shifted, bloodstained bed and all, into fresh lodgings.

"Hey, Vic?" Erin called.

"Yeah?" Vic replied.

"You okay?"

"Yeah. Got clocked pretty good. I think it was a piece of that damn oxygen tank. How'd that bastard get a flare into the ER, anyway?"

Erin shrugged. That was a question the hospital security folks would be asking themselves. At the moment it didn't seem too important.

"I was only down for a few seconds," Vic grumbled. "But I missed all the fun. How's your dog?"

"Something's wrong with his paw," she said. "It could be just a sprain, or it might be broken. I need to get him to the vet."

"You're not looking so great yourself," he observed.

"I've been worse."

"No shit. You think maybe you should stop getting lit on fire?"

"Good idea."

"How'd you know he was in the ceiling?"

"I figured he'd have a way in," she said. "Not the door; that'd be too obvious. He must've been in one of the other rooms in the ward, probably next door. He lay there until he saw a chance of sneaking out of bed. Then he climbed into the crawlspace and worked his way over. He rigged an oxygen bomb from the stuff in his room and set it off with the flare he smuggled in."

"Good thing we switched off Corcoran's O2," Vic said. "It could've been an even bigger bang and it would've taken his face right off."

"Don't be awful," Teresa said. She flinched as the nurse probed the gash on her face.

"That was a brave thing you did," Erin said, stroking Rolf's head.

"What'd she do?" Vic asked. "I missed that part, too."

"She whacked Pritchard with a bedpan," Erin said.

"Outstanding," Vic said, grinning at Teresa. "I didn't know you were a badass. And you're gonna have an awesome scar to show off."

"Don't listen to him," the nurse said. "We'll get this cleaned out and put in a few stitches. It's a clean cut. That must have been a very sharp blade, and that's good. It means there really won't be much of a scar. Let's get you to the ER and we'll take care of this."

"Carnes, go with her," Erin said.

Carnes hesitated. "I'm supposed to be watching you," he said uncertainly. "She doesn't need me."

"Go," she repeated.

"Sorry, ma'am," he said. "I don't take orders from you."

Erin raised her voice. "Lieutenant Lewis?" She'd just spotted the ESU officer leaving the restroom at the end of the hallway. He had a handful of paper towels pressed against his nosebleed.

"What is it?" Lewis asked, walking quickly toward her.

"Can you order Carnes to escort Miss Tom—Miss Lopez?" She caught herself at the last moment.

Lewis looked from Erin to Teresa and back. He nodded. "Carnes? New assignment. Keep an eye on Miss *Lopez*."

"Yes, sir," Carnes said.

"How're you doing, Lieutenant?" Erin asked.

"This?" Lewis indicated the bloodstained mass of towels. "It's nothing. When the window in that door blew out, I caught some shrapnel and it knocked me down. Sorry I wasn't quicker getting back inside. But you handled things fine."

"Not really," she said. "Everybody got hurt."

"But nobody but that hitman got killed," Lewis said. "I got a look at Webb. He's pretty much fine, Lord knows how. That crappy old trench coat of his is a write-off, I think, but the guy inside it is tougher than he looks. Mild blast concussion and some first-degree burns is all."

"What about Corcoran?" she asked. She'd been pretty out of it, and concerned primarily with Rolf, in the first minutes of cleanup and triage.

"Not even singed," Lewis said. He threw an admiring glance at Teresa's retreating form. "She shielded him with her own body, if you can believe it. That's one hell of a lady, if you ask me. She's lucky to be alive."

Erin nodded. "Pritchard's dead," she said.

"Yeah," Lewis said.

"You sure?" Vic asked. "That's one hard man to kill."

"I've seen a few bodies, Neshenko," Lewis said. "That man is not getting up again. Excellent shooting, O'Reilly. And the shoot was as clean as they come. Clear-cut, by the book, and you had to do it. That son of a bitch didn't give you a choice."

"Damn right," Vic said.

After a few minutes, Webb came back into the hallway. As Lewis had said, his trench coat was a wreck. Pieces of shrapnel from the oxygen tank appeared to actually be fused with the fabric. He put his hands in his pockets and surveyed the battered remnants of his squad.

"That could have gone worse," was his verdict.

"Really?" Vic said. "How, exactly?"

"We could all be dead."

"That's true," Vic said. "But if we were, someone else would have to do the paperwork."

"That's an interesting point," Webb said. He pulled out a pack of cigarettes and actually had one in his hand before remembering where he was. He slid it back into the pack and returned it to his pocket with a sigh.

"Are you all right, sir?" Erin asked.

"Oh me? Perfectly fine." Webb smiled thinly. "I employed a self-defense method I learned on the playground when I was a boy. I dropped to the floor, curled into a ball, and hoped I wouldn't get kicked too hard."

"I don't think they give you the Medal of Valor for that, sir," Vic said.

"No," Webb agreed. "But I might live to collect my pension. I wasn't about to start shooting at an explosive device, so it wasn't really clear what good I could be doing at that moment."

"Erin was taking out the bad guy," Vic said.

"O'Reilly's good at killing people," Webb said sourly.

"Not as good as Pritchard was," Erin said. She shuddered as some of the earlier events started catching up with her nervous system.

"You were right," Webb said. "He got admitted as one of the casualties from the apartment fire. We'll need Arson to finish investigating, but I'd bet a week's pay and a carton of Camels he lit it. Your brother worked on him. I sent one of the nurses to track him down. He should be showing up any—oh, here he is now."

Doctor Sean O'Reilly Junior burst through the doors, then pulled up short when he found himself staring down the wrong end of Parker's AR-15.

"He's fine, Parker," Erin called.

"But you're not," Sean said, kneeling beside her. "Good Lord, kiddo. You look like a parking lot after the Fourth of July. Scorch marks everywhere. Did you get checked out?"

"Yeah," she said. "I'm okay, but Rolf's paw is banged up. As soon as they let me out of here, I need to get him to the emergency vet."

"You treated a Caucasian male, mid-forties," Webb said to Sean.

"That's right," Sean said. "He didn't have any ID on him and he wasn't responsive. That's not unusual with burn victims. Serious burns are a nasty shock to the system. And this guy was in bad shape. It wasn't just the burns. He had a deep laceration in his left wrist, a penetrating stab wound."

"I know," Erin said. "A steak knife made the cut. And he had tooth marks."

"He'd been bitten," Sean said, surprised. "It looked like canine dentition."

Erin said nothing. Sean's eyes traveled to Rolf's head, still resting in her lap.

"Oh," he said.

"Tell us about the burns," Webb said.

"He had fresh second-degree burns on large portions of his right arm and face," Sean said. "But I noticed some older scarring, too. I thought that might help us ID him later. He didn't seem to be in too much pain; he was mostly just disconnected. Sometimes the fire destroys the nerve endings, so burns don't hurt as much as they should. I patched up his punctures and did what I could for the burns. They were bad but not life-threatening. Then I sent him here to start recovery."

"Didn't you get the BOLO for a dark-haired Irishman with fresh burns?" Erin asked.

Sean blinked. "Yeah, now that you mention it," he said. "Hold on, you're telling me that's who this was?"

Erin nodded.

"It never crossed my mind," Sean said. "If he'd come in on his own, that would've been one thing, but he was in an ambulance with another victim. Our people brought him here! And I never would've thought he'd attack the hospital!"

"He came to kill another patient," Erin explained.

"A ceiling tile is out next door," Webb said. "He jury-rigged an oxygen canister as a bomb, lugged it up there, and dumped it on the other side."

"Nearly killed all of us," Vic said.

Sean looked like he wanted to throw up. "God, Erin, I'm so sorry," he said. "I had no idea. Are you sure—"

"For the fifteenth time, I'm fine," Erin said loudly. "Or I will be, once I get Rolf seen to. Can I go to the vet now, sir?"

"You just killed a man, O'Reilly," Webb said. "You need to stay here until you give the Captain your statement. Then there's the breathalyzer and blood tests, and you need to surrender your weapon. You know the drill."

"I'll take Rolf to the vet," Vic said quietly. "Your dog knows me. I didn't fire a shot, so I don't have to hang around."

Erin hesitated. "I ought to be there," she said.

"It's just his paw," Vic said. "That mutt's hardcore. Do you think he wants you fussing all over him? It'd just embarrass him."

"Okay," she said reluctantly. "But be careful. If it's broken, you could make it worse moving him. Don't let him put any weight on it."

"Copy that," Vic said. He knelt beside her. "How do I tell him to jump, again?"

"*Hupf,*" she said.

"Okay, Rolf," Vic said, extending his arms. "*Hupf!*"

Rolf clambered wearily up to stand on three paws. His hindquarters tensed as he looked for where he was supposed to jump. Vic ducked his head under the dog's body, wrapping his arms around Rolf's legs. Then he stood up. A very startled Rolf went with him, draped across Vic's broad shoulders.

"Nothing to it," Vic said. "I bench lots more than this. I could carry two of him."

"Give me a call as soon as you know his condition," Erin said. "I've turned my phone back on."

"Copy that," he said again. "Stop worrying. You'll get frown lines in your face and then you'll be ugly and the Irish guys will stop trying to sleep with you. On second thought, that's a great idea. It'll solve half our problems. Frown away."

"Up yours, Neshenko," she said, but without any real malice.

"That's the end of it," Webb said quietly as they watched Vic carry Rolf out of ICU. "Every major O'Malley is accounted for. All of them except Pritchard are in custody, and Pritchard's dead."

"I've heard that before," Erin said.

"This time it's true," Webb said. "I think we'd better leave you and Carlyle under protection at least overnight, though."

"It's not like we've got a home to go back to," she said.

"I'm sorry about that," Webb said.

"It'll be fine," she said. "The fire didn't spread to the upstairs. The worst thing will be smoke damage. But the building's a mess. It'll need months of repair work, and this is a lousy season for it. Maybe Carlyle and I should take a vacation."

"That's a good idea," Webb said. "As long as nobody knows where you're going."

"That shouldn't be too hard," she said, "since we don't know yet. Shit, I still need to call him. If he's watching the news, he'll be going out of his mind. And that's assuming Pritchard didn't make a stop at the safe house on his way here!"

"Relax, O'Reilly," Webb said. "Take the paranoia down a notch. I've been in touch with the Marshals. They're fine, and so is Carlyle. It's over."

Chapter 22

After that it was the familiar tangle of red tape. Erin handed over her Glock, along with a few samples of body fluids, and answered a bunch of questions. Nobody seriously thought the shooting hadn't been justified—the bombed-out wreckage, Teresa's bloodied cheek, and several eyewitnesses were in her favor—but the protocols had to be observed, especially since it wasn't her first shooting incident.

The Captain from the 13th Precinct turned up, since Bellevue was in his Area of Service. Captain Holliday also made an appearance to support his detectives. Then there were firefighters, hospital security personnel, and of course the reporters. Erin even saw Holly Gardner's familiar blonde hair, fortunately in time to duck her.

It was a good thing there weren't any more O'Malley thugs on the loose. So many people were coming and going that it was essentially impossible to keep a close eye on all of them. Twig and Parker stuck with Erin, which was some comfort, but she knew if someone really wanted to take a shot at her, the best ESU could do was avenge her death.

Teresa Tommasino was gone. Carnes had escorted her out of the building and into a taxi. Where she went after that was anybody's guess.

"She wouldn't tell me," Carnes reported to Lewis, "and I didn't want to ask. She said the Mob would be after her if they knew, and secrecy was her best defense. Who *is* that lady, anyway?"

"Nobody to worry about," Erin said. "She's on our side."

"I'm glad of that," Lewis said.

"Me, too," Parker said. "She took that guy on with a bedpan! That girl's a keeper, you ask me. Not bad looking, either."

"I'm going to tell your wife you said that," Twig said.

"A guy can look and dream," Parker said. "But y'know, even with a name like Lopez, I could've sworn that chick was Italian, not Mexican."

"You're a cop," Carnes said with a sly smile. "Don't all the brown people look the same to you?"

"Don't even joke about that," Lewis said. "Especially with all these reporters around."

Erin's phone buzzed. When she saw Vic's name on the screen, she almost dropped it in her eagerness to answer.

"How's Rolf?" she asked.

"Hello to you too," Vic said. "He's fine, Erin. Just broke a bone in his paw, that's all."

She gripped her phone so hard its edges dug into her fingers. "A broken paw isn't fine, Vic!"

"Relax," he said. "It's not like they're gonna cut it off or anything. I've broken bones in my hands. Happens all the time. Boxer's fractures, mostly. It happens when you don't make your fist right, or when you hit a guy wrong and smack into bone. It's the fifth metacarpal or whatever it's called, and it's not a big deal."

"Vic?"

"Yeah?"

"I don't give a shit about your hands right now."

"Right. So, your dog's got a cast on his leg, but it's mostly so he doesn't mess around with it. Doc says he'll be as good as new in eight weeks."

"That's two months!"

"Yeah. It could've been worse. Erin, he could've been killed. So could you. Hell, so could I! So maybe look for the silver friggin' lining?"

She let out a long breath. "You're right, Vic. Sorry. I've been worried. You know how it is."

"He's had worse," Vic reminded her. "At least nobody shot him this time."

"I know. I just... the vet told me he couldn't take much more wear and tear, so every time something happens I think maybe that's it, you know?"

"I copy. On that subject, how's your head?"

"My head?"

"Yeah. You know, that thing on top of your neck that keeps feeding you bad ideas?"

"Nothing's wrong with my head."

"You clonked it on the floor again, didn't you?"

"Not very hard."

"It didn't need to be hard. You've had, like, three dozen concussions. You're gonna end up like a boxer that's been KO'd too much, only without the cauliflower ear."

"It doesn't even hurt," Erin lied.

"Whatever. Look, I've got your dog here. He's got a cast on his leg, one of those collars around his neck that makes him look like a desk lamp, and he's giving me this look that says he's sick of me. Where do you want him?"

"Can you get him back to the safe house without anybody following you?"

"Who's gonna follow me? The veterinarian? Nah, I understand. I'll be careful."

"If I'm not there, hand him off to Carlyle."

"Copy that."

"And Vic?"

"Yeah?"

"I'm not going to be in to work for a little while. I'm taking some time."

He thought about that for a moment. "That's probably a good idea," he said. "Let Rolf heal up a bit, get your own head in order. But for the love of God, go somewhere nice. Don't just cross the river into Newark. Go to Disneyland or a national park or something."

"How about Vegas?"

"Are you nuts? The Mob runs Vegas!"

"I was joking, Vic."

"You're not as funny as you think you are."

"And you're even uglier than you think. Take care of yourself till I get back, Vic."

"You too. I still don't like you, but I've gotten used to you. I don't want a new partner."

* * *

It was well after dark by the time Erin finally got away from the hospital. What she wanted was to get behind the wheel of her trusty Charger, go home, and take a long, hot bath. Maybe even a bubble bath. The scented soap could finally get the smell of smoke out of her hair and skin.

What she got was another ride in the beat-up van, its moldy-marijuana odor worse than ever, with a crew of tired, grouchy ESU officers who smelled every bit as bad as Erin herself. She ended up at the safe house, which didn't even have a bathtub, let alone a bottle of bubbles. But Carlyle was there, and so was someone else.

"Hey there, kiddo," she said, dropping to one knee to greet her K-9. Rolf had been lying next to the living-room couch, watching the Marshals and Carlyle play cribbage. When he caught sight of Erin, he struggled to his feet and hobbled over to her, tail wagging frantically. His soulful brown eyes showed the indignity of the protective cone around his neck, but every bit of his body language told her he was ready and eager to dive right back into the fray, cast or no cast.

He tried to thrust his head into the angle between Erin's arm and her body, but his cone got hung up on her and brought him up short. He snorted irritably and tried again, unsuccessfully.

Erin leaned in and cupped his cheek inside the cone. She kissed his forehead, ignoring his dirty, smelly fur. He carefully extended his tongue and licked her face.

"That boy's a real trooper," Calley said.

"Yeah," Erin said, and to her own surprise burst into tears. She retreated to the bathroom, hoping the Marshals hadn't seen. She stripped off her filthy clothes and climbed into the shower. The showerhead was a cheap piece of steel that split the incoming water into hard little droplets that stung when they hit her skin. The hot water took too long to get going, and then became scalding. The shampoo was a little freebie bottle someone had once liberated from a motel bathroom. She didn't care. Just getting clean felt amazing.

She wrapped a towel around herself and another around her hair when she got out. She ducked into the bedroom and found, to her surprised delight, a suitcase containing some of her own clothes. She put on a set of navy blue sweats with a big yellow NYPD emblazoned on the front and came back out into the living room feeling almost human again.

"Now that's how you dress for undercover work," Parker said, grinning. "Nobody would ever know you're a cop."

"I'd like to talk to Carlyle for a minute," she said. "Alone."

Calley nodded. "We'll step next door," he said. "You have a gun?"

"My backup piece," Erin said, drawing her snub-nosed .38 from the pocket of her sweatpants.

"Call if you need us," he said. "If you don't have time to call, just start shooting and we'll figure it out."

Erin waited until her guardians were gone. She sat on the couch, trailing a hand down to scratch Rolf behind the ears. He'd need his own bath, but she couldn't figure a good way to do that in this apartment while keeping his cast dry. She'd have to take him to a groomer.

Carlyle came and sat next to her. "Feeling better, darling?" he asked.

"Yeah. Where'd my clothes come from?"

"I talked to Marshal Calley and loaned him my keys. He made a run to our flat to fetch some of our things. I hope I've not forgotten anything important. What's the news?"

"Pritchard's dead."

"You're certain?"

"I shot him. Four times, close range."

"I see."

"He went for Corky. He almost got him, but Teresa and I stopped him. That woman... she's changed. Corky did something to her."

Carlyle's mouth twisted wryly. "A great many things, I'd imagine," he said.

"She's determined to look after him," Erin said. "And I actually think she can do a pretty good job. She's tougher than she was, and resourceful."

"I know it," Carlyle said. "Corky told me about a wee incident involving a Mafia lad."

"I don't want to know any more about that," she said. "The main thing is, with Pritchard out of the way, all Evan's people are off the board. We'd be able to go home, except..."

"Aye," Carlyle said. "Except."

"Webb ordered me to take some time off after my assignment finished," she said. "A couple weeks, at least. And Rolf's paw needs time to heal."

"What're you thinking?"

"How about a trip out of town? Someplace warm, maybe?"

He smiled. "You're thinking of our jaunt to the Bahamas, aye?"

"I was, yeah. Only maybe this time there won't be an assassin waiting in my bedroom when we come home."

"Small chance of that. Richie O'Malley's not up to anything of the sort."

Erin froze. "Richie?" she said. "What do you mean?"

"Evan's son," Carlyle said. "Richard."

"Yeah, I know who he is," she said. "Why isn't he in jail with the others?"

"Didn't you know, darling? He's not directly connected to any of his da's operations."

"Bullshit! Evan was going to put him in charge of the drug trade!"

"I don't know what Evan was planning to do, but he'd not done it yet," Carlyle said. "But you needn't fret yourself."

"I'll fret myself plenty!" Erin burst out.

"Why? The lad's nobody. He's useless to everyone but himself, and small use even then. There's a reason Evan didn't trust him with the running of the family. You think it's an accident I was next in line to the throne and not his own blood?"

"I don't care if he's an idiot! We threw his dad in jail! He's going to hate us! Don't you remember Alfie Madonna? These guys *live* for revenge!"

"What would you have us do, darling?" Carlyle asked gently. "Richard's broken no laws. Your people have nothing to hold him for. He's alone, without resources. The coppers have frozen Evan's accounts and seized his assets. All the lads he'd go to for help are incarcerated. If he knows what's good for him, he'll cut his losses. I'd not be surprised if he left New York altogether for greener pastures."

"I hope you're right," Erin said. She buried her face in her hands. "I don't know what I was thinking, expecting this to end. It never ends! It's just one damn thing after another!"

Carlyle laid a hand on her shoulder. "Your idea of travel's a fine one," he said. "But I'd not recommend that place in the Bahamas. It's Evan's, after all. Your government's discussing its status with the locals even now, I'll warrant, and it's just possible a few rough lads may be hanging about down there. Nay, I'd recommend a different destination. Have you ever been to Hawaii?"

"Are you kidding? I've hardly been to New Jersey."

"Then it's high time you went," he said. "Maui's lovely, even in December. A bit of island paradise is just what you're needing. I'll make some calls and set everything up."

"I can't afford to go to Hawaii," she said.

"I can," Carlyle said cheerfully. "A day or two for me to arrange it and we'll be on our way. We can make arrangements for the repairs to be done on the Corner while we're gone. Just think of it. We'll be sipping drinks on the beach watching the sun set over the Pacific horizon. It'll be grand, darling."

Chapter 23

Erin O'Reilly lay back on the beach, resting on the soft towel. The sun was sliding down the western sky, laying a golden path across the water. The temperature was eighty degrees, something her New York senses would take a while to accept. She listened to the soft, throaty growl of the ocean as the waves rolled slowly in.

Rolf lay at her feet. He was getting used to the cast on his paw, and Erin had trusted him enough to take off his cone, but he still gave the impression of being much put-upon. He settled his chin on the ground and heaved the heavy sigh only a dog could.

Carlyle walked toward her, clad in light cotton trousers and a Hawaiian shirt patterned with blue flowers. He was carrying a cocktail glass in each hand, filled with a cloudy concoction Erin didn't recognize.

"What've you got there?" she asked.

"Irish whiskey, Irish cream, and Hazelnut liqueur over ice," he said, handing one to her. "It's called a Celtic twilight. It struck me as appropriate."

"That's pub owners for you," Erin said, taking a sip. "A drink for every occasion. This is damn good."

"I couldn't get Glen D, sadly," he said, sitting down beside her. "But I've done the best I could. You're looking right lovely."

"You'd say that to any girl in a swimsuit," she said. The suit was nothing spectacular; just a one-piece black number with a halfway-modest neckline. She didn't do much swimming or sunbathing, as a general rule. Her previous vacation with Carlyle had been the last time she'd had it on.

"Hardly," he said. "What do you think of Maui?"

"It's beautiful," she said. "I love the way the light just glows. And the way the air feels... it's amazing. I'm glad Rolf could come with us."

"There's advantages to flying privately," Carlyle said. Rolf had been able to ride in the cabin with Erin on the plan he'd chartered.

"Yeah, but it costs a fortune."

He shrugged. "Money's only good for what it can buy."

"That sounds like something Corky would say."

He chuckled. "It does, aye. I hope the lad's keeping all right."

"He'll be fine, with Teresa looking after him."

"I'd imagine so. James Corcoran with his devoted lover and nursemaid. I'd never have thought it."

"If she's changed, so has he," she said.

"Aye, so he has," Carlyle said. "Just like the rest of us. How does it feel?"

"What?"

"Victory."

Erin wrinkled her forehead. "Is that what this is?"

"It's the closest we're likely to get to it," he replied. "You should enjoy the fruits, darling. You've accomplished a great deal. There's many a dangerous man warming a cell. There's unfortunate lasses you've freed from enslavement. There's a drug network that's been dismantled, and a network of corruption exposed."

"Yeah," she said hollowly. "And Phil Stachowski's never going to walk again. Corky's in the hospital. People are *dead!* Your bar got ruined, Rolf got hurt, the hospital got bombed. And that's not even counting those innocent people in that apartment fire. Was it worth it?"

He took her hand and smiled. "I'm no accountant," he said. "Particularly in matters of the soul. Don't go taking the weight of all the world's sins on your own shoulders. Every one of us made our own choices, and we're the ones must live with the consequences. For myself, you saved me from damnation, and for that I'm grateful, now and forever."

"Bullshit," Erin said. "You saved yourself."

"Perhaps," he admitted with a soft smile. "And while I'd like to think I've been of some service to you, I'm still very much in your debt."

She tried to match his smile. "Then you're welcome," she said.

"I spoke with Ian," he went on. "The lad's overseeing the contractors working on the Corner. He'll make certain the work's done, prompt and proper. The lad's doing some thinking, too."

"What about?"

"He's planning to ask Cassie Jordan to marry him."

"She'd be nuts to turn him down," Erin said. "He's one of the best guys I know."

"Agreed," Carlyle said. "But he'll be making a change in his circumstances. He'll be a family man. He'll need to keep more predictable hours. Also, Cassie doesn't like him carrying a gun. She thinks it's bad for him and might be keeping his mind on things best left in the past."

Erin nodded. "Does he know what he wants to do?"

"He's expressed an interest in learning more about New York's Bravest."

"FDNY?" She was startled, but realized she shouldn't have been. "Is this because of the fire at the Corner?"

"That's what put it in his head, I'm thinking," Carlyle said. "He told me it had all the thrill of combat, with none of the bullets. Corky knows some lads in that line."

"Of course he does."

"So if the lad does decide to pursue that vocation, he'll find his way in easily enough."

"What about you?" Erin asked, coming up on one elbow and turning to face him. "What are your plans?"

"That's something I've been hoping to talk with you about," Carlyle said, speaking slowly, almost reluctantly. "As you know, I've found the life of a publican to my liking. It's an honorable trade, and one I know well. I think I'll like it better without the trappings of crime. What do you think?"

"I think if that's what you want to do, you should do it," she said. "It's your life. You've had it on hold long enough, in hock to Evan O'Malley. You should live it for you now."

He shook his head. "Nay, that's not it at all. You've a say in this too."

Erin laughed. "I'm Irish. We can always use a good pub. You're not worried I'll get bored with you, are you?"

"I hope not," he said. "Listen, Erin. There's something I've been working toward asking you. The time never seemed right, what with all the gunfire and explosions and whatnot, but it's quiet now. I've no right. But as I've said, the world runs on favors, so I'm hoping you'll do me the one I'm about to ask."

"Ask away," she said. She was a little confused now, and trying not to be worried. There was something unusual in Carlyle's eyes. He actually looked scared, more frightened than when he'd faced down Gordon Pritchard or Siobhan Finneran.

He stood up and reached into the pocket of his trousers. He cleared his throat and blinked a couple of times. Erin waited, wondering where he was going with this.

"I've been trying to think how best to ask," he said. "Words usually come easy to me, but not right now. Erin, you know what a mess I've made of my life. As you'll recall, my da was killed when I was fourteen. I went into the Brigades, all hot for vengeance, and wasted my childhood building explosives. Then, when I met Rose McCann, I thought I'd found a way out, a path to a normal life. But you know how that ended.

"When she died, I gave up on my life. I didn't come to America to find a new one, but to run away from the old. I'd scarce arrived when by blind fate I ran into one of the bastards who'd murdered my Rose. He deserved all I did to him and more, but the doing put me in Evan's power. I've been a gangster ever since.

"I've done terrible things. I've caused pain and misery, placed my soul in mortal peril, and all for nothing. When you came into my life, I was all but lost. You didn't trust me at first, nor should you have, but we've forged a friendship and more. You gave me a purpose, a meaning I'd scarce imagined. I'd die for you, darling. You know that."

"I know," Erin said, shifting uncomfortably. "And I've told you, I don't want that. I want you to live for me, not die for me."

"That's just the point," Carlyle said. "I'm too old, too broken, too wretched a lad to ask it, but it's what's in my heart."

Carlyle went to one knee in front of her. His hand came out of his pocket, holding a little velvet-lined box.

"Erin O'Reilly," he said, "will you marry me?"

He flipped the lid open. A gold ring shone in the Pacific twilight, the setting sun reflected in the facets of a very large emerald, cut in the shape of a heart. The band was an intertwining Celtic knot which ended in a pair of golden hands cupping the heart.

"Oh my God," Erin said. It was a stupid thing to say, a cliché, but somehow she'd never expected this to actually happen.

"You know everything about me," he said, still kneeling. "The good and the bad. If you'll have me, I promise I'll try every day to be a better man than the day before. It's no secret I want children, but if that's not something you're wanting, it's your choice to make. I'll be your friend and your lover, your ally and companion. There's better men than I in this world, but there's none love you so dearly. I understand I've rather sprung this on you, so if you're needing time to think on it, take all you're needing. And if you don't feel the same, you've only to say. Yes or no, it's entirely up to you."

"Stop talking," Erin said. "Of course it's yes."

She might have been able to keep back the tears, if she hadn't seen Carlyle's eyes. His were shining with surprised joy. She realized he hadn't truly believed she'd say yes. That doubt should have made her angry, but it didn't.

She held out her left hand, fingers extended. He slipped the ring onto her third finger. It fit perfectly. Ring size wasn't the sort of detail Morton Carlyle would get wrong. She stared at the sparkling gemstone.

"I don't even want to know how much this cost," she said.

"As you'd say, darling, forget about it," he said. "As it turns out, I know a lad in the trade."

"Of course you do. Just tell me one thing."

"What's that?"

"Tell me it's not stolen."

He laughed. "Nay, darling, fairly bought and paid for. My outlaw days are behind me."

Erin was laughing and crying. "Then come here," she said and opened her arms.

He came to her. They lay together on the beach as the sun went down and the last twilight faded. They talked and laughed and promised and planned.

Rolf watched and listened for a while, then got up and limped a short distance away where he could get some quiet, undisturbed sleep. Soon he was breathing hard, his paws twitching in a dream of chasing bad guys.

And Erin O'Reilly, for the first time in a very long time, allowed herself to hope.

Here's a sneak peek from Book 26: Headshot

Coming 12/16/2024

"Are you lost, ma'am?"

Vic Neshenko had on his public-relations face. He wasn't smiling—Vic's smile tended to unsettle civilians—but he wasn't scowling either. If you ignored his twice-broken nose, the scars on his knuckles, and his overdeveloped musculature, you might even think he looked concerned and helpful.

Erin O'Reilly wasn't fooled. She folded her arms and glared at him. At the other end of the leash that dangled from her right hand, Rolf copied her stare. The Shepherd's tail waved slowly back and forth, like a mountain lion deciding on the perfect moment to pounce.

"I think I'm exactly where I'm supposed to be," she said.

"I don't think so, ma'am," Vic said. "You see, this is the Major Crimes office. Even if you need to report a major crime, you need to talk to the sergeant at the front desk. You must have passed him in the lobby. I'd show you down myself, but I'm a detective with the NYPD and I really do have a lot of work to do.

It's your tax dollars paying my salary, ma'am, and I'd hate to see them wasted."

"Ha ha," she said. "You're a riot, Vic. I missed you too."

He cocked his head. "You know, from just the right angle you look a little like some lady I used to work with," he said. "Except the resemblance isn't really that strong. You're a lot tanner, you look like you've been getting enough sleep, and maybe you've been eating healthy. Nobody'd mistake you for a detective."

"I haven't been gone that long," she said.

"You kidding?" he retorted. "It's been three friggin' months! Three months you left us here, holding our dicks!"

"I thought if you did that more than four hours you were supposed to consult your physician," Erin said.

Then Vic did smile. It didn't scare Erin; under his thuggish exterior was one of the best friends she'd ever known. "You look good," he said, opening his arms. "Get over here."

She crossed the office and gave him a hug. It was surprisingly tight and even a little emotional.

"I missed you, you big lug," she said. "You look the same as you did."

But it wasn't true. Vic looked tired. He had dark rings under his eyes. Despite some questionable personal habits, he'd almost always showed up for work clean-shaven, but now he had about three days' stubble on his chin. But there was something else about him, something hard to define. Erin stepped back to arm's length and studied his face, seeing that elusive something lurking at the back of his eyes.

"What?" he said, the smile slipping off his face. "I feel like you're about to bust me for shoplifting or something. I swear, Detective, I didn't do nothin.'"

"You look... happy," she said.

"Well, yeah," he said. "What'd you expect?"

"I missed something," she said.

"You missed a lot," Vic retorted. "Three months! You take off in December for Hawaii or some godforsaken place, you get a lot of sun, you probably get laid a lot, which I don't wanna hear about, or even think about, you come back with the deepest tan you've ever had in your pasty Irish life, and you think everything's just the way you left it? C'mon, Erin, do the friggin' math! Who don't you see in this office?"

"Lieutenant Webb," she said at once.

"Besides him," Vic said impatiently. "He's at the monthly CompStat meeting."

Then Erin got it. "I feel like an idiot," she said. "Zofia! The baby! She must've had it. Did everything go okay?"

Vic's smile came back, warmer and more genuine than she remembered it. "Yeah," he said. His hand went into his hip pocket and came out with his phone. He thumbed the screen and brought up a photo of NYPD Officer Zofia Piekarski lying in a hospital bed with a newborn baby in her arms. The baby looked confused, which Erin supposed was a natural reaction to being born. Piekarski looked tired, sweaty, and radiant.

"Mina Angelica Piekarski," Vic said proudly. "It's short for Wilhelmina, but we're not ever calling her that. Mina means 'resolute protection,' did you know that? Great name for the kid of a couple cops."

"I didn't," Erin said. She grabbed Vic's hand and gave it a good hard squeeze. "And you're absolutely right. Congratulations, Dad!"

He grimaced. "I'm not used to that yet," he said. "Anyways, Zofia's on maternity leave. I got two weeks too, but then I had to come back. Poor Webb was getting snowed under trying to manage the office all on his own. I think he actually missed us, if you can believe it. Not that he'd ever admit it."

"Of course not," Erin agreed. "I'm sorry I haven't been in touch. You should've called!"

"And interrupt your vacation?" he replied. "You needed to get away from it all. Besides, I haven't had time to talk much, or think about anything. It's been pretty crazy, what with Mina and our lousy half-squad trying to close cases."

"Catch any interesting ones?"

"Nothing worth talking about. Just assholes killing other assholes. SSDD."

"Same shit, different day," she agreed.

"Something's different about you, too," Vic said, and it was his turn to study her. "I'm not talking about the tan. Did you change your hair?"

"It's a little longer, I guess," she said. "I need to get it cut. If I grow it out too long, it gives the perps too much of a handhold."

His eyes traveled down her. Then he saw her left hand. He blinked.

"Holy shit," he said.

"What, this?" Erin nonchalantly held up her hand. On her ring finger, a gold ring with a big emerald glittered.

"You dumped that gangster, found Mr. Right, and got married in Vegas!" he exclaimed.

Erin punched him in the shoulder almost as hard as she could. It had basically no effect, and felt like hitting a heavy training bag filled with cement. She winced. "I did not dump 'that gangster,'" she retorted. "He proposed on a beach in Maui at sunset. It was beautiful and romantic and I said yes, you damn knucklehead. Another crack like that and I won't invite you to the wedding!"

"You sure about that?" he asked.

Erin shook her head. "No, I was kidding about the wedding invite. Of course you're invited, and if you try to beg off I'll cuff you and drag you there."

"No, I mean the other thing. Carlyle. You sure this is what you want?" His eyes were serious.

"I've never been more sure of anything," she said. "And he's not a gangster, Vic. Not anymore. All that's behind him. He's just a bar owner now."

"Didn't his bar burn down?"

"The renovation's almost done," she said, brightening. "We got a good line on some really solid contractors. Corky Corcoran gave us the recommendations and they've really come through. Most of it's finished. The Barley Corner will be reopening soon. And the upstairs apartment's fine. We were able to move right in when we got back Sunday evening."

"Congratulations," he said. "I guess."

"For the bar repairs or for getting a fiancé?"

"Both," he muttered. "But remember what I said about him a while ago?"

"That if he broke my heart you'd break his arms?"

"It's still true."

She grinned. "I don't think he's forgotten."

"How about the mutt?" Vic asked, turning his attention to Rolf. "Last time I saw him, he had on a cast and one of those stupid cones. He was pretty well out of commission."

Rolf appeared mildly offended at the suggestion he would let something as insignificant as a broken paw even slow him down, let alone take him out of action.

"All better," Erin said.

"Thank God for that," Vic said. "We can use him. With Zofia benched on account of the whole mom thing, we're still down one body, even with you back in the rotation. What I figure is, as soon as the Lieutenant gets back—"

He was interrupted by his phone. Erin noted he'd changed his ringtone to the theme music from "The Terminator."

"Speak of the devil," he said, glancing at the screen and setting the phone to speaker. "Neshenko here, sir. Guess what? You don't have to worry about leaving me in charge anymore. I've got some adult supervision now. Some hotshot Detective Second Grade just turned up, walking in like she owns the place."

"Hello, sir," Erin said.

"O'Reilly," Lieutenant Webb said. "Glad you're back. And great timing. I'm stuck in this purgatorial meeting for another... God help me, three hours. I just stepped out for a minute, and I need to get back in, so I'll keep this short. I need you to get to McQuillan's Bar in Hell's Kitchen."

"Sounds like my kind of place," Erin said. "A good Irish bar?"

"I don't know about that," Webb said. "You'll be investigating the scene along with a rep from IAB."

"Internal Affairs?" Vic demanded. "What do we want with those weasels?"

"That's for you and O'Reilly to sort out," Webb said. "You'll understand when you get there."

"Give me something more than that, sir," Erin said. "Why IAB? Is a cop a suspect?"

"No," Webb said. "He's a victim. I've been told there's an NYPD officer lying dead in the restroom, shot by his own gun."

"Vacation's over," Vic said to Erin.

"We're on our way, sir," Erin said into the phone.

Ready for more?

Join the Clickworks Press email list
for the latest on new releases, upcoming books and
series, behind-the-scenes details, events, and more.

**Be the first to know about new releases in the Erin
O'Reilly Mysteries by signing up at
clickworkspress.com/join/erin**

About the Author

Steven Henry learned how to read almost before he learned how to walk. Ever since he began reading stories, he wanted to put his own on the page. He lives a very quiet and ordinary life in Minnesota with his wife and dog.

Also by Steven Henry

Fathers
A Modern Christmas Story

When you strip away everything else, what's left is the truth

Life taught Joe Davidson not to believe in miracles. A blue-collar woodworker, Joe is trying to build a future. His father drank himself to death and his mother succumbed to cancer, leaving a broken, struggling family. He and his brother and sisters are faced with failed marriages, growing pains, and lingering trauma.

Then a chance meeting at his local diner brings Mary Elizabeth Reynolds into his life. Suddenly, Joe finds himself reaching for something more, a dream of happiness. The wood¬worker and the poor girl from a trailer park connect and fall in love, and for a little while, everything is right with their world.

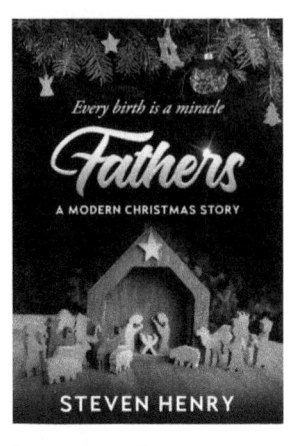

But suddenly Joe is confronted with a situation he never imagined. What do you do if your fiancée is expecting a child you know isn't yours? Torn between betrayal and love, trying to do the right thing when nothing seems right anymore, Joe has to strip life down to its truth and learn that, in spite of the pain, love can be the greatest miracle of all.

Learn more at clickworkspress.com/fathers.

Ember of Dreams
The Clarion Chronicles, Book One

When magic awakens a long-forgotten folk, a noble lady, a young apprentice, and a solitary blacksmith band together to prevent war and seek understanding between humans and elves.

Lady Kristyn Tremayne – An otherwise unremarkable young lady's open heart and inquisitive mind reveal a hidden world of magic.

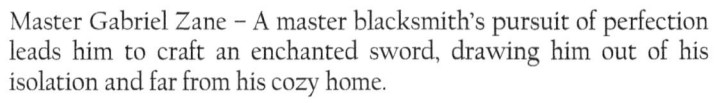

Robert Blackford – A humble harp maker's apprentice dreams of being a hero.

Master Gabriel Zane – A master blacksmith's pursuit of perfection leads him to craft an enchanted sword, drawing him out of his isolation and far from his cozy home.

Lord Luthor Carnarvon – A lonely nobleman with a dark past has won the heart of Kristyn's mother, but at what cost?

Readers love *Ember of Dreams*

"The more I got to know the characters, the more I liked them. The female lead in particular is a treat to accompany on her journey from ordinary to extraordinary."

"The author's deep understanding of his protagonists' motivations and keen eye for psychological detail make Robert and his companions a likable and memorable cast."

Learn more at tinyurl.com/emberofdreams.

More great titles from Clickworks Press

www.clickworkspress.com

The Altered Wake
Megan Morgan

Amid growing unrest, a family secret and an ancient laboratory unleash long-hidden superhuman abilities. Now newly-promoted Sentinel Cameron Kardell must chase down a rogue superhuman who holds the key to the powers' origin: the greatest threat Cotarion has seen in centuries – and Cam's best friend.

"*Incredible. Starts out gripping and keeps getting better.*"

Learn more at clickworkspress.com/sentinel1.

Hubris Towers: The Complete First Season
Ben Y. Faroe & Bill Hoard

Comedy of manners meets comedy of errors in a new series for fans of Fawlty Towers and P. G. Wodehouse.

"*So funny and endearing*"

"*Had me laughing so hard that I had to put it down to catch my breath*"

"*Astoundingly, outrageously funny!*"

Learn more at clickworkspress.com/hts01.

Death's Dream Kingdom
Gabriel Blanchard

A young woman of Victorian London has been transformed into a vampire. Can she survive the world of the immortal dead— or perhaps, escape it?

"*The wit and humor are as Victorian as the setting... a winsomely vulnerable and tremendously crafted work of art.*"

"*A dramatic, engaging novel which explores themes of death, love, damnation, and redemption.*"

Learn more at clickworkspress.com/ddk.

Share the love!

Join our microlending team at
kiva.org/team/clickworkspress.

Keep in touch!

Join the Clickworks Press email list
and get freebies, production updates, special deals,
behind-the-scenes sneak peeks, and more.

Sign up today at clickworkspress.com/join.

Milton Keynes UK
Ingram Content Group UK Ltd.
UKHW021905230924
448765UK00015B/263/J